Your ...

Three spirited ...
find the men ...

Hazel, Iris and Daisy, the spirited Springfeld sisters, are expected to marry well. But they have other ideas. Hazel, the clever one, wants someone to appreciate her for her intelligence. Iris wants to be loved for something other than her good looks, and sporty Daisy is too busy having fun to think about things as boring as marriage. But each in turn will find the right man to match their highly individual personalities.

Read Hazel's story in
Wagering on the Wallflower

Available now

And look for Iris's and Daisy's stories

Coming soon!

Author Note

Only one thing was expected of aristocratic young women in Victorian England—to get married, preferably to someone with equal or higher status. But what happens if you are hopeless at social chitchat, can't dance and have a habit of tripping over your feet?

That's the fate of Hazel Springfeld, an intelligent woman, born in a time and into a class where intelligence was not one of the qualities admired in a woman.

I loved writing Hazel's story. Despite being considered a wallflower, she's spirited, clever and more than a match for Lucas Darkwood, the man who sees her merely as a means to win a wager.

I enjoy hearing from readers, and you can contact me via my website or on my Facebook page.

EVA SHEPHERD

Wagering on
the Wallflower

HARLEQUIN®
HISTORICAL™

Recycling programs
for this product may
not exist in your area.

ISBN-13: 978-1-335-50614-6

Wagering on the Wallflower

Harlequin Enterprises ULC
22 Adelaide St. West, 40th Floor
Toronto, Ontario M5H 4E3, Canada
www.Harlequin.com

Printed in U.S.A.

After graduating with degrees in history and political science, **Eva Shepherd** worked in journalism and as an advertising copywriter. She began writing historical romances because it combined her love of a happy ending with her passion for history. She lives in Christchurch, New Zealand, but spends her days immersed in the world of late Victorian England. You can follow her on evashepherd.com and Facebook.com/evashepherdromancewriter.

Books by Eva Shepherd

Harlequin Historical

Young Victorian Ladies
Wagering on the Wallflower

Breaking the Marriage Rules

Beguiling the Duke
Awakening the Duchess
Aspirations of a Lady's Maid
How to Avoid the Marriage Mart

Visit the Author Profile page
at Harlequin.com.

To the lovely ladies at Academy Group—
especially the ones who enjoy romance novels.

Chapter One

London—1885

For many people, hell was fire, brimstone and red-faced devils poking you with sharp, pointed pitchforks. But not for Lady Hazel Springfeld. For her, hell was being forced to wear an overly fussy pink ballgown and having to spend the evening being dragged around the dance floor by a boorish man, while mocking society ladies tittered behind their fans.

Yes, she was in hell. But it was a hell she was going to have to endure. After all, what choice did a young lady of twenty-three have? This was her fifth Season. Her fifth year of trying to find a suitable husband. Her fifth year of being ignored by all the attractive eligible men, who flocked round the pretty girls like bees around the honeypot. Her fifth year of being pursued by men like Lord Halthorpe, who were prepared to overlook her flaws and focus instead on the substantial financial sum they would acquire as part of her marriage settlement.

While being left on the shelf was becoming increasingly likely, it was also becoming increasingly attractive. If it was a choice between being left on the shelf or marrying Lord Halthorpe, then Hazel would happily climb up on to the highest shelf and remain there for the rest of her life.

She smiled to herself, imagining what her shelf would be like. It would be a delightful refuge away from everyone who had ever accused her of not being graceful enough, pretty enough or suitably demure enough to attract a man. It would contain all the latest scientific journals and books on astronomy, chemistry and physics. And she could sit up there all day long, reading to her heart's content, without anyone passing judgement on what was or wasn't correct behaviour for a genteel young lady.

Yes, the shelf was starting to appear rather enticing.

Lord Halthorpe sent her a gap-toothed smile. 'Good to see you smiling, my dear. I take it you're enjoying this dance.'

'Mmm…' she replied, doing her best to avoid telling a lie.

'I think we might be in for some rain later,' he murmured in her ear, causing her to draw back quickly to stop his walrus moustache from tickling her cheek.

The weather. That old standby for social chit-chat. Hazel suppressed a sigh and tried to ignore the smell of brandy and cigars coming off his breath. She was at least going to have to try to make polite conversation. Especially as her mother was watching from the edge of the dance floor, concern etched on her face.

'Yes.' She forced herself to smile. 'Earlier today I noticed nimbus clouds were moving in, suggesting we're in for some rain within the next twenty-four hours, and the drop in the atmospheric pressure probably means there will be an increase in the strength of the wind as well. Perhaps not storm conditions, but definitely a weather event of some significance.'

Hazel knew she shouldn't do it. Hadn't her mother told her often enough that men do not like clever women? She had promised her that tonight she would try, really, really hard, to act suitably mindless, but oh, the tedium that came with talking about the weather, how pretty the flowers looked or how lovely the ballroom had been decorated. Just once, she wished she could have a conversation with a man that didn't cause her to feel she was being crushed under the momentous weight of boredom.

Lord Halthorpe looked back at her with a familiar expression of suppressed irritation, one that confirmed her mother's claim that showing any signs of intelligence was not the way to capture a man's heart.

'Hmm, yes,' he mumbled, his strained smile as artificially held in place as his waxed moustache. 'I say, that's a lovely ribbon you've got in your hair, my dear. Matches your blue eyes.'

Hazel replied with an equally false smile, then joined him in wincing as her feet once again crushed his toes.

Poor Lord Halthorpe had now joined the ranks of men whose feet had been reduced to a state resembling mashed potatoes under Hazel's unruly feet. Making mindless chit-chat wasn't the only social skill she had failed to master. When it came to dancing, having the proverbial two left feet would be a vast improvement on the clodhopping hooves she possessed.

'I'm so sorry, Lord Halthorpe.'

'Not at all, my dear. My fault entirely,' he said through gritted teeth.

Hazel had to give him some credit for his high pain threshold. Or was it simply that he knew how much she was worth? Perhaps the thought of getting his hands on the dowry that came with marrying the Earl of Spring-feld's plain, frumpy eldest daughter was enough to make him impervious to pain.

Hazel knew that her dowry was by far her most attractive feature for men like Lord Halthorpe. It certainly wasn't her looks he was attracted to. She was painfully aware that her nose was too long, her face too round and plump, and as for her hair, birds' nests were more orderly than the unfashionable riot of curls that passed for her crowning glory. The attributes of which she was most proud were not the ones men generally admired. She could quickly calculate mathematical problems in her head, could grasp scientific principles faster than any man she had met and was a quick learner in all academic subjects in general. But who cared about that?

Finally, the waltz came to an end. Lord Halthorpe bowed and escorted her off the crowded dance floor.

'Allow me to get you some refreshments,' he said with another bow, then limped off as quickly as he could into the milling crowd. More likely, he was heading for a private spot where he could investigate the state of his mangled feet.

Her mother joined her, smiling her encouragement. 'I think you've made a catch there, Hazel. Lord Halthorpe seems quite taken with you. I'm confident that this Season you will most definitely get a proposal.'

Hazel had to admire her mother's optimism. 'We all know what he's really taken with and it's not me. In fact, I suspect everyone in this room knows the only reason he's dancing with me is because he can think of no better way of settling the substantial debts on his estate other than marrying an heiress.'

Her mother frowned. 'Don't talk about yourself like that, Hazel. You're a highly accomplished young lady. It's just that you hide your charms and don't let men see just how lovely you really are.' She reached up and attempted to push a few escaped locks of Hazel's frizzy brown hair back into her coiffure.

'And Lord Dallington has been watching you all night as well.' Her mother's smile grew brighter. 'I suspect he'll be asking you for the next dance.'

Hazel's mood sank from dispirited to despondent. Lord Halthorpe was bad enough, but Lord Dallington was impossible. The man was sixty if he was a day and his florid complexion and bulbous nose suggested he was fonder of his brandy and port than was good for him.

Had she been reduced to this? Being sold off to an ageing dullard who could bore the birds out of the trees? Her mother smiled at someone across the room. Hazel followed the direction of that smile. When she saw the recipient the temperature of hell rose by a few degrees. Lord Dallington was smiling back at them, his large, yellowed teeth visible even at this distance, and he was making his way across the crowded room towards them.

This was asking too much. Lord Dallington was even more desperate for money than Lord Halthorpe. She had been forced to dance with him at her last ball and he had made it clear that he was very interested in asking for her hand, although she knew what he was really interested in was getting his hands on her dowry.

Her parents would never expect her to marry someone against her will, but with each passing Season they were getting increasingly worried that she might never marry and would suffer the ignominy of being an ageing unmarried woman. She didn't want to disappoint them, but Lord Dallington—that was surely asking too much. Dancing with him was bad enough, never mind marrying the man. It was time to take some evasive action.

'I'm sorry, Mother, I need the water closet. Right now.'

Ignoring her mother's wince of disapproval, she departed. Fast. She elbowed her way through the crowd of elegantly dressed men and women, to the accompaniment of *ouches* and *Well, I nevers*, proving that the dance floor wasn't the only place where people weren't safe from her crushing feet.

Taking a quick, furtive glance over her shoulder she saw that Lord Dallington was also pushing through the crowd, his eyes firmly fixed on his prize. He wasn't going to let her, and her money, get away that easily. She quickly scanned the ballroom, looking for a safe refuge from the determined Lord.

Could she hide behind one of the large potted ferns

lining the edges of the room? Would anyone notice if she secreted herself under one of the linen-covered refreshment tables? But Hazel knew herself well enough. Instead of finding refuge, she was more likely to draw attention to herself by sending the ferns crashing to the floor or plates laden with tonight's supper flying across the room as she upturned the table.

And there was no point hiding out in the ladies' retiring room. It wouldn't surprise her if Lord Dallington and Lord Halthorpe staked out the room, both reluctant to let such a valuable heiress escape.

But she had to get away. She had already suffered enough tonight. Ignoring more outraged looks and disapproving comments, she continued to elbow her way through the crowd, her desperation rising with every step. She needed to find a place to hide. And she needed to find it quickly.

Lucas Darkwood needed a mate. Not just any mate, but a mate with specific qualities: an excellent pedigree, high stamina and the potential to breed profusely and regularly.

It was the search for such a mate that had brought him to Lady Clarmont's ball. He ignored all the debutantes vying for his attention and headed straight for the card room. That was where he would find the Earl of Bromley, the man who could provide him with the mate he required.

If Lucas Darkwood had been the sort of man to admit to having faults, the only one he would have owned was a determination to succeed, no matter what. At school and university his competitive nature had seen him win every sporting event he entered and excel academically. And that determination continued when he entered the world of business and finance. He would not come second, no matter what.

And that was why he needed the Earl to provide him with a mate who would ensure he continued to be victorious.

Breeding racehorses was his latest passion. He now owned several brood mares with impeccable pedigrees, and his stallions were among the best in the country. But he wanted the Earl's horse. She had already given birth to Ascot winners, even when bred with second-rate stallions. If Lucas mated her with his stallion, he knew they would produce superior horses that would be unbeatable. Particularly as he had secured the services of the country's best trainers and jockeys.

Unfortunately, the Earl knew how determined he was and he was taking advantage of, for once, having Lucas just where he wanted him.

He entered the study, which had been converted to a card room for the ball. It provided a refuge for men who, like himself, did not care for idle chatter, or the dancing and matchmaking that was taking place in the ballroom.

Bromley was seated at the baccarat table and signalled for Lucas to join him. It seemed Lucas would have to endure a few rounds of cards while he spoke to the Earl, even though baccarat bored him. It relied too much on luck. Lucas took pleasure in winning only when it was due to his own skills, not the roll of a die.

'Have you given any consideration to my latest offer?' Lucas asked as he sat down.

The cards were dealt and Lucas placed a bet, hardly looking at his hand.

Bromley stared intently at his cards, trying to calculate whether he had a winning hand or not.

He finally placed a bet and turned to Lucas. 'You know I don't need the money, Darkwood. You'll have to come up with something better than that if you're to get my mare off me.'

Lucas swallowed down his anger. The Earl was obviously enjoying having Lucas at his mercy and taking full advantage of such a rare event. 'And what do you suggest? Name it and it's yours.'

The Earl looked up from his cards and gave what could only be described as a rapacious grin. 'Anything?'

Lucas nodded.

'That's an interesting offer,' Bromley said. 'Let's see. It would have to be something substantial to make me part with such a prize.'

Lucas could almost see the Earl's mind working, trying to come up with something that would satisfy his need to get revenge for past defeats. Lucas's reputation for winning at all costs angered many men and had made him a lot of enemies, including the Earl of Bromley. The son of a wealthy, self-made man, Lucas came from a family that owned more land and capital than many of the aristocrats seated around this card table. Since his father's death he had further increased that fortune and knew that caused resentment among people who thought that the aristocracy were the only ones entitled to wealth and the power and privilege that came with it.

The Earl was not going to miss the opportunity to try to take Lucas down, to remind him that he did not possess a title and was not *one of them*, but whatever scheme he came up with, Lucas was confident he would come out triumphant. Didn't he always?

While Bromley was considering how he could get the better of Lucas, the door to the card room flew open and a somewhat dishevelled young woman burst in and flattened herself against the wall behind the door. Every head in the room turned in her direction, including the Earl's, and a few titters were heard.

The young woman registered the laughter, looked around the room and her already flushed cheeks turned a brighter shade of red. Her blue eyes behind her round tortoiseshell glasses darted around the room in what appeared to be desperation. Several strands of brown hair had escaped from her ornate hairstyle and were standing up from her head at somewhat comical angles.

She had every appearance of a woman being chased by a marauding band of ruffians. But Lady Clarmont was hardly likely to have invited a gang of thieves and vagabonds to her ball. She was reluctant enough to even invite Lucas, but had no choice. The Clarmonts saw themselves as being at the very pinnacle of society. Lady Clarmont often boasted of how she had been granted the honour of dining with Queen Victoria herself on numerous occasions. Despite that lofty position, they weren't the only aristocratic family present in debt to Lucas. And as their lack of solvency and the extent of their debts were something they would prefer to be kept secret, they were forced to put aside their snobbery against people without a pedigree and accept Lucas into their circle.

'I'm sorry, I was just…' The young woman took a peek out of the door, emitted a loud gasp and flew across the room, out of the French doors and on to the terrace. But not before dislodging an aspidistra plant on the way and sending it, along with the porcelain pot, crashing to the floor. 'I'm sorry' was heard from the terrace.

The titters turned into loud laughter, with everyone taking delight in their ridicule of the young woman's unusual behaviour. Everyone, that is, except Lucas.

Lord Dallington entered the room and looked around. It was now obvious why the young woman was in such a hurry to escape. Fighting off a band of ruffians would be preferable to spending time with that buffoon.

'Lost something, have you, Dallington?' one smirking male guest enquired, to the accompaniment of giggles from a group of ladies in the card room.

The old codger looked around a few times. 'Has anyone seen Hazel Springfeld? She's promised me the next dance.'

'I believe she was seen heading down the hall a few minutes ago,' Lucas said before anyone else could answer. 'If you hurry, you might catch her.'

'Thank you, Darkwood. I wouldn't like that lovely dowry—I mean, that lovely young lady to get away. She's quite the cash cow.' He winked, not registering Lucas's look of disgust, then headed off down the hall.

Once again, the room exploded with laughter and loud chatter at the young lady's expense.

'I think that's one–nil to the heiress.' Lord Bromley laughed.

'I suppose you have to feel sorry for her, the poor thing,' a woman seated at the table added, smiling at Lucas, her voice containing none of the sympathy her words suggested.

Lucas ignored the young woman and looked over his shoulder towards the French doors.

'So, who is she?'

'She's the eldest daughter of the Earl of Springfeld,' Bromley said, signalling for another card. 'The younger daughter is reputed to be a beauty, but that one…' Bromley tilted his cards in the direction of the terrace and barked out a laugh. 'What can one say? But she's worth a pretty penny so she's in much more demand than her looks certainly deserve, at least from men like Dallington who need her money. I've also heard she's a bit of a bluestocking.' Bromley gave a false shudder which caused the young lady to giggle again.

'And lord preserve any man who dances with her,' Bromley continued. 'He'd better come wearing workman's boots if he wants his feet to survive the ordeal.'

Everyone at the table, except Lucas, joined in on the laughter. The casual cruelty of these people should not surprise him. He knew it grew out of boredom and a sense of privilege that had never been challenged, but it still disgusted him and was one of the reasons he chose to avoid such social occasions. But unfortunately, until he had secured his mare, he was going to have to endure their company a bit longer.

'I've heard her mother has hired a string of tutors to try to turn that particularly ugly duckling into a swan, but to no effect.' Bromley laughed again and signalled to the dealer that he wanted more cards.

'If I was a gambling man, which I am,' Bromley looked around the table to ensure everyone got his joke, 'I wouldn't put my money on any tutor being able to improve that ageing duck before it's too late. And if she runs away from men who actually want to court her, then there's not much chance of her bagging a husband this Season, that's for sure.'

Lucas drew in a deep breath and exhaled slowly. Bromley was almost as much an imbecile as Lord Dallington. 'If she's being chased by the likes of Dallington, then one can hardly blame the young lady for making no effort to attract his attentions,' he said, failing to keep the disdain out of his voice. 'If anything, it shows that she is eminently sensible for making no effort and should be admired, not disparaged.'

'Oh, and I suppose if it was the likes of you after her, then the ugly duck would suddenly transform herself into a beauty, full of charm and grace.' Bromley looked around the table so the other men could share his joke.

Lucas shrugged. It hardly mattered as he was unlikely to be chasing after Lady Hazel or any other young woman in search of a husband. He was after a horse, not a wife. He was just as determined to gain one as he was to avoid acquiring the other.

Bromley stopped laughing and stared at Lucas. 'I dare you.'

'You dare me to do what?' This conversation was becoming increasingly irritating.

'I dare you to put your money where your mouth is. If you can transform that…' he pointed his cards at the terrace '…by the end of the Season into something that can capture a man's attention, and not just ones like Dallington who are after her dowry, I'll make you a gift of that brood mare you so desperately want.'

'Don't be ridiculous,' Lucas shot back.

'What, are you not up to the challenge?' Bromley smirked at him. 'You said for me to just name my price. Well, I've named it. If you think it's too hard for you, then it looks as though you won't be getting my horse.'

Bromley's smirk became even more malicious as the other men broke into raucous laughter, causing Lucas to grind his teeth in anger. He hated to see a woman mocked in such a manner. No one deserved to be on the receiving end of such ridicule, nor did they deserve to be the subject of such an offensive challenge.

'Take it or leave it, Darkwood, it's the only offer I'm prepared to make,' the Earl said, encouraged by the laughing men. 'If, by the end of the Season at least, one man has expressed his regard for the girl because he's smitten with her and cares not a fig for her money, then you can have my mare.'

Lucas glared at him, hardly able to believe that the Earl would stoop so low as to make sport of a young lady in this offensive manner.

'What's the problem, Darkwood? Is it that conscience

of yours that's bothering you? Well, why should it? If you succeed, the young lady will have a beau. Something she's unlikely to get on her own. You'll be doing her a favour. And you'll win my mare.'

Lucas looked over towards the French doors. It was an outrageous proposal, but he had to admit the Earl had a point. Would it actually harm the young lady if he helped her find a suitable beau and saved her from men like Dallington?

'I see I've piqued your interest.' Bromley laughed. 'But there has to be a penalty if you lose, something of equal value to my mare.' He thought for a moment, then rubbed his hands together with barely contained excitement. 'If she doesn't manage to attract a genuine beau, then you'll marry the girl yourself.'

The volume of the laughter increased and included much back slapping from the assembled men. Lucas looked around the table at their self-satisfied faces, flushed with amusement and port. Their cruelty disgusted him. But why should he be surprised? He had known many of these men since school days. They had enjoyed taunting younger and weaker students back then and they obviously hadn't changed one iota. As a boy with no title he, too, had been the subject of cruel taunts. Many had even tried to use violence to put the upstart in his place, something they quickly came to regret.

His sympathy lay entirely with Hazel Springfeld. No one deserved to be mocked the way these men were mocking her. It would serve them right if he did transform her into a desirable young woman, one they admired rather than scorned. But were the stakes too high? If he lost, he would have to marry the girl and one thing he most definitely did not want to do was marry anyone, ever.

But then Lucas never lost to anyone, ever.

'You're on,' he said, reaching over the table and shaking the hand of the surprised Bromley.

Chapter Two

'Do you require some assistance?'

A deep, masculine voice caused Hazel to look towards the doorway. And there before her was a sight that caused the air to leave her lungs, her heart to do something she knew was physiologically impossible—to stop beating inside her chest—and for her mouth to drop open.

Standing in the doorway, lit from behind by the twinkling chandeliers, was a vision. One that had presumably descended from on high. Hazel gazed up at him. At five foot eleven, most men were shorter than her, but at several inches over six feet this was a man she could definitely look up to.

Look up to and admire. She closed her mouth and took in his beautiful face. With olive skin, striking grey eyes and hair so black it almost appeared blue in the subdued light, he was undeniably the most handsome man she had ever seen. And this godlike creature, with his strong, clean-shaven jawline and lovely, sculptured lips was staring straight at her, waiting for her answer.

Hazel closed her mouth, which had somehow once again fallen open, and swallowed. Her heart, which had improbably stopped beating, now resumed, thumping loud and clear against the wall of her chest. 'Um, no, I'm fine, thank you,' she stammered.

She expected that to be enough to cause this impossibly handsome stranger to depart and leave her alone, because men like him most certainly did not pay any attention to girls like her. But he didn't leave. Instead he stepped out on to the terrace to join her.

'I get the impression you're hiding from Lord Dallington, which I must say makes you a very sensible young lady. But you won't be able to hide from him all night. When it comes to chasing down his quarry, whether it's foxes, hares or young women, Dallington is relentless.'

Hazel suddenly remembered why she was hiding, something she had momentarily forgotten, distracted by the sight of Mr Handsome. She exhaled loudly and her shoulders slumped.

Eventually she was going to have to return to the ballroom. Eventually she was going to have to endure being cornered by that insufferable bore. And there was a risk that tonight was the night when he would ask for her hand. Hazel shivered, as if the temperature of the late-summer night air had suddenly plunged to that of midwinter. It was a horror she was going to have to eventually face, but one that Hazel was determined to delay for as long as possible.

'You could continue to hide out here for the rest of the ball,' the handsome stranger continued, looking upwards. 'But by the look of that sky it's going to rain soon.'

Hazel also looked up and could see that the nimbus clouds had moved in and neither the stars nor the full moon were now visible. He was right about that as well. Rain was all but inevitable. But she would much rather take a drenching than dance with Lord Dallington.

'Or I can escort you back into the ballroom for the next dance and I promise I will do my best to protect you from the attentions of the relentless lord.'

Hazel lowered her head from staring at the sky, unsure whether she had heard him correctly. Had he just offered to dance with her? Why on earth would he do that? Why would a man who looked like him, who was as suave as him, who could have any woman he wanted, offer to dance with her? It made no logical sense.

Slowly she turned to face him, cautiously trying to assess what he was up to.

Was he another impoverished aristocrat who had heard about her exceedingly generous marriage settlement?

His well-tailored evening suit, which she had to admit displayed his broad shoulders, slim waist and long legs to perfection, appeared new. Although that really meant nothing. The aristocracy were notorious for not paying their tailor's bills, so despite his immaculate appearance he could still be poor.

But even if he was penniless, with looks like his, there must be many other heiresses who would gladly throw their inheritance in his handsome direction.

Or was he a cruel man who wanted to have some fun

at her expense? His face did not appear cruel. Anything but. It was a strong face, disconcerting in its dazzling good looks, but his full lips did not contain that hint of a smirk that usually signalled a man was using her for his malicious amusement.

'Well? Shall we?' He reached out his hand towards her.

She stared at the proffered hand. There was still no logical reason why this man would ask her to dance. It made no sense. A few raindrops fell, splashing on the tiled floor of the terrace, signalling that the weather was about to change, and they were about to be caught out in the deluge. She could not remain hiding on the terrace for much longer. It seemed she had no choice but to accept his offer.

Tentatively, she placed her hand in his, as if approaching an open flame and in danger of getting singed.

'So, before we take to the floor, let me introduce myself. I'm Lucas Darkwood.'

Lucas Darkwood.

This was getting more and more illogical. Even she had heard of Lucas Darkwood. The fire on her cheeks grew more intense as she remembered overheard comments about Lucas Darkwood. He was reputed to be a notorious womaniser, with countless mistresses, including ones from some of the highest ranks of society.

He was also known to be one of the wealthiest men in England, with a multitude of business interests in rail and shipping, vast estates in several counties, and a palatial manor house in Kent which his father had bought from a bankrupt aristocrat.

Well, at least that answered one question. He most definitely did not need her money. But as for the most important question, Hazel still did not have an answer. Why would a man who was reputed to have many other women in his life want to dance with someone like her?

His black eyebrows rose in question and Hazel remembered her manners. 'And I'm Lady Hazel Springfeld. Pleased to make your acquaintance.'

His hand closed over hers and he bowed. A strange quivering sensation overcame her, starting where his hand was touching hers, rippling up her arm and lodging itself in her fluttering chest.

'Well, Lady Hazel Springfeld, shall we return to the ballroom before the rain gets any heavier?'

As if in a daze Hazel allowed him to lead her off the terrace and into the card room. Several of the men stopped what they were doing and stared at them, avidly watching their progress as they walked through the room. A group of women standing near the door smiled at Mr Darkwood, then smirked at Hazel and giggled behind their hands. They were doubtlessly thinking exactly what Hazel was—what was a man like Lucas Darkwood doing with a woman like Hazel Springfeld?

They reached the crowded ballroom and he led her out on to the dance floor. Then she woke from her dazed state and found herself in the middle of a nightmare. What on earth was she doing? Did she really want to massacre this poor man's feet? Did she really want to humiliate him, not to mention herself yet again, by her clumsy behaviour? Did she really want to make a fool of herself in front of *him*?

Fear making her immobile, she froze on the spot.

He took hold of her hands as if she were a puppet and he the puppetmaster, placed one hand on his shoulder and kept hold of the other. Hazel was so pleased she was wearing gloves. How would she have ever coped if skin had been touching skin? It was bad enough that he was so close to her. So close she could feel the warmth radiating from his body. As for her own body temperature, that was starting to reach a dangerous level and she was sure her cheeks had turned an unflattering shade of deep crimson.

He took a step forward. She didn't move. He almost crashed into her. Only his quick action of placing his hands on the small of her back stopped them from tumbling to the ground.

This was a disaster. He must be able to see that. He must realise he had made a mistake, a mistake that could only be rectified by leading her back off the dance floor.

But that wasn't what he did. Instead he once again took her hands, placed one on his shoulder and kept hold of the other.

'Relax, Lady Hazel. This is just a dance.'

Just a dance.

That was easy for him to say. For her it was a form of torture that should be reserved for the seventh level of hell.

'I am relaxed,' she said, aiming for a carefree laugh that came out sounding strangled and almost hysterical.

'Look at your hands. I don't think that is what relaxed looks like.'

She cast a glance in the direction of the hand on his shoulder, which had somehow managed to grip the fabric of his black evening jacket and twist it into a knot, as if she was a drowning woman clasping at the last available straw. Then her gaze moved to the hand clasping his. She was gripping him so tightly his long fingers were bunched up into a tangled pile. She must be just about crushing the poor man's hand, although his face showed no sign of pain. It seemed his pain threshold was even higher than Lord Halthorpe's. That was some consolation—at least when she crushed his feet, he'd be able to endure the agony.

'Take a few slow breaths.' His voice was soothing—dare she think it, seductive. No, she would not dare to think that.

'Block out everything else from your mind. Just concentrate on the music and let it flow over you. Pretend no one is watching. There's just you and the music, no one else. Then allow yourself to move to it. I'll lead you. You don't have to do anything, just surrender yourself to the music and to me.'

He drew in a deep breath and exhaled slowly.

'Yes, all right,' she squeaked, trying to ignore the effect of his voice on her nervous system at the thought of actually doing what he suggested, surrendering herself to him.

'Do it,' he commanded and once again took a deep breath in demonstration.

She followed his example and they breathed together, in and out, deeply and slowly.

'Now listen to the band and let the music wash over you.'

Her eyes closed, she listened to the music and continued to draw in long, slow breaths.

Suddenly they were moving round the ballroom. He was right. She was relaxed and all she heard was the music as he glided her across the parquet floor. Hazel allowed herself to smile and opened her eyes. This actually felt good. She was actually dancing like a woman who knew what she was doing.

He pulled her in slightly closer. His hand moved further round her waist. A small gasp escaped when his chest touched hers. He was so close her breasts were skimming against his jacket.

What was happening? Why was he doing this? Why was she reacting like this? Her smile quivered. The sound of the band faded, drowned out by her pounding heartbeat. She registered the hardness of his body against her own, that lovely scent of him, all warm masculinity. She forgot to focus on the music, forgot to breathe and her feet forgot what they were supposed to be doing.

The feeling of his toes being crushed under her feet also crushed any illusion she might have had that she knew how to dance and bought her crashing back to reality. She was not a graceful woman being whirled round the dance floor by a handsome suitor. She was plain, clumsy old Hazel Springfeld, doing what she did best, reducing a man's feet to mashed potatoes.

'I'm so sorry,' she blurted out and took a quick step away from him, desperate to escape this embarrassing situation. Pulling him with her, she unbalanced them both. Her feet twisted underneath her. In desperation, she tried to right herself, but to her horror she was falling, backwards, towards the floor. This was worse than simply crushing a man's feet. She was going to make a complete spectacle of herself and drag him down with her.

A strong arm surrounded her waist, breaking her fall. She froze, waiting for him to lift her back to her feet. Suspended in mid-air, leaning back over his arm, she continued to wait, mere inches from total humiliation, completely at his mercy. If he let her go, she would be sent sprawling across the dance floor. She looked up at him, her eyes pleading with him to show her some mercy. She might be a buffoon with the social graces of a hippopotamus, but even *she* did not deserve to be humiliated in this way, even if it was all her own clumsy fault.

He looked down into her eyes. For a moment she almost forgot about her precarious position. The noise of the ballroom faded. The thought of all those laughing people left her mind. All she could think about was those intense, smoky grey eyes gazing down at her, their mesmerising power driving out all other thoughts.

'I think we've just invented a dance move,' he said, still holding her over his arm, his eyes still holding her captive. 'By next Season I'm sure everyone will be doing the backwards dip,' he added as he lifted her to her feet.

Too surprised to think, she once again surrendered to his lead and they continued to whirl around the floor, as if her ungainliness had indeed been a deliberate dance step.

How could someone be so confident, so sophisticated, so uncaring about what others thought? Hazel wished she had just a modicum of his self-assurance. But then, it must be easy to be so confident when you're the best-looking man in the room.

The tune ended and for once Hazel was disappointed a dance was over. He escorted her off the dance floor and her pleasure instantly died when she spotted Lord Dallington heading her way, across the crowded ballroom.

Hazel looked around, scanning the room for the nearest means of escape.

'Don't worry, Lady Hazel, I'll deal with the persistent Lord.' He placed his hand gently on her arm. 'Just go along with whatever I say.'

Too confused by the hand touching her, she remained glued to the spot as Lord Dallington bustled up to them, nodded to Mr Darkwood and then smiled at Hazel, his yellowed teeth causing her to cringe.

'Lady Hazel, I believe you promised me the next dance,' Dallington said, bowing low.

Hazel had made no such promise and she was sure that Lord Dallington knew it. He extended his arm and Hazel looked desperately at the doorway. If she started running now would she be able to make it out of the ballroom before he caught up with her? And where was she going to hide now that the rain had started? The terrace was out of the question.

'You must be mistaken,' Mr Darkwood said, taking a step towards Lord Dallington, causing him to take a quick step backwards. 'Lady Hazel has promised every remaining dance to me.'

'I have?' Hazel asked. He sent her a quick wink, causing Hazel to gulp. 'Oh, yes, that's right, Lord Dallington, I'm afraid I have.'

'What? Every dance? That's most improper.' He glared at Mr Darkwood. 'That would suggest that the two of you were courting.'

Lord Dallington's outraged expression suggested that, like Hazel, he thought such a thing was an absurd idea and she, too, was curious to know what Mr Darkwood was up to.

They both looked at Mr Darkwood. He made no reply.

'So, what are your intentions towards Lady Hazel?' Lord Dallington said, managing to combine incredulousness with annoyance. 'Are you courting her? Is that what you're saying?'

Hazel didn't particularly like being discussed as if she wasn't present, but she, too, wanted to know what Mr Darkwood's intentions were and she waited expectantly for his answer.

He looked down his nose at the irritated Earl. 'You could say that, if you choose to.' He took Hazel's hand and placed it on his arm. 'Now if you'll excuse us, Lord Dallington, the band is about to start again. Shall we, Lady Hazel?'

He really was going to dance with her again. In a state of confusion, she stumbled forward as he led her back on to the dance floor. He had given Lord Dallington a decidedly ambiguous answer, one that also went no way towards answering Hazel's question—what was Mr Darkwood up to?

Chapter Three

It was a risky strategy, but a challenge of this magnitude demanded risk taking. Lucas was determined to win this bet. He *had* to win this bet—too much was at stake. And the best way he could do that was to keep Lady Hazel to himself for as long as it took to transform her into the sort of woman that any man would want. And that was not going to happen while she was being relentlessly pursued by men like Lord Dallington—that was simply turning her into a laughing stock. Nor would other men see her as a desirable catch if she spent the ball running away like a frightened rabbit desperately searching for a bolthole.

He looked down at the woman on his arm. She sent him a tentative smile. He hoped that smile wasn't because of what he had just said to Lord Dallington. Perhaps he should not have given Dallington the impression that they were courting. But if she was harbouring that misconception, if she did think that he had any intentions of marrying her, he was sure that delusion would disappear once he found her a suitable beau, a man who was right for her, one who she could happily spend her life with.

Not that acting as a matchmaker was part of the conditions of his bet. All he had to do was ensure that Lady Hazel attracted the attentions of a man, any man, as long as it was one not after her dowry. Nowhere did it stipulate the man had to be suitable. But to foist her off on to just anyone would be unfair. She had done nothing wrong and she was obviously a nice young lady, if a little awkward and self-conscious. She deserved to be treated with respect. So, drawing the attentions of someone suitable, someone she was equally attracted to, would be an extra stipulation he would add as part of winning this wager.

'So, shall we take our places for the quadrille?'

She stopped walking. Her body went rigid, as if he had asked her if she'd like to enter the gladiatorial arena and wrestle with a few lions.

It seemed turning Lady Hazel into a woman who attracted a man's attention for the right reasons was going to take some time. If he was going to help her become a better marriage prospect, the first thing he was going to have to do was get her to relax when she was on the dance floor and see dancing as something to enjoy, not a punishment to be endured.

At the moment, with her rigid body, furrowed brow and tightly pinched lips, she did not look like a woman about to partake in something that was fun, but one that demanded the utmost concentration if one was to survive the harrowing ordeal.

'Remember, Lady Hazel, breathe slowly and deeply,' he said with a voice gentle enough to soothe a skittish colt. 'Forget about everything and everyone else and lose yourself in the music.'

She nodded in agreement, her face still tight with concentration.

'Before we join the others, perhaps we should start by taking some deep breaths.'

He drew in his breath in demonstration and she followed his example. Slowly her expression lost its tension and her rigid body became less stiff. She drew in another deep breath and smiled at him. It was no longer a tentative smile, but a genuine, warm, friendly smile. A lovely smile that transformed her face. His gaze lingered on her smiling lips. He hadn't noticed before, but she really did have beautiful lips, plump, soft rosebuds in an inviting shade of pink. For a moment he imagined kissing those lips, imagined her kissing him back.

She bit the edge of her bottom lip and he realised he was staring in an improper manner. This would not do. It was unacceptable to look at any innocent young lady in such a suggestive manner and even more so when it came to Lady Hazel Springfeld, a respectable young lady who was as far removed from the type of woman he usually associated with as it was possible to get. And, following that conversation with Lord Dallington, it was most certainly both improper and unwise to be thinking about kissing Lady Hazel. He did not want to give her the wrong impression. If she really did think he was courting her, this complicated situation could become even more convoluted, to say the least. Once he had won his bet it would be essential that he was able to extricate himself from Lady Hazel as smoothly as possible without causing her any harm.

He looked around the room to find a suitable couple with whom to dance the quadrille, determined to put any thoughts of Lady Hazel's lips out of his mind. He spotted the Earl and Countess of Winfield. The Countess was a motherly type who would not object to Lady Hazel's somewhat unusual dancing manner and the Earl wouldn't dare object to his feet being stood on, not if upsetting Lady Hazel would result in the Earl suffering an even greater assault in the form of his wife's reprimand.

He took her arm and led her across the dance floor to join the older couple.

'I haven't thanked you for saving me from Lord Dallington,' she said as they took their places. 'That really was kind of you.'

'Please don't mention it,' he said, looking straight ahead to ensure he did not repeat his earlier improper behaviour.

'So, are you going to tell me why you did that?' She waved her hand back to the side of the dance floor where the discussion with Lord Dallington had taken place. 'As I said, it was very kind of you to help me out, but I can't help but wonder why?'

Lucas continued staring across to the far side of the room, guilt this time preventing him from looking at Lady Hazel. He could not tell her the truth. She was sure to be offended if she knew she was the subject of a wager.

'Well?' she asked, an impatient note coming into her voice.

He turned to look down at her and she was once again wearing that pinched expression.

'Lord Dallington is a terrible old buffer. No woman deserves to be stuck with a grasping old buffoon like him. You could do much better than him, Lady Hazel.' It was the truth, even if it wasn't the entire truth.

She shrugged one shoulder. 'Perhaps I don't want to do any better. Perhaps I don't want to marry at all.'

Lucas gazed into her big blue eyes, staring defiantly up at him behind her tortoiseshell glasses. He could detect no coquettishness in her reply, but he hoped her words were mere pretence. If it was true that she had no intention of marrying, it would make this challenge even more difficult. How was she going to attract a beau if she was not in pursuit of a husband?

'But doesn't every woman wish to be married?' he asked, hoping she would give him a shy smile and admit that it was so.

'Not always. Not when the sacrifice is too high,' she stated emphatically. 'I don't want to have to spend my life stuck on some country estate with only an endless round of balls and tea parties to amuse me. I'd be bored senseless.'

This was not good. That was exactly the life that most aristocratic men would offer their future wife. He could only hope she was just saying that because, at the moment, it was a prospect that was eluding her and she was putting on a brave face.

'What sort of life would you like then?'

That lovely smile returned and her big blue eyes sparkled. 'What I'd really like to do is go to university and study science.'

Lucas stifled a groan. Lord Bromley was right. She was a bluestocking. That was not a quality that members of the aristocracy generally looked for in a wife.

'Women are going to university now, you know,' she continued with growing enthusiasm. 'They can't graduate, but some have been allowed to attend lectures. That's what I'd love to do.' She gripped his arm and smiled wistfully. 'We're living in such a time of change, one where scientific discoveries are being made all the time. It would be so wonderful to be part of it.'

Lucas admired her enthusiasm, but it was not the sort of enthusiasm that would find her a husband. Although if she looked the way she was looking now it would certainly help. Her eyes were twinkling with pleasure, her cheeks had turned a pretty shade of pink and she was once again smiling that warm, inviting smile.

The grip on his arm loosened and she huffed out an exasperated breath. 'But that's just a dream. You're right, I am expected to marry and there's every likelihood it will be to some man like Lord Dallington who scorns study.'

'Well, not necessarily. There must be some men who are interested in such things.'

She laughed, a laugh that was more annoyed than amused. 'Can you point to one man in this room who would tolerate a wife who wanted to devote her time to further education? Can you point out one man who would not dismiss science and the pursuit of knowledge as a complete bore? I've yet to meet any man at one of these society events who is the slightest bit interested in chemistry or astronomy or physics. All any of them want to talk about is the weather, the latest gossip, shooting, hunting and fishing, and the next ball they plan to attend.'

Lucas looked around the room. She was, unfortunately, right. And that presented an enormous problem for him. How was he going to get any of these men to see her as a potential bride for any reason other than her money when she was such a determined bluestocking?

Lord Bromley had certainly known what he was doing when he had made this bet. Lucas was expected to somehow transform a bluestocking, who couldn't dance, abhorred gossip and had an aversion to small talk, into a coquette who could glide across the floor, flirt and gossip along with the most accomplished women and attract the attention of men who cared nothing of her dowry. Somehow, he was going to have to change her passion for education and scientific discoveries into a passion for a man, marriage and a conventional life to a conventional man. It looked as though winning his brood mare was becoming increasingly elusive, but then, he had never been one to back down from a challenge, no matter how insurmountable.

The band began to play and they moved forward for the first set of the quadrille, which thankfully was executed without Lady Hazel causing any mayhem, although she did stride towards the other two partners with her arms swinging, as if she was setting out on a

brisk cross-country walk rather than moving elegantly
to the music.

He twirled her around and she headed off towards
the Earl of Winfield. Lucas cringed when she all but
collided into him, but the Earl managed to save the
situation, halt her progress and twirl her around so
she could set off in the opposite direction, albeit in a
manner that didn't quite conform to the precise steps
of the dance.

Lady Hazel was also apparently aware that the steps
were not as they should be. She stared down at her feet
as she marched towards him, as if mentally giving them
a talking to and telling them to behave.

He took her hand and spun her gently in a circle.
'Remember, breathe, relax, enjoy the music and dance
as if no one is looking at you.'

She gave him a timorous smile, then looked back
down at her feet.

'And don't look down. You want to be able to see
where you're going.' He placed his hand gently under
her chin and tipped it up. His finger lingered a moment
longer than was essential, stroking the soft skin, and he
stopped moving. Now he seemed to be the one who was
forgetting the precise steps of the quadrille.

They twirled again and he sent her on her way back
towards the Earl. This time she followed his instructions and kept her head high. She also seemed to be listening to the music and was almost moving in time to
the rhythm. Hopefully, she would get through the entire set without tripping, falling or colliding with any-

one, and none of the men would be forced to suppress a wince of pain.

After executing a perfect twirl, she returned to his side and smiled up at him, giving every impression of a woman who was enjoying herself, or at least relieved that nothing had yet gone wrong.

The music came to an end, and they simultaneously exhaled their held breaths. It seemed neither of them were following the simple instruction to breathe, but for him, with so much riding on transforming Lady Hazel into a desirable young woman, was there any surprise that he would be experiencing some anxiety?

'You still haven't told me why you left Lord Dallington with the impression that we are courting,' she said as he took her arm to lead her off the floor.

He shook his head. 'I believe I have already given you an explanation.'

'No, you haven't. Not really. There are lots of other things you could have said to discourage him, without giving him the impression that we are courting.'

He paused, ostensibly to let another couple get past them on the busy dance floor, but really to try to think of an answer that would not upset her, one that would not reveal his secret and one that would certainly not cause her to think they were in fact courting, or, heaven forbid, that he saw her as a potential marriage partner.

He struggled to find an answer and had to admit she was right. Why on earth did he choose to let Dallington think they were courting? It made no real sense.

'Well, it worked, didn't it?' he finally said. 'I doubt

if you'll have to run and hide from Lord Dallington again.'

That settled, he took a step forward, but she didn't move.

'That's not the point,' she said. 'Why make him think that we're courting? Don't get me wrong, I know that you didn't mean it. And you don't need to worry—even if Lord Dallington told anyone what you said, no one is going to believe that you would really want to court me. So, you're quite safe. I just want to know why you said it.'

He shook his head. That was definitely something that had to change. She could not think of herself in such derogatory terms. 'I could say the same thing. No one would believe that a woman as intelligent as you would want to be courted by a man like me. You'd be far too sensible.'

She rolled her eyes, showing him she did not believe a word he said. Lucas could only hope that what he was saying was the truth, that she was indeed a woman far too sensible to even consider him as a potential marriage partner. If she wasn't as sensible as he assumed, then he had made a very big mistake taking on this bet. He just hoped it would not be something he would come to regret.

Chapter Four

Something was going on, but what it was, Hazel had no idea. There had to be a reason why Lucas Darkwood was paying her so much attention. He did not appear to have noticed, but the entire time they had been on the dance floor, women had been looking in their direction. Hazel could almost read their minds. They were all thinking the same thing as her—what was a man like him doing dancing with a woman like her?

Why wasn't he dancing with one of those beautiful young debutantes? Why would he be spending so much time with her when all those other women were trying to attract his attention? And, most curiously of all, why had he given Lord Dallington the impression that they were courting? That was a question he seemed to be avoiding answering.

Hazel knew she didn't possess any of the skills that a young lady was expected to have, but there was one thing that she did have—an enquiring mind. When presented with a seemingly unsolvable question, she took delight in exploring it and coming up with an answer, and she was determined to get to the bottom of the question that was Mr Darkwood.

In the meantime, there was no harm in her enjoying herself. Something that had never happened at a ball before, and she had attended, and endured, so many over the last five Seasons that she had lost count.

Dancing with him had been lovely. Just lovely. She had almost felt elegant when he had whirled her around and held her close, and that was such a wonderful experience, who really cared what his reasons were. For now, she would just enjoy herself and leave the conundrum of what he was up to for a later time.

She looked up at him and smiled. He nodded, but did not smile back, but Hazel was not surprised. She had not seen him smile once since he first introduced himself. He was polite. He was charming but so serious, and there was something behind those grey eyes that raised further questions in her mind. Like a darkening grey sky just before a storm, there was the hint of intensity to them, such depths, one might almost say suffering. What could have happened to this man to make him so sombre? He had everything a man should want— money, good looks, power—and he could presumably have any woman he desired. Wouldn't that be enough to make most men exceedingly happy?

But she would not think of that either, not now. Instead, she would just enjoy the moment. And she *was* actually enjoying herself. She was no longer in hell. Purgatory, perhaps. After all, being held in Mr Darkwood's arms was somewhat disconcerting, particularly as it was causing some rather disturbing, rather unfamiliar reactions. All that fluttering and throbbing going on in various parts of her body were definitely a new experience. Ones she chose not to think too deeply about, not now at least. That, too, she would save for analysis at a later time.

Despite her odd reactions, despite her confusion, being with Mr Darkwood was infinitely better than the hell of dancing with Lord Dallington or Lord Halthorpe. She shuddered at the thought of how this evening might have ended—with a proposal from one of those frightful old men. Yes, despite her confusion, this was infinitely better.

'Are you cold, Lady Hazel?' Mr Darkwood asked. 'Would you like me to get your shawl?'

'No, no, I'm perfectly comfortable.'

She looked up at him again and smiled. He looked down at her and held her gaze and those strange feelings in her body were reactivated. Ones that most definitely could not be described as comfortable. She swallowed and told her body to behave itself. Quite obviously she was attracted to this man—how could she not be?—but she knew the feeling would not be mutual. He wouldn't be going all mushy inside every time she looked at him.

And thank goodness for that. She would hate to think how her tormented body would behave if he really was attracted to her. Her poor heart was taking enough of a pounding as it was, and as for her cheeks, they wouldn't stop bursting into flame every time he looked at her. Not to mention what was happening in parts of her body that should not be mentioned or even thought about in polite society. If he were to look at her with real affection, she was sure she would either spontaneously burst into flames in the centre of the dance floor or melt in a puddle at his feet.

'In fact, I'm definitely not cold,' Hazel said, rapidly fanning her burning cheeks. 'It's rather warm in here, don't you think?'

'Would you like some refreshments to cool down?'

She nodded her head in gratitude. She definitely needed to cool down. 'That would be lovely, thank you.'

He nodded and moved through the crowd towards the supper table set up in the corner. Unlike Hazel, who'd had to elbow her way through the jostling guests when trying to escape Lord Dallington, the crowd parted before Mr Darkwood, like the miracle of the Red Sea parting before Moses.

Hazel sighed. He really was quite miraculous. Then she mentally castigated herself. Surely that thought was going too far and was possibly even blasphemous. She was turning into some sort of moonstruck young woman, swooning over a handsome man. And that just simply was not her. She was known as the sensible one of the three Springfeld sisters. Plus, he wasn't interested in her in *that* way. So she had to try to at least act like a mature woman of twenty-three and not a silly debutante at her first ball, especially as there were more dances left on the card and he had promised to dance every one of them with her.

The crowd closed up behind him and he disappeared from view. Her smile faded. Quite possibly, that would be the last she would see of him.

Many other men in the past had used the excuse of getting refreshments to escape from Hazel Springfeld and her notoriously injurious feet.

One of those pretty young debutantes who had been sending him coquettish smiles above her fluttering fan would capture his attention and that would be that. Oh, well, it had been nice while it lasted, Hazel consoled herself.

But, no. The crowd parted again and there he was, striding towards her like a magnificent vision, two glasses of punch in his hands. It seemed another miracle had occurred.

He handed her the drink and Hazel made sure not to touch his hand as he passed it to her. There'd been enough disconcerting physical contact tonight already.

She gripped the glass of punch with gratitude, desperate for a cool drink. The crowded room, with its candles burning in the numerous chandeliers and in the sconces lining the walls, was very warm and she had built up quite a thirst during the dances.

Although that was not the real reason for Hazel's raised temperature. She knew her cheeks were now an unfashionable shade of deep red and her body was decidedly hot more as a result of the man standing beside her than the effect of the room or the dancing.

She forced herself not to gulp down the drink and tried to take more ladylike sips, the way the other women in the room were doing.

Once again, Hazel smiled her gratitude at him for all that he had done for her this evening. He had been kindness itself from the moment they had met. He had rescued her from Lord Dallington, then brought her in from the terrace before she got a soaking from the rain and had kindly danced with her. Whatever his reasons for doing so, it would be selfish to expect more from him. It was time for Hazel to return the favour. Rather than question his motives, the kinder thing to do would be to reluctantly set him free.

'You don't have to actually dance with me for the rest of the evening,' she said. 'You've succeeded in saving me from Lord Dallington. I saw him leave while we were dancing the quadrille and Lord Halthorpe seems to have disappeared as well. So I'm quite safe. But thank you so much for all that you've done.'

He took another sip of his drink and looked at her over the glass. 'Do you not want to dance with me again?'

Of course I do. Dancing with you has made this the most wonderful, if disconcerting, night of my life.

'I'm just wondering what others might think. I wouldn't want to cause tongues to start wagging about us.' She looked around the room as if in concern. As if tongues would ever wag about Hazel Springfeld and a man. Laugh, yes. Wag, never.

'And you worry about such things?'

Hazel had not worried before. Had never had cause to worry. The only time people paid her any attention was when they were making mocking comments about her lack of grace and beauty. And as for setting tongues wagging, well, she was never expected to be the subject of any gossip because she was never expected to have the opportunity to be caught up in a scandal.

She lifted one shoulder, unsure how to answer. 'It's just, you know, people do talk.'

'Personally, I've never cared whether people talk about me or not, but if it does worry you, perhaps I shouldn't monopolise all your attention.'

Oh, monopolise me as much as you want.

Hazel sent him what she hoped would pass as a co-quettish smile, but suspected that, as in all the feminine arts, she failed dismally.

He looked around the room. 'Is there someone else here tonight that you would rather dance with?'

How could there be anyone else on this planet she would rather dance with than Lucas Darkwood? Every woman in the room must be envying her, something that had never happened before and was unlikely to ever happen again.

She shook her head, wanting to scream out, *no, no, no.*

'If there is, then perhaps I could introduce you.'

'No, there's not.' Hazel's reply came out louder than intended, revealing her panic at the thought of him leaving her. 'I believe I already know all the men in the room,' she added in a more restrained tone.

She might be feeling somewhat awkward in his company, but if he was prepared to stay with her a little longer, then how could she possibly object? After all, being with him was like a fairy tale come true. Whatever his reason, if this impossibly handsome man had decided to stay with her a bit longer, she would be a fool to not gratefully accept it without question.

'I would love to dance the last two remaining dances

with you,' she said, hoping her voice didn't sound as desperate as she felt. 'And I promise to breathe, move with the music, look up, enjoy myself and not care what anyone thinks.'

'Are you sure? You aren't worried about people talking?'

She gave a small laugh, which she hoped came out girlish and light-hearted. 'Not at all. I'm going to try to be more like you and not worry about what people think.'

'In that case...' He took the empty glass from her hand, placed it on a nearby table and led her back through the crowd and on to the dance floor.

'But you are right,' he said as he took her hand for another waltz.

Hazel nodded. She had no idea what he was referring to, but at the moment everything felt absolutely right.

'I shouldn't be the only one to dance with you. At our next ball I will ensure that other men get the pleasure of your company.'

Hazel could have pointed out to him that this was her fifth Season. If those men wanted the pleasure of her company, they'd had ample opportunity to take it. But she cared little of that. All she could think of was the other part of what he had said. *Our next ball*. Did that mean he expected to see her at another ball, that this wasn't the end? She did hope so.

He led her around the floor and she admonished herself not to think of the future, to just enjoy the present. Whether she saw him again did not matter right now. Right now, she was in the arms of the most handsome man in the room, the most handsome man she had ever met. He was whirling her round the dance floor and she was dancing like a woman who never mangled men's feet, who was never gauche or boring. Even if she wasn't exactly the belle of the ball, while she was in his arms, she could almost imagine that she was.

The waltz finished and they lined up for a country reel, a playful, lively dance designed to get everyone on the floor at the end of the night, even those who were elderly or, like Hazel, had no sense of rhythm or style. By the end of the dance, Hazel was laughing and clapping along with everyone else, and joined in the loud cry of disappointment when the band stopped playing.

When Mr Darkwood led her off the floor, she was positively beaming with happiness. The last two dances had been a complete success. She'd got through them without causing any disasters, without overly embarrassing herself, and every man she came into contact with had managed to survive the experience with his feet intact. That had to count as a triumph.

Usually she greeted the end of a ball with immense relief and couldn't wait for her mother to escort her to the family coach and take her home. But tonight, it was all over far too soon. She wished she could continue dancing on and on and never stop.

He led her to where her mother was waiting with the other mothers.

'Mr Darkwood,' her mother said, with a slight curtsy, apparently needing no introduction. The slightly disapproving look on her mother's usually polite and friendly face suggested she not only knew who Mr Darkwood was, but also knew about his reputation.

'Lady Springfield,' he said with a bow. 'May I return your daughter to you.'

Her mother gave him a tight smile. Hazel continued smiling despite her mother's wary expression and the sidelong looks she kept giving Mr Darkwood. She was no doubt thinking the same as Hazel had been all night—what was this handsome man up to? But who cared? Hazel had had the most enjoyable night of her life.

The formalities over, they said their goodbyes. Hazel's brother Nathaniel joined them and her mother hurried them out of the ballroom and through the crowds still gathered around the entranceway saying their goodbyes.

Rows of coaches were lined up in front of the house, coachmen jostling for the best position, while chatting guests waited. The coach bearing her father's crest, driven by a coachman dressed in the family livery of gold and crimson, halted in front of the house. The footman jumped down to lower the steps and helped Hazel and her mother inside.

Still smiling, Hazel looked out of the window as the carriage jolted forward and drove through the London streets, still busy even at this early hour of the morning.

Hazel wondered if any of the occupants of the other coaches they passed on the road had had as wonderful a night as she had. She doubted that very much and almost felt sorry for them for what they had missed out on.

Throughout the journey her mother kept staring at her with a curious look. Tomorrow, Hazel was sure she would be hit with a barrage of questions, ones that she would probably be incapable of answering. But now was not the time to think of that. Now was the time to luxuriate in what had just happened.

It had been a dream of a night and Hazel was still in a dreamlike state that she hoped would never end. Mr Darkwood had mentioned their next ball, but that was surely just an idle comment made in passing. She did not know whether she would ever see him again, but one thing she did know for certain—it would be a long time before she stopped thinking about her night in the arms of the wonderful Mr Lucas Darkwood.

Chapter Five

As for Cinderella, the ball was over for Hazel. She wasn't dressed in rags. No one expected her to clean out the fireplaces and her two sisters were beautiful, not ugly, but the next morning it was back to plain old reality after her magical night with a handsome prince.

Despite what he had said about dancing at their next ball, she doubted she'd ever see the handsome Mr Darkwood again. But at least she did have last night and that was a memory she would cherish for ever. It no longer mattered what his motive had been for dancing with her. All she was going to hold close to her heart was the fact that a handsome, charming, rather wonderful man had whirled her round the dance floor and flattered her with his attention.

She entered the breakfast room and for once Hazel could enjoy her breakfast with the family without having to apologise for anything she had done the previous night. She had danced almost every dance rather than skulking in the corners. She had not tripped over once.

Well, except for that time that Lucas Darkwood caught her before she crashed backwards to the ground, but he had saved her rather delightfully on that occasion. She had not upturned any of the decorations. Well, except for the aspidistra in the card room, but her mother hadn't seen that. And she had not embarrassed herself by trying to get into a conversation about topics no one other than her wanted to talk about. Well, except for discussing meteorology with Lord Halthorpe, but her mother didn't know about that either.

Humming to herself, she served a generous breakfast from the silver tureens lined up on the sideboard. She sat down at the table, removed the silver napkin ring, shook out her linen napkin and gave her parents, her two sisters and her brother a cheerful *good morning*.

Her father nodded to her briefly over *The Times*, shook the paper with a decisive rustle, then went back to reading, while her mother frowned at her.

'Your father and I think we need to discuss what happened last night, Hazel.'

Oh, it seemed they had heard about the aspidistra and the meteorology discussion.

'It was lovely that you were dancing so often, but was it wise to dance so much with Lucas Darkwood and why on earth did you turn down Lord Dallington in favour of that gentleman?'

Hazel stared at her mother, her fork suspended in mid-air. Was that really a question she was being asked and how long did her mother have to listen to the long list of reasons?

'Well, let's see...' She lowered her fork and tapped

her finger on her chin as if she was truly considering the question. 'Lucas Darkwood is young, probably barely thirty, while Lord Dallington is old enough to be my grandfather. Mr Darkwood is fascinating company, while Lord Dallington is a boorish old buffoon. Lucas Dark—' Her mother held up her hands to stop Hazel's list making.

Her sister Iris winked at her and suppressed a smile. 'And from what Hazel said when she returned last night, Mr Darkwood is handsome, charming and a wonderful dancer, while Lord Dallington looks a bit like a suet pudding that's been left hanging for too long and galumphs round the dance floor like an ageing walrus.'

Her mother glared at Hazel's younger sister. 'That's enough, Iris. Don't encourage her.' She then turned to Hazel and sent her a sorrowful smile. 'I know this is not suitable for a young lady to hear, but Lucas Darkwood has somewhat of a reputation...' her mother frowned and blinked a few times '...when it comes to the ladies,' she continued in a lowered voice.

Her father's newspaper rustled again as if to underline the point.

'No respectable woman should be seen with him. It will diminish your...' She looked up at the ceiling and bit her top lip, and Hazel was sure she was trying to think of a less vulgar way of saying it would lower Hazel's value on the marriage market.

'It might discourage potential suitors who will wonder about your eligibility as a future bride.'

'No, it won't,' Nathaniel said, rapidly buttering his toast.

All attention turned to her brother.

'If anything, it will have the opposite effect,' he said as he added a large dollop of marmalade. 'When Hazie was dancing with Darkwood it sent all the ladies a-twittering. They were all wondering why he had singled her out to dance. Apparently, he rarely attends balls and he never asks a lady to dance. And several men asked me about Hazie. So, if anything, I think his attention was good for her marriage prospects.'

Their mother frowned in concentration. 'Really, do you think so, Nathaniel? Do you think it will have improved Hazel's prospects?'

Her brother nodded and took a loud bite of his toast.

Their mother looked at her husband, who lowered his paper and gave his wife a considered look. She nodded as if they had just conducted a conversation by telepathy.

'Well, I suppose a few dances won't do any harm,' her mother conceded. 'And it was in a very public place so no one can question your virtue.'

'And no one can even think Darkwood is after Hazie's dowry,' Nathaniel added, buttering another piece of toast, having devoured the last in a few sizeable bites. 'He hardly needs it. I've heard he's as rich as Croesus.'

'Don't discuss money, dear,' her mother said, even though everyone at the table knew that if Hazel did find a husband, it would be her money that he would be after.

'And more importantly, Hazie had fun,' her youngest sister Daisy added. 'And that's much more important than finding a husband.'

Hazel and Iris smiled at Daisy in agreement, while

the furrow between their mother's eyebrows grew deeper.

'No, no, dear. You don't understand at all. Marriage is important to a young lady and it really is essential that Hazel find a suitable husband before the end of this Season.'

The chatter died and everyone continued eating their breakfast, concentrating intently on the food in front of them. Hazel knew what they were all thinking. Next Season, Iris would have her coming out. She was everything Hazel wasn't. She was beautiful and graceful and when she entered a room all the men suddenly started acting as if no other woman was present. Plus, whoever married Iris would get the same financial endowment as the man who married Hazel. So why would anyone in their right mind look at Hazel when Iris was available?

'Anyway, it was nice of him to dance with me, but I'm unlikely to ever see him again,' Hazel said, breaking the uncomfortable silence and hoping that the family would move on to discussing another topic.

Nathaniel obliged and began regaling them with a funny story about something that had happened when he had been inspecting the family's Dorset estate. The conversation and laughter became increasingly loud and no one noticed a footman had appeared bearing a silver tray until he coughed, neither discreetly nor quietly.

Hazel's father lowered his paper, read the card, then handed it to her mother, who read it once, stared up at Hazel, then read it again, her hand clasping at the lace around her neck.

'It seems Mr Darkwood wants to take you driving in Hyde Park this afternoon,' her mother said, her voice shocked, her eyes wide, as if the card suggested Mr Darkwood wanted to sell Hazel into white slavery.

Everyone at the table stared at her mother, then all heads turned towards Hazel, who could feel her face flushing.

Iris and Daisy both made grabs for the card, but Nathaniel got there first.

'Well, well, Hazie, it seems you *will* be seeing Darkwood again and rather soon.' He smiled and handed her the white card bearing the masculine handwriting.

Hazel stared at the card as if it could answer the myriad questions whirling through her mind.

Why would he want to see her again so soon? What on earth did he want from her? What would they talk about? How was she supposed to behave? What would she wear?

'I *suppose* a drive in Hyde Park will be all right,' her mother said, looking to her husband for confirmation. 'Although it does suggest that he has intentions towards you.'

Hazel swallowed and looked over the table at her mother.

'And even if he doesn't,' Nathaniel added, pulling the card out of Hazel's fingers, 'absolutely everyone will see them. Hazie is going to be the most popular woman in London. Every eligible bachelor in England will finally be aware of just how wonderful a catch she is. It has just taken being seen with Lucas Darkwood to open their eyes.'

Another look was exchanged between her father and mother and her father gave an almost imperceptible nod.

Hazel stared at them, her mouth suddenly dry. They couldn't possibly be going to agree to this. Last night had been wonderful and she was looking forward to cherishing that precious memory. While she fancifully thought about how delightful it would be to see him again, the reality of doing so was decidedly unnerving.

And she still had no idea what he was up to. She had gone over and over his motives last night, while she lay in her bed, considering them from every angle and had finally settled on one answer. It might not be the correct one, but it was the one she liked the best. He had simply behaved like a charming gentleman. He had seen a lady in distress and had wanted to save her from a marauding band that consisted of Lords Halthorpe and Dallington. She had decided to cast Mr Darkwood in the role of a dashing, modern knight in shining armour who had ridden to her rescue.

But that did not explain why he wanted to see her again today. Her logical brain knew this was no fairy tale. There had to be more to this. He had to have some secret reason that could not possibly have anything to do with wanting her company and certainly not because he had any *intentions* towards her.

How disappointing. The fantasy was so much nicer. Now she would once again have to try to work out what he was actually up to.

And then there was the disquieting prospect of spending more time with him, just the two of them in his carriage, sitting side by side. The mere thought of it set Hazel's cheeks aflame. Last night she had experienced some rather unsettling physical reactions to being in the arms of Mr Lucas Darkwood. How was her poor body going to behave if she was seated close beside him in a carriage with no means of escape? She shuddered to think.

'His timing could have been better,' her mother muttered, taking the card off Nathaniel and reading it again. She looked up at Hazel over the card. 'I have an appointment with my dressmaker this afternoon, so I won't be able to chaperon you.'

'Oh, that's a shame,' Hazel said, both relief and disappointment rushing through her. 'I won't be able to go.' She did want to see him again, Hazel could not deny that. She *really* wanted to see him again. But life would definitely be easier if she didn't have to endure the anxiety of actually spending more time in his company.

Her mother shook her head and placed the card on the table. 'No, you can take your lady's maid. I'm sure that will suffice, especially as you'll be in a public place.'

That was worse than being accompanied by her mother. Her French maid hardly spoke a word of English. She had never had to chaperon Hazel before, as a chaperon had never been needed before. Hazel was sure Marie-Clare would consider keeping an eye on Mr Darkwood's behaviour somewhat beneath her. It would be as if she were effectively alone with him.

Alone with Mr Darkwood. The mere thought of it sent Hazel's nerves into peculiar spasms.

'So, what do you think you'll wear?' Iris asked. 'And

do you think you should get Marie-Clare to restyle your hair?'

Hazel touched her hair. Her lady's maid had styled it in the same way she did every day, in the way Hazel demanded, parted in the middle and tied back in a tight bun. It was a functional, efficient style which kept her wild curls under control. Well, that was the intention, although by the end of the day a few pesky curls had usually managed to escape their confinement.

And as for her clothes? She looked down at her plain brown skirt and cream blouse. Should she change, put on something more feminine, more alluring? Or would that just make her look ridiculous? Would it give him the wrong idea?

She did not want to appear to be under any illusions. It was extremely unlikely that he was actually courting her. There had to be some other reason why he had asked her to take a drive in Hyde Park. And she would only make herself look ludicrous if she tried to deck herself out like a young maiden expecting to be wooed.

'I believe the way I am dressed will suffice.'

'I agree,' her father said, speaking for the first time as he folded up his paper. 'You will look demure and refined, and it will send a message out to anyone watching that you are not one of Lucas Darkwood's many women who flaunt themselves in society. Everyone will know that Hazel Springfeld is a good girl.'

Hazel was unsure whether that description was quite apt. Usually, she was castigated for talking too much, particularly about subjects no one wanted to discuss. She knew people tended to describe her as clumsy and gauche rather than demure and refined. And as for being a good girl, well, she'd had few opportunities to be anything other than good.

While the rest of the family went back to chatting, laughing and eating their breakfast, Hazel sat in silence, her appetite gone as she contemplated the day to come. She was going to see him again in a few hours. She was going to spend more time in the company of the most handsome, charming man she had ever met. Such a prospect was both overwhelmingly exciting and overwhelmingly terrifying in equal measure, and Hazel knew she had just a few short hours to pull herself together if she was to survive this ordeal without making a fool of herself in front of that handsome man.

Chapter Six

Lucas knocked on the door of the Earl of Springfeld's Belgravia town house. A liveried footman escorted him into the entrance hall and he was hit by a barrage of noise. One young woman was walking down the hall wrestling with a disorganised pile of sticks that appeared to be croquet mallets and tennis rackets. At the same time as she was grappling with the bundle in her arms she was yelling up to the young man at the top of the stairs, something about riding their bicycles to the croquet court. Another young woman was dancing around with a yapping pug dog, who seemed to be attempting to drown out the voices of the other young woman and young man with its persistent barking.

The footman, who was seemingly immune to the cacophony happening around them, asked Lucas in a raised voice to wait a moment while he was announced. The young man at the top of the stairs spotted Lucas and rushed down, several steps at once, grabbed his hand and gave it a hearty shake.

'I'm Nathaniel, Viscount Wentworth, Hazel's brother. I'm very pleased to make your acquaintance. May I introduce my youngest sister, Lady Daisy.'

The young girl with the croquet sticks tried to perform a small curtsy, but failed as her bundle clattered to the marble floor. Nathaniel and Lucas both bent to retrieve her mallets and tennis rackets. They were joined by a second sister, who kindly relieved Lucas of the sticks, gave a quick curtsy and tried to control the little dog snuffling around his feet.

The footman reappeared and ushered a relieved Lucas into the drawing room. He was introduced to the Earl, who had not been at last night's ball, and once again greeted his wife, who was as effusive as her husband was taciturn.

While the mother was chatting amicably, Hazel stood up, then sat down again, then commenced twisting the ribbons of her reticule in her hands, as if she was unsure how she was supposed to behave. Nathaniel and the two younger sisters burst into the room, chatting and giggling at once, having disposed of the mallets and pug dog. Nathaniel helped himself to a large piece of cake and sat down beside Hazel on the sofa.

The two sisters squeezed in on the same sofa, then all four of them stared up at him, as if expecting their guest to provide them with some form of entertainment.

The mother rescued him, directing him towards a chair, and smiled at him reassuringly as she chatted about the weather and last night's ball.

He looked around at the smiling group. It was obvious he was in the midst of a happy, loving family.

Pain gripped his chest. He fought not to wonder what it would have been like to be born into such a family. What sort of man would he be if he had grown up surrounded by such warmth and laughter? His own family life was as far removed from this cheerful setting as it was possible to get. No wonder Lady Hazel Springfeld was such an open and happy young woman who laughed and smiled so easily.

She might not have been blessed with great beauty and charm, but she was indeed a lucky young woman to have such a family. He could only hope that when she did eventually marry it would be to an equally joyful young man, and the two of them would establish a household and family just as happy as this one. Having had no experience of such a family life, that was something he knew he would never be able to offer a young lady. It was another good reason why he would never marry.

He coughed to try to relieve that annoying ache in his chest that for some reason was refusing to budge and turned down the offer of tea. While he was pleased for Lady Hazel, such a household was not for him. It was too noisy, too excitable, too effusive. He was used to solitude, to the quiet of his own company, and that was the way he wanted to keep it. A man like him could never be at home in a household such as this.

The family chatter whirled around him as he made the suitably polite answers to the various questions that Hazel's mother put to him. Once sufficient time had passed, he stood up and bowed to the Earl and the Countess.

'Shall we, Lady Hazel?' he asked, offering her his arm.

She stood up, looked down and saw what she had done and began unravelling the ribbons of her reticule that had tangled themselves around her fingers.

Everyone in the family watched Lady Hazel's antics, her mother with an affectionate smile, the father with a look of concern for his daughter, the sisters and brother with indulgent smiles. It seemed they were used to Lady Hazel's awkward behaviour and neither judged nor condemned her for it. It was a far remove from the way his own father would have reacted if he had ever dared to do anything that suggested he was anything less than perfect. One thing was for certain: his father would not have reacted with affection, concern or indulgence.

Finally free, she sent him an embarrassed smile, took his waiting arm and Lucas led her out to the hall, where the pug dog ceased scratching at the door and greeted them with his small wagging tail. The lady's maid was also waiting and, ignoring the butler who was trying to perform his duties and escort the couple out, the Earl and Countess of Springfeld, the other three Springfeld children and the pug dog all made a noisy procession through the entrance hall to Lucas's open carriage, waiting at the doorstep.

The Countess kissed Lady Hazel's cheek and pushed a few stray curls back into her bun and whispered something in her ear. Then Lucas helped her up into the open carriage. The family remained standing on the doorstep, still chattering away, waving and calling out their effusive goodbyes as the carriage drove off. Anyone would think they were heading off on a major sea voyage, rather than a quick jaunt round the park. But perhaps that was the way happy families behaved. He wouldn't know.

They turned the corner, leaving the family behind, and despite the noise of the bustling city and the sound of the horses' hooves on the road, after the commotion of the Springfeld household, the carriage now seemed painfully quiet. The lady's maid pulled a book out of her bag and lowered her head, her face disappearing under the rim of her wide bonnet. She was giving every appearance of someone who did not want to be disturbed, leaving the two of them effectively alone.

'Are they always like that?' Lucas asked, breaking the silence. 'Always so boisterous.'

Lady Hazel laughed lightly. 'Oh, no, of course not. They're usually much louder. My brother and sisters were on their best behaviour today because they wanted to make a good impression.'

'Well, they certainly made an impression.'

She laughed again, taking delight in her family's antics. 'So, how many siblings do you have?' she asked.

Lucas's body tensed. He did not want to discuss his family. He did not want to even think about his father or his childhood, but she was looking at him with obvious curiosity. It would be rude not to answer. 'I'm an only child.'

She frowned and blinked several times. 'Oh, I can't imagine that. Was it very lonely growing up or did you have lots of cousins and friends and so on to play with?'

'No, but I was not lonely,' he replied, with more sharpness than he intended. 'I have never been lonely and have never had difficulty in finding all the company I could wish for.'

She blushed and looked straight ahead and he instantly regretted his tone. He had not meant to be so brusque. But nor did he have any intention of discussing his family or analysing why her reference to loneliness should have unsettled him so much.

'Yes, I've heard you're never short of company,' she said quietly, no longer laughing. He looked at her serious face. Was she referring to his reputation for having a stream of constantly changing female companionship? Or, worse, was she accusing him of using those women to stave off loneliness? Yes, he would admit that sometimes the company of a woman would momentarily drive away that gnawing pain in the pit of this stomach, the one that could overwhelm him and cause him to feel as though he was drowning. That was often the reason he went in pursuit of temporary female companionship, but he did not use those women and how dare she think it. Those women came willingly to his bed and, if they meant little to him, it was a feeling that was completely mutual.

They drove along in silence, both lost in their thoughts, and Lucas cursed himself for his terseness. He had no idea of what she was thinking and, even if she was judging him, her opinion should not matter one bit. He did not care what anyone thought of him and he certainly did not care whether Lady Hazel Springfeld approved or disapproved of how he lived his life.

But he needed her to enjoy herself, to smile and laugh the way she had last night. It would not do to have a miserable Lady Hazel sitting beside him, her lips pursed with the disapproving moue of a chastised child. She needed to give the appearance of a happy, carefree young woman so she would draw the attention of the men riding and walking in Hyde Park.

'I'm pleased you could join me this afternoon, Lady Hazel,' he said, keeping his voice as light as possible. 'It's a pleasant day for a ride, is it not?' That old standby, the weather, would have to do for conversation. Especially as he did not want to discuss his family and he most certainly did not want to discuss the company he usually kept.

She sent him a polite smile, albeit a somewhat pinched one. 'Indeed it is, although I must admit I was surprised to get your invitation.'

That knot in his stomach returned, but this time it felt decidedly like guilt over his motivation for the invitation. 'I thought it would be something you would enjoy.' His response was true, but only a small part of the truth.

She nodded her head slowly, staring at him as if trying to work him out. But there was no way she could possibly know the real reason for his invitation. She surely had no idea that he wanted to show her off to as many eligible young men as possible in the hope that she would attract the attention of at least one man who would make an acceptable suitor.

'Thank you,' she murmured as if not completely convinced.

The carriage turned into Hyde Park and they rode along the tree-lined pathways, joining the parade of people in open carriages, on horseback and strolling along the paths. Everyone was dressed in their finest clothes. The latest carriages were on display, many bearing the owner's crest. An afternoon drive in Hyde Park was the perfect opportunity to be seen, to show off your wealth and for the available young women to attract the attention of the young men.

Lucas rarely, if ever, took his carriage into the park, preferring to ride his horse alone in the early morning before it became crowded with the promenading ladies and gentlemen. Unlike most members of the aristocracy and nouveau riche, he did not see the point in displaying his wealth and power by riding out in his finest new carriage. And as he was not in the market for a bride, he did not need to scrutinise what was on offer in the parade of available young women.

But it was the perfect place to show off Lady Hazel to potential beaux. Although it seemed Lady Hazel had no intention of playing her part when it came to making sure she was noticed.

He looked at her sideways and took in her plain skirt and blouse, and her even plainer hairstyle. Rather than being dressed to attract a man's attention, her attire seemed to mark her out as a woman who was not on the hunt for a husband.

While the other young women in the park were dressed in an array of bright colours, wearing hats bedecked with ribbons, feathers and other fripperies, and twirling their lacy parasols in a manner designed to catch the eye, Lady Hazel was unadorned and dressed modestly. Although he had to admit this style suited her much more than the unfortunate, overblown gown she had been wearing last night, with its large puffed sleeves, ruffles, lace, ribbons and assortment of bows.

Today's clothing flattered her fuller figure so much more. Its simplicity drew his eyes, not to the dress, but to her curves under the skirt and blouse. Full feminine curves. She was not the type of woman he usually preferred, but he could definitely see the attraction of a more womanly figure.

Not that he should be thinking about what Lady Hazel's body looked like under her clothes. Appreciating her curves would not help in his goal of finding her a beau and winning his brood mare. In fact, he should not be even thinking about her curves at all, or what she looked like either in or out of her clothing, as tempting as it was to speculate.

She turned and sent him a quizzical look, causing his head to snap face forward and for him to move uncomfortably in the seat. Had she read his mind? Had she realised he was imagining what she looked like naked? Did she know he was wondering what those curves would be like when unconstrained by her garments? What her soft skin would feel like?

He coughed to clear his throat and to drive away those inappropriate thoughts. Of course she wouldn't know what he had been imagining. She was not a mind reader.

'I think we should be honest with each other, Mr Darkwood,' she said quietly, causing Lucas to once again cough away an uncomfortable lump that had formed in his throat. Perhaps she *was* a mind reader.

'Honest, Lady Hazel?' Honest was the last thing he

wanted to be. He did not want to be honest about what he had just been thinking. In fact, there was little he did want to be honest about. Everything about this invitation, everything about his behaviour was dishonest. He drew in a slow, deep breath and reminded himself that even if he was being dishonest with this innocent young woman, his actions would not cause her any harm.

He sat up straighter in the carriage. In fact, he would be helping her. When he won his bet, he would get that prized horse and she would have met a suitable young man who would commence courting her and hopefully one day marry her and give her the love and happiness she deserved. No, he had nothing to feel guilty about, he reminded himself and coughed again to relieve that gripping sensation in his chest.

'Last night you danced with me to save me from Lord Dallington and I am very grateful to you for that,' she said. 'But that odious man is nowhere in sight today. So why did you really invite me for this carriage ride? It wasn't simply because it's a pleasant day.'

'I invited you because I enjoy your company.' That at least had an element of truth to it. He did enjoy her company, even if it wasn't the main reason for his invitation.

She tilted her head on the side as if not quite believing him.

'Hmm,' she murmured.

It was obvious Lady Hazel was suspicious of his motives, did not believe that a man would invite her to ride with him simply because he enjoyed her company. That was something he was going to have to change.

He turned in the carriage to face her. 'When a man

sends you an invitation, should you not just take it at face value and accept that he has no other motive than merely wanting to spend time with you?'

She shrugged her shoulders, obviously still sceptical. He looked deep into her eyes to convince her of his sincerity. 'Lady Hazel, you are a lovely, interesting and intelligent young woman who is delightful company. I am honoured that you accepted my invitation to accompany me today.' And in that, Lucas was telling the truth. Not the whole truth admittedly, but still the truth.

Chapter Seven

Hazel tried to hold his gaze. While his handsome face made one want to stare at him adoringly, there was something ominous behind his metallic-grey eyes. Like the face mask of a suit of armour, they presented a barrier to the rest of the world, warning one not to get too close.

He was different today. Last night he had been all charm itself, but today it was as if a barrier had come up. Had something upset him? She supposed that her family had been a bit effusive and when he had been in their home he had been looking somewhat uncomfortable. Or perhaps it was because she had asked him about his family, or, worse than that, mentioned the company he kept.

She realised she was staring at him and was forced to blink several times, then look away, out at the parading people and the majestic oak trees quivering slightly in the light wind.

And if it wasn't his steel-grey eyes that had caused her consternation, his words would have done so anyway.

He'd said she was intelligent. All right, she could cope with that. It wasn't the first time a man had said she was intelligent, although it wasn't usually said in a complimentary manner. Interesting? That could be a compliment or an insult, so she was all right with that as well. But lovely? Delightful? When had anyone outside the family ever described her as either lovely or delightful? Not once that she could recall and she wasn't sure how to react.

Perhaps all she should do was follow his advice and take it at face value.

He thought she was lovely, delightful and he enjoyed her company.

Hazel turned that idea over in her mind to consider whether it could possibly be true, wanting to believe him. Then dismissed it as absurd. The man could have any woman he wanted. He was fabulously wealthy, fabulously handsome, just fabulous in every way. Any one of the unmarried women circulating in Hyde Park today would be more than happy to attract the attentions of Lucas Darkwood. In fact, a great many of the fashionable young ladies walking along the paths were trying to do exactly that. Not that Hazel blamed them. How could they not look at such a magnificent man? Last night he had looked superb in his formal evening suit and today he looked just as handsome in his charcoal frock coat, black waistcoat and the maroon cravat that looked so dashing against his tanned skin.

Hazel stifled a sigh as yet another young lady turned in the direction of their passing carriage and sent a coquettish smile in the direction of Mr Darkwood.

No, she couldn't blame them, but it was still somewhat annoying.

These women were the sort that he should be taking for a drive in the park. Even if he did think her lovely and delightful, what chance did she really have? None, that was the easy answer to that question. All these young ladies were much more lovely, much more delightful, and Mr Darkwood could have his pick.

So, she turned the question round in her mind again. What was the real reason he had invited her on this jaunt round Hyde Park?

That was what Hazel should be thinking about, not speculating about the secrets of his eyes or the reasons for his confusing compliments.

She already knew it couldn't be her dowry. So, could it be her family connections? She *was* the daughter of an earl, after all, and that title did mean something.

She took a quick sideways look in his direction. He wouldn't be the first man without a title who wanted to align himself with an aristocratic family and the Springfelds could trace their ancestry back countless generations. But if he did want to marry an aristocrat there were plenty for him to choose from. England was dotted with innumerable aristocratic families in need of money, who would happily marry their daughter off to a wealthy man, title or no. Yes, he must want to align himself with her father, the Earl of Springfeld, for his connections.

Hazel nodded to herself. Yes, that seemed to make sense. Businessmen often wanted an aristocrat on their company's board to increase its prestige and credibility.

Making a play for an earl's unattractive daughter would be a good way of getting the father's attention and interesting him in a business proposition.

She decided to check out her hypothesis.

'I believe you're in business, Mr Darkwood. That must be fascinating. What type of businesses do you own?'

He raised his eyebrows, presumably surprised at her question. 'I have shipping and rail companies, various mining companies in England and abroad, land, trading concerns and an interest in several other industries.'

'Fascinating. My father was just saying this morning that he was looking for some reputable businesses in which to invest.'

'Perhaps I'll discuss that with him some time.'

His voice sounded uninterested, but wasn't that what salesmen reputedly did, pretended that they weren't really concerned so they wouldn't put people off by appearing overly eager? Of course they did.

Yes, that was most likely what he was up to. It wasn't really her he wanted to spend time with. It was her father. Why had she not thought of that earlier? It made perfect sense. Hazel sat back in the carriage and smiled with satisfaction as relief washed through her.

She had been a bundle of nerves since his card had arrived this morning and that bundle had become even more tautly tied since his arrival. And as for sitting beside him in this small carriage, that had caused her nerves to twitch and tingle, her supposedly intelligent mind to repeatedly go blank and her stomach to act as if it had been weeks since her last meal.

She moved slightly in her seat to put a bit more distance between them. Her quivering nerves needed a rest and that wasn't going to happen when she was so close that his thigh was almost up against her leg, his shoulder was nearly touching hers. She looked down at his leg. It would be so easy to just move her hand slightly and touch his thigh, to stroke the muscles that she could see under the fabric of his trousers.

Hazel gulped and looked straight ahead. Where on earth had that inappropriate thought come from? She looked at Marie-Clare, willing her lady's maid to do her job and act as chaperon. Although how Marie-Clare was to chaperon Hazel's thoughts and force them to behave in an appropriate manner she had no idea. That was a job only Hazel could do.

Her head rigidly facing forward, she reminded herself that Mr Darkwood was only here because he was using her as a means to an end, as a way of getting access to her father. He wasn't here to be subjected to her inappropriate thoughts even if he had no knowledge of them. Shame on her.

Now that she knew the real reason why they were driving through Hyde Park she should be just sitting back, enjoying the ride and letting him make all the moves. Moves on her father, of course, not her. She gave a small, embarrassed cough at the absurdity of thinking he would actually make a move on her.

'Lovely weather, isn't it?' She laughed nervously, trying to shift her thoughts away from anything inappropriate, like Mr Darkwood's thighs, eyes or any other part of his body.

He raised an eyebrow and looked down at her. 'Why is lovely weather funny?'

'Oh, it's not.' She laughed again, her cheeks growing even warmer. 'But I suppose me talking about the weather is funny. Usually when people talk about the weather I can't help but give them a rundown on why the weather patterns are behaving in a certain way and what meteorological forces are in play.'

'So, why didn't you do that today? Do you think such things would be above me?'

'Oh, no, not at all. I just don't want to bore you.'

He raised his eyebrows again. 'Try me. Go on, give it your best. See if you can completely bore me until I fall asleep. I dare you.'

Was he teasing her? Flirting with her? No, of course not. He was out to woo her father, not her. But he had asked her to bore him and boring a man was something she was well versed in.

'Well, if you insist. To put it simply, last night's nimbus clouds did what was expected, which is why we had that rain overnight. And the lower atmospheric pressure explained the accompanying increase in the wind velocity. But that wind caused the clouds to disperse, taking with them any remaining moisture, and with the clouds gone, an increase of solar energy could be transferred to the earth, meaning we have a warm, sunny day.'

'And the showers have made everything smell fresh and clean.'

'Indeed.' Hazel inhaled deeply. The trees probably did smell fresh and clean, but all her senses could register was that intoxicatingly masculine scent of the man sitting next to her. Her laughter caught in her throat as she registered musk, leather and the hint of citrus from his shaving soap.

Heat flooded her body. A reaction that could not be explained away by the level of the solar energy.

She closed her eyes and held her breath. If she stopped breathing maybe she could ignore his scent and the way her body was reacting in such a disturbing manner.

But ceasing to breathe was not an option. Slowly she exhaled and gasped in another shallow breath, trying to ignore the clean scent of his soap and that underlying hint of something much more primal.

But try as she might, neither her mind nor her body could ignore the effect he was having on her.

She forced her scattered thoughts to gather themselves and to think about this logically.

Yes, he smelt wonderful. And, yes, it was causing her mind and body to become agitated, but it changed nothing. He still meant nothing to her and she was just a means to an end for him, a way of getting in with her father. Maybe she should see her reactions as worthy of a scientific research project. Putting it all in a scientific context would stop her from reacting in such an overly emotional manner. She could try working out why men smelt so different from women. And why that smell was so alluring. It must have something to do with biology, attraction, something that all animals possessed so they could attract a mate.

Hazel swallowed. No, perhaps that was not a good

area for study. The last thing she wanted to think about right now was animals mating. And as for mating with Mr Darkwood...

Hazel's hand shot to her mouth as if she had said that thought out loud. He sent her a quizzical look. She lowered her hand and tried to smile through her embarrassment.

'Yes, the trees do smell lovely,' she said, aware that her voice sounded strangled. She swallowed again to try to soothe her dry throat and squirmed uncomfortably in her seat.

He was still giving her a curious look. 'So, I take it you've always liked to know how things work.'

Yes, as long as it isn't trying to work out why you smell so wonderful.

'Yes, I suppose so.'

'That's rather unusual for a young lady.'

'Yes. I know. I was supposed to have a conventional education for a girl, you know—painting, embroidery, playing the piano and singing—but none of my lessons turned me into the accomplished woman I was supposed to become. My watercolours tend to resemble stick figures undergoing a particularly gruesome form of torture. My embroidery invariably ends up a tangle of brightly coloured threads and my singing has been compared to a couple of street cats fighting. And I suspect that was a compliment.'

He leaned back his head and laughed. Hazel looked at him in surprise. She doubted she had ever made a man laugh before. Well, perhaps her brother, but he didn't count, and men often laughed at her, but none had laughed as if they found her amusing. It was rather a nice feeling and she found herself relaxing and smiling back at him.

'So, how did you learn about nimbus clouds and solar energy and…?' He waved his hand around as if to encompass the entire natural world.

'I used to sit in when my brother was having his lessons. His tutor realised I was picking up the subjects faster than Nathaniel, so he started giving me lessons as well. Then I was gripped. I started reading everything I could about science. I love chemistry, physics, astronomy. I just wish…' She frowned and gritted her teeth.

'You just wish what?'

'I just wish women were allowed to have the same educational opportunities as men. And I wish an educated woman wasn't seen as some sort of social outcast whose company was to be avoided at all costs.' She looked over at him to gauge his reaction. 'Does that shock you?'

'Not at all. I think everyone should be allowed to live the way they want, to achieve their own potential in the way that is right for them.'

She looked at him with curiosity. It was not a view held by most men, particularly when it came to young ladies. Most men simply wanted women to look pretty but say little and, if they did have opinions, they were expected to keep them to themselves.

'Is that what you've done?' she asked. 'Lived the way you want to?'

He looked at her, his dark brows drawn together.

'Yes, I believe so,' he said, his voice terse. 'It's true that I have everything I want in terms of money, power, prestige, wom…' He paused. 'Let's just say my every need has always been catered for so I can live however I want.'

'You don't sound very happy about it.'

His brows drew closer together and his forehead furrowed deeper. He stared at her as if considering her statement and the tension returned to his shoulders. Perhaps she shouldn't have said that. It was a touch too forward, even for her.

'Happiness is not something I usually think about,' he said and breathed in deeply through flared nostrils as if this was a subject he was not prepared to discuss.

'Although how can I not be happy today?' he continued in a lighter tone. 'Who wouldn't be happy riding in a carriage under all this glorious solar energy and without a single nimbus cloud in the sky threatening to ruin our day with a significant weather event.'

Hazel looked back at him, both surprised and pleased. He had actually heard what she had said and taken it in. That was another first. She had made him laugh and now he had listened to her. Both novel experiences when it came to men.

Her smile returned and she sat back in the carriage, contentment washing over her. This was starting to be fun. Another novel experience. She had never had fun before when in a man's company, but then, up till now, the only men she had spent time with were the likes of Lord Halthorpe and Lord Dallington.

'So, you've told me about the weather—what other facts can you tell me about the park?' he asked.

She raised a teasing eyebrow and continued to smile at him. 'Are you making fun of me or have you suddenly discovered an interest in science?'

'Well, I'm definitely not making fun of you, so it must be the latter.'

It almost seemed as though he was flirting with her, but a small part of Hazel wasn't completely convinced. However, for now she would take him at his word and not worry about what was real and what was pretence. He was pretending to be enjoying her company until he could talk to her father about whatever business proposition he had and she was pretending she didn't know and was enjoying the novelty of being courted.

'Hmm. Well, what can I tell you?' She looked around. 'See those trees, they're just starting to lose their summer green and beginning to change to their autumn foliage. That's because in late summer there's less energy coming from the sun and the trees have stopped turning sunlight into food in the form of chlorophyll. It's the chlorophyll that makes them appear green. Now that it's being broken down, the chemical composition of the leaves is changing, so they'll soon take on the autumn colours of yellow, orange, red and brown.'

She turned and looked at him. 'Is that enough of a lecture, or do you want to know about the conversion process of the chemical components of oxygen and carbon dioxide within the leaves?'

He smiled at her, sending a pleasant yet disconcert-

ing shiver rippling through her body. His smile really
was magnificent and he should do it more often. It transformed his face, making him no less handsome, but so
much less formidable.

She stared at his mouth, unable to look away from
those perfect white teeth and those full lips curving upwards. His smile was so rare, and therefore more precious and for Hazel it was as if she was being bathed
in warm sunshine.

'It's all fascinating, but perhaps we'll leave the con-
verting bit for another day.'

Her cheeks burned and she looked away to try to
cover her confusion. Another day? There would be no
other day. Once he had her father's attention there would
be no point in paying any attention to the daughter.

'You are making fun of me,' she said.

'Never, Lady Hazel. And even if I was, which I'm
not, why should you care what anyone else thinks? If
people do make fun of you it's only because they realise
you're much more intelligent than they are and they
cover up their own inadequacies by trying to make you
feel bad about yourself. You shouldn't let them win by
ever thinking less of yourself because you were born
with a quick intelligence and a passionate nature.'

A passionate nature? Lovely, delightful and now a
passionate nature. Hazel was unsure whether she could
cope with any more compliments. They were nice to
hear, but when they caused her cheeks to burst into an
unbecoming shade of red and for her to fidget in a manner that was generally assumed to be unbecoming in a

young lady, it might perhaps be better if he kept such things to himself.

Hazel was saved from having to make a reply when a man pulled up on his horse beside the carriage. She looked up and saw Lord Bromley smirking down at them.

'Why, Darkwood, didn't expect to see you here today,' he said, trying to rein in his horse. 'Are you going to introduce me to your young lady?'

Hazel had been introduced to Lord Bromley on several occasions, but it seemed he did not remember. It appeared that now she was in Mr Darkwood's company she was suddenly someone worth meeting.

Mr Darkwood introduced them with apparent reluctance. Despite everything he said about not caring what people thought, was he uncomfortable at being seen with her in public? If that was the case, then why did he invite her to go for a drive in Hyde Park? If he wanted to avoid drawing attention, he was going about it the wrong way.

'So, will we be seeing you at Lady Danson's ball, Lady Hazel? If you're going to be in attendance, then you'll have to save a dance for me.'

Hazel noticed the malicious glint in Lord Bromley's eye as he spoke to her and she was sure he winked at Mr Darkwood. Was he in on Mr Darkwood's plan to ingratiate himself with Hazel so he could get on the good side of her father?

'That's if Lady Hazel can spare a dance,' Mr Darkwood said before Hazel had a chance to answer. 'I believe her card is already quite full.'

Lord Bromley tipped his hat. 'A pity, but I'll look forward to seeing you there. Good day to you, Lady Hazel, Darkwood.' With that he rode off, still smirking.

'I would avoid dancing with Lord Bromley if I were you. He has quite a reputation,' he said in a terse voice.

The pot calling the kettle black was a saying that popped into Hazel's mind. Was there anyone with a reputation as bad as Mr Darkwood's? She doubted it. If only half of the rumours she had heard were true, he had a decidedly blackened reputation. But such a thing would be most impolite to point out.

'But I, too, will be going to the ball and would be honoured if you saved at least one waltz for me,' he added, in a more conciliatory tone.

Given that Hazel's dance card was completely blank and was likely to stay that way all evening, she could easily save him a waltz or two, and maybe the quadrille and several reels as well, so she nodded her agreement.

She looked out at the passing parade of carriages and people walking and smiled to herself.

Another ball to look forward to. Another night dancing with this handsome man. Hazel knew it was all a bit of a fantasy. The man was not really attracted to her, the mere thought of it was ludicrous, but how could she possibly turn down the opportunity to spend one more evening in his company? All she had to do was remember that she meant nothing to Mr Darkwood and he meant nothing to her.

She looked at him and smiled. That should be easy to

do. She certainly had no intention of doing something silly like actually falling for the man. It would all just be a bit of fun and no harm would be done.

Chapter Eight

'A present has arrived for you, Hazie,' Iris said, rushing into Hazel's room without knocking. She held out the box tied with a ribbon, then sat beside Hazel on the needlepoint stool in front of the dressing table and peered down as Hazel opened the box.

Inside were four silver hair combs and a card saying they were from Lucas Darkwood.

'Oh, Hazie, they're lovely. You'll have to wear them in your hair tonight.'

Hazel continued staring at the beautiful combs, sitting in the red-velvet-lined box. She ran her finger along the delicate flowers and ivy etched into the silver which wound their way around sparkling turquoise stones. They were more elegant than anything she would normally wear. It would almost seem like an insult to put them in her unmanageable hair. But then, would it be even more of an insult to not wear them? Hazel was unsure. A man had never bought her presents before.

She looked up at her sister. 'Is it appropriate to wear

them tonight? I hardly know the man. What will Mother and Father think if I wear his gift to the ball?'

Iris shrugged. 'They won't think anything. I was in the hall when they were delivered so they don't know anything about them. And of course it's appropriate. They're beautiful and will look lovely, as long as you ask Marie-Clare to dress your hair in a suitable style.'

They both looked up at Marie-Clare, who was brushing down the gown Hazel would be wearing tonight. She took the combs out of Hazel's hand, inspected them, then looked at Hazel's hair and nodded.

'You're going to look beautiful, the belle of the ball,' Iris said. 'I'll leave Marie-Clare to work her magic.' She kissed her sister on the cheek and departed.

It would indeed take a magician to transform her into a beautiful belle of the ball. Just looking acceptable would be enough for Hazel.

Marie-Clare unclipped Hazel's hair and brushed it out with more vigour than Hazel felt was entirely necessary, her head being pulled back with every stroke. It was as if she was trying to tame a wild animal, but presumably that was how she saw Hazel's riot of curls.

Then she began twisting and plaiting and doing a range of things, the purpose of which Hazel had no idea. Finally, she pushed in the combs.

'*Voila!*' Marie-Clare stood back to admire her work. '*Mademoiselle* is *très* beautiful.'

Hazel looked at her reflection in the oval looking glass and could hardly believe what she was seeing. Marie-Clare had indeed transformed her hair. Instead of the usual wild, unruly locks that could only be controlled by tying them in a tight bun, her hair was sitting like a soft, opulent cloud on her head, with a few wispy curls around her face.

Hazel picked up the hand mirror to observe the silver combs, which were artfully placed and made an attractive contrast to her dark brown hair. She turned her head from side to side to see the effect.

Marie-Clare was perhaps exaggerating to say she looked beautiful, but it certainly was an improvement. It seemed Lucas Darkwood had better taste than Hazel did and also had a better idea of what would suit her.

Her stomach flipped as a thought occurred. Perhaps Mr Darkwood hadn't selected them at all. Perhaps he had a lady friend helping him. Rumour had it that he had numerous women in his life, and even her father, a man who did not listen to gossip, had suggested that such a thing was true. Maybe one of his mistresses was helping him in his quest to curry favour with the Earl of Springfeld by buying gifts for the dowdy daughter.

She pushed away that thought. There was no evidence to support it and, even if it were true, what did it really matter? Lucas Darkwood meant nothing to her. She meant nothing to him. Tonight was just going to be a fun evening, nothing else, and now she would be wearing some rather stunning combs in her hair while she did so. Her father would also be attending tonight's ball. There was every likelihood that Mr Darkwood would make time to talk to him and that would be that. His attentions towards her would come to an end and there would be no more pretty gifts.

She should just make the most of it while she could.

Marie-Clare helped her into the fluffy concoction of tulle and lace that was her ballgown. During the day Hazel could get away with wearing plain, practical clothing, but for balls she was expected to dress up in the latest style. But even she could see that puffy, leg-o'-mutton sleeves that were all the fashion only made her shoulders look bigger. As for the padding on her hips, she most certainly did not need that. She had enough padding of her own. But fashion demanded padding, so padding was what was added, even if, instead of giving her the desired hourglass figure, she looked more like a plump partridge ripe for the pot.

As she stared at herself in the full-length looking glass it became even more evident that Mr Darkwood had to be up to something. Her hair might now be lovely, thanks to Marie-Clare, but the woman staring back at her was not one that any man in his right mind would want to court. And Lucas Darkwood most certainly gave every appearance of being in his right mind.

Hazel shook her head to drive out those thoughts. It did not matter.

Cinderella was off to another ball. Why should she care that Prince Charming was more concerned with securing a business partner than he was with slippers and princesses? She would be having fun tonight no matter what his reasons. For five Seasons she had either sat abandoned on the edge of the dance floor, or reluctantly danced with men like Lord Halthorpe and Lord Dallington. Her final Season was nearly over. She would soon be up on the shelf and there would be no more balls. So, there was no harm in pretending she really was being wooed and enjoying herself while she could.

Hazel stood at the top of the stairs, on the arm of her father, and looked down at the glittering site below her. For once, excitement and anticipation were coursing through her body, not dread and despair.

Was it just her mood, or did the ballroom look more splendid than usual? She had attended several balls at Lady Danson's over the last five Seasons, but had never noticed how the crystal chandeliers containing a multitude of small candles sent glittering lights sparkling over the guests. Nor had she previously noticed the way the aroma of fresh-cut flowers from the glorious floral displays scented the air. And had those large, exotic palms always lined the walls? It was as if she was looking down on a beautiful, enchanted garden.

She smiled and looked at the crowd assembled below them. The elegant women, wearing gowns of every colour, made a beautiful sight as they whirled around the floor on the arms of men dressed in their black evening suits, white shirts and ties. And musicians, seated on a balcony above the ballroom, were playing the most divine music. It really was a fairy tale setting and she couldn't wait to join the crowd below and dance the night away.

She quickly scanned the room and saw her pretend Prince Charming standing in the corner looking up at her. Her breath caught in her throat as she gazed down at his handsome face. How had she forgotten how literally breathtaking he was? She placed her hand on her stomach to still the fluttering and tried to remind her jittery nerves that this was all just pretend. It meant nothing. She was just here to enjoy herself and there was no reason for her to get the slightest bit agitated.

Their names were announced and her father led Hazel and her mother down the stairs. Hazel almost tripped on the first step, momentarily forgetting to move her feet, her eyes were fixed so firmly on Mr Darkwood.

Her father smiled at her and patted her hand in reassurance. She smiled back at him and for a moment imagined that he was leading her down the aisle to her expectant husband-to-be. She looked at the man, now standing at the bottom of the stairs waiting for them, and pushed that ludicrous idea out of her head. That was simply going too far. Fantasising that Mr Darkwood was courting her was just a bit of fun. Thinking that he was going to marry her was somewhat delusional.

Instead she lifted her head high, remembered what Mr Darkwood had said about breathing and not looking at her feet, and tried to descend with as much grace as she could, on legs that had taken on a jellylike consistency. As much as she loved having him look at her, her entrance would be much easier if she wasn't weakened by knowing that those grey eyes were watching her every move.

Or were his eyes fixed on his real object, her father? Whatever. It didn't matter. She was going to spend one last night with Mr Darkwood and, despite her nerves, she was going to enjoy herself.

He joined them, bowed formally and asked if he

could have Hazel's hand for the next dance. Her parents
exchanged a look, then her mother nodded her consent.

'But please remember, Mr Darkwood, it will not do
if my daughter dances every dance with the same man,'
her mother admonished.

'Of course, your Ladyship.' Mr Darkwood nodded.
'I will ensure that Lady Hazel has the opportunity to
dance with as many young men as possible.'

*Oh, no, don't do that. I want to dance every dance
with you*, Hazel thought, smiling at him as he took her
arm and led her out on to the dance floor.

'Your mother is right, Lady Hazel,' he said as he
placed his hand on her waist and took hold of her gloved
hand. 'There are many other young men who I am sure
would be delighted to dance with you.'

Hazel chose not to point out to him the absurdity of
this comment. If there were many other young men who
wanted to dance with her then they'd had five Seasons
in which they could have asked her, but they hadn't.

'I'll introduce you to several suitable men. As your
mother so rightly pointed out, it would not be right for
us to dance together too many times.'

Hazel wanted to cry out *please ignore my mother,
she doesn't know what she's talking about, we can
dance every dance together and no one would care*.
But she supposed he wanted to spend some time talking to her father this evening and it would be selfish of
Hazel to keep him to herself. Although being selfish
was exactly what she wanted to be.

Remembering her lessons from the last ball, she took
in a series of slow, deep breaths, relaxed and let the

music flow over her. They glided across the polished wooden floor and Hazel's fantasy that she was a princess in a fairy tale felt complete.

'You look lovely tonight, Lady Hazel,' he said as they moved easily together as one.

And Hazel indeed did feel lovely. She smiled up at him. 'Thank you for the combs, they're beautiful.'

'My pleasure. And you seem to have mastered the steps of the waltz.' They twirled around again, and once again Hazel easily avoided his feet.

Warmth rushed through her at his compliment and for once her temperature hadn't risen because she had embarrassed herself, but because she felt so happy.

'I've had a good teacher.' It was tempting to add that being in his arms felt so good it was like dancing in a dream. But such an admission would only make him uncomfortable and reality might come crashing in and ruin the fantasy.

Far too soon the waltz came to an end. He escorted her off the floor towards a group of men and introduced her. They were men whom she had met before, but it seemed none of them had remembered her, because they greeted her as if they were being introduced for the first time.

One man, whose name she immediately forgot, asked her for the next dance. Hazel looked at Mr Darkwood, hoping he'd repeat what he had said to Dallington last night, that every dance on Hazel's card was promised to him. But he said nothing. With reluctance she allowed the young man, whose name she still could not remember, to lead her on to the dance floor.

Despite not being with Mr Darkwood, she managed to remember his instructions about relaxing and just going with the music. And it worked. The young man's feet remained untrampled, she did not collide with any other dancer, trip, fall or cause havoc of any kind. Keeping her head high and not looking at her feet was also easy to achieve, as she spent the entire dance looking to see where Mr Darkwood had gone. She had expected him to take the opportunity to talk to her father, but he hadn't. Instead he was standing on the side of the dance floor watching her.

Why would he be watching her? Why was he not talking to her father or even asking some other young woman to dance?

It didn't really make any sense at all. Perhaps he did want to dance with her and had only reluctantly acceded to this young man. Perhaps this wasn't just a fantasy. Perhaps, just perhaps, the attraction was mutual. Could such a thing be possible?

The dance came to an end and the young man led her off the floor, back to where Mr Darkwood was standing with the same group of men. Hazel waited in anticipation. If he asked her to dance, it would support her theory that this wasn't just a fantasy. But instead, another of the young men, whose name she had also forgotten, asked her to dance.

Hazel swallowed her disappointment as they took their places for the quadrille, although she knew she really had nothing to be disappointed about. Once this would have been a dream come true, to be asked to dance by a succession of eligible young men. But it was not what she wanted. She only wanted to dance with her Prince Charming. If only Lord Dallington was present, or Lord Halthorpe. Then Lucas Darkwood could once again rescue her, like the damsel in distress she wanted to be.

She smiled at the young man and even found herself making small talk with each man as they changed partners throughout the quadrille and circled each other. It appeared small talk was rather easy to do when your mind was only half on the conversation, while the other half of your attention was fixed on the man watching you from the side of the room.

Was he ever going to ask her to dance again? That was the only reason she had been so excited about attending this ball. The Season was nearly over. Once Mr Darkwood had spoken to her father, she might not see him again and she so wanted to be held in his arms, for as many dances as possible. She had never tried subterfuge, coquettishness or any of those other tricks that women used to get a man's attention, but desperate times called for desperate measures. It seemed Hazel was going to have to exercise some sluggish feminine wiles.

The young man escorted her back off the floor and Hazel took Lucas Darkwood's arm. 'The next dance is the mazurka. I don't really know the steps and I'm afraid I might need a little help,' she whispered to him. 'I know it's forward of me, but would you dance the mazurka with me?'

'I'd be delighted to,' he responded, to Hazel's immense relief. It was true that she had avoided the mazurka in the past—its complex steps allowed for too many opportunities for her to generally cause bedlam.

He led her out on to the dance floor and Hazel couldn't stop herself from beaming. He took her hand, the music started and her smile died. She remembered why she avoided the mazurka. It did have complicated steps. It required her to keep up with the music, to avoid colliding with the other partners. So far tonight she had avoided making a fool of herself and now she was going to do exactly that, in front of the one man she did not want to think badly of her.

Like a statue, she remained rigid, immovable, while the other couples danced around them. Her mind was a blank. She could not even remember the basic steps of the mazurka, never mind the complicated twirls and jumps.

'Are you all right, Lady Hazel?' he asked as she remained rooted to the spot.

'I don't really know how to dance the mazurka.'

He raised an eyebrow and she knew exactly what he was thinking: *Then why did you ask me to dance with you?*

Because I'm a nincompoop, that's why.

'Then we don't need to dance,' he said. 'Would you prefer to take some refreshments?'

'Oh, yes, please.' Even better. They could spend some time together chatting and hopefully she would make him smile and laugh again.

He led her off the floor, weaving through the couples who were prancing and jumping as if born to it. They walked through to the adjoining room, where long tables covered in stiff white linen were laden with food and bowls of punch.

Mr Darkwood handed her a glass of fruit punch, which she drank with relief.

'I'm sorry about that, I forgot that I don't really know how to dance the mazurka.'

'Nothing to apologise for,' he said, taking the empty glass from her hand and refilling it. 'Did you enjoy the other dances, with the Earl of Burnside and Viscount Henley?'

Was that what their names were?

'Yes, and they managed to survive the dances with their feet intact,' she said with a laugh.

He nodded. 'And you looked completely at home on the dance floor. I'm sure more young men will be anxious to dance with you.'

I don't want to dance with other men. I only want to dance with you. Hazel felt like stamping her foot with impatience.

'Will we be dancing again tonight?' she asked, trying her hardest to keep the note of desperation out of her voice. 'Perhaps not the mazurka, but there will be another waltz soon, and a quadrille, and a polka. I'm pretty sure I know all the steps to the polka.'

She pulled out her dance card and pencil and looked up at him. He took the pencil from her hand and wrote his name beside the next dance and handed back her card.

'I believe you should leave some space free for other men who want to dance with you. It would not do if I took every remaining dance.'

'But you didn't care about that at the last ball,' she said, pushing the dance card in his direction, desperation making her forget her manners.

'Last time I was saving you from Lord Dallington. Tonight, you have the attention of several eligible young men.' He frowned slightly. 'You don't object to the Earl of Burnside or Viscount Henley, do you?'

But I don't want their attention. I only want your attention, Hazel wanted to scream at him.

'No, of course not,' she said instead.

'And your mother has asked me to leave some dances for other men.'

'But I'm sure my mother won't object if we have a few more dances.' She held out the dance card towards him, ignoring that voice in her head telling her that her behaviour was shameless.

He took her dance card and placed his name next to two more dances.

'Oh, and that one as well.' Hazel pointed to the last dance on the card. That was the most important one. She wanted to spend the last dance in his arms so she could hold that memory in her heart and savour it for ever.

He raised his eyebrows and she held her breath, hoping he would not object. When he wrote his name on the space left for the final dance, she slowly exhaled.

She was tempted to clutch the card to her chest, so happy to be having four more dances with him. Instead she lowered the card and smiled. She now had a memento of this wonderful night to treasure. She would be able to read his lovely name, again and again, and remember this magical night.

'So, as you've promised me the next dance, shall we?' He removed the now-empty glass from her hand and placed it on the table. Unable to get that silly grin off her face, she placed her hand lightly on his extended arm and, as if floating on air, she was escorted back to the ballroom.

The rest of the ball went past in a happy whirl. Between each dance with Mr Darkwood, other men asked to stand up with her, which once would have made her extremely happy. Never before had she danced every dance on the card and with such eligible young men. But now, all she wanted was for those dances to be over so she could be back in Mr Darkwood's arms.

Making her excuses, she skipped the second-to-last dance and headed to the ladies' retiring room to freshen up. If it was to be her last dance with Mr Darkwood, she wanted to make sure she looked her best, was as composed as possible and possibly, just maybe, he'd remember her with some affection, if and when he looked back on this night.

Almost giddy with pleasure, Hazel looked at her smiling face in the gilt-edged looking glass. This must be how young women usually felt when they attended a ball. This joyfulness during a social occasion was an unfamiliar experience for Hazel. She examined her face, which looked different. She had to admit, she almost looked pretty. Her cheeks were flushed, but with pleasure, not embarrassment, her eyes were sparkling and even her hair had miraculously stayed in place. She touched the combs and delicious pleasure rippled through her. His gift would be another memento of this wonderful night.

Two other young women entered the retiring room and Hazel smiled at them, wanting to share her happiness with everyone she met.

One young woman looked her up and down. A shiver of wariness rippled through Hazel. Was their unfriendly demeanour because they envied her? That, too, was a novel experience. Young women usually either pitied or mocked Hazel, but envy? Never. But tonight was different. Who wouldn't envy a woman who spent so much of the evening in the arms of the most handsome, most charming man at the ball?

She smiled at the two women and greeted them politely, forgiving them their disapproving looks. Tonight she could be magnanimous because nothing was going to dampen her pleasure.

The young ladies did not return her smile.

'This is the young woman who is the subject of that bet I was telling you about,' one young woman said, causing her friend to giggle behind her gloved hand.

Hazel's stomach lurched. What were they talking about? She could tell these women were up to something, were wanting to play a mean trick. Hazel knew envy could make young women behave in an unpleasant manner. She should ignore them. But she couldn't stop herself from asking. 'Bet? What bet?'

'Oh dear, I suppose I shouldn't have said anything,' the young woman said with feigned embarrassment, placing her hand across her smiling lips.

'What bet?' Hazel asked again, her unease evident from the tremor in her voice.

The young woman's lips curled into a sneering smile. 'Well, if you insist on being told. Lucas Darkwood and Lord Bromley have placed a bet on you. If Mr Darkwood can get a man to show you the slightest bit of regard by the end of the Season, and not just be chasing after your substantial dowry, he will win Lord Bromley's brood mare, but if he loses he'll have to marry you himself.'

As if the air had suddenly left the room Hazel was unable to gasp in a breath. Her head started spinning and a strange thrumming noise in her ears was making her wonder if she had heard correctly.

'Don't look so offended,' the young woman said, tilting up her chin. 'You did insist that I tell you, so you've only got yourself to blame if you don't like what you hear.'

She took her friend's arm and they left the room. Before the door had closed behind them, they broke into loud giggling.

Hazel grabbed the washstand, the room seeming to spin with the floor disappearing beneath her feet.

She had always known that she meant nothing to Mr Darkwood, but had been prepared to ignore it so she could indulge herself in a fantasy. The thought that he was only paying her attention because he wanted to ingratiate himself with her father was something she could tolerate, but this, being part of a bet, was contemptible.

He had placed her in a bet up against a brood mare.

Hazel had been humiliated before, had been the subject of a man's cruel joke before, but never had she been subjected to something as nasty or as demeaning as this.

She looked at her reflection in the mirror. Her flushed face was now ghostly pale. The combs in her hair were no longer flattering. They looked ludicrous, as if they were mocking her.

She pulled them out, dislodging several locks of hair while she did so. Instead of being a memento of an enjoyable evening they were now an emblem of something cruel and heartless. She tossed them on to the washstand beside her dance card.

That, too, was now mocking her. Only moments before she had been gazing at it with such affection, had been looking forward to preserving it, keeping it as a memento, something to be read again and again with pleasure. What a fool she was.

She picked up the card, ripped it into tiny pieces and threw them on the floor.

This was a level of cruelty of which she had not expected him capable. She was one half of a bet, the other half being a horse. If he had wanted to mock her, make the world see exactly what he thought of her, there would be few more insulting ways for him to do it than to bet her against a horse.

How he must have laughed when he took on that bet. How he must be laughing at her every time he danced with her. Did he make cruel comparisons between the looks of the two sides of the wager? Did he see the way she danced as being akin to the lumbering of a horse? She could almost hear the laughter between him and

Lord Bromley. No wonder Bromley had been smirking when he met them in Hyde Park. Taking one horse out for a ride so he could win another, more attractive horse, she imagined them saying.

Both men were beneath contempt, but Mr Darkwood even more so. He was the one who had acted as if he was enjoying her company, while mocking her the entire time. He was the one who had sent her a beautiful present, which, in her deluded state, she had been so happy to receive and had taken such delight in wearing, as if they were a token of his affection.

She looked down at the combs, which not long ago she had admired for their beauty. How dare he treat her this way? She had expected to be upset when the ball was over, knowing that it would probably be the last time she would see Mr Darkwood. Instead, she never wanted to endure the company of that vile man ever again.

Except, she had all but forced him to ask her for the last dance. How could she face him now that she knew he was laughing at her? The temptation to run away and try to hide from her all-consuming shame was overwhelming.

It was so unfair. She had done nothing wrong. He was the one who should be feeling ashamed, not her. She would not let him laugh at her a minute longer. He might be mocking her, but she would hold her head high and not let him see how much he had hurt her.

Grabbing the combs, she pushed them back in her hair, not caring whether they sat neatly or not. There was no reason why she should have to hide or run away, so she wouldn't.

With as much dignity as she could muster, she left the ladies' retiring room, determined to get the last dance over and done with and for no one, including Mr Darkwood, to ever know the enormity of the pain she was feeling inside.

Chapter Nine

Daisy and Iris stared back at her, their wide-eyed, open-mouthed expressions reflecting her own outrage. Despite the late hour, Hazel had found them waiting expectantly in her bedroom when she returned home. Seated on her four-poster bed, they were excited to hear all about the ball. Instead of delighting them with tales of being spun around the dance floor by the dashing Mr Darkwood, she had shocked them with the revelation of his abhorrent behaviour.

'The man's a complete cad,' Daisy said, lowering her hands from her cheeks.

'Yes, a scoundrel of the worst sort,' Iris added. 'What did Father say when you told him? I imagine he wanted to have the rogue horsewhipped.'

'I didn't tell him,' Hazel said. 'And I won't. You're the only people who I'm going to tell.'

Iris shook her head, her brow furrowed with concern. 'But you must have said something to Mr Darkwood, told him exactly what you thought of his appalling actions. I hope he was suitably shamefaced.'

Hazel blinked, determined not to cry and to ignore the pain gripping her stomach. 'No, I decided the best thing to do was to pretend I didn't know so I could at least hang on to the last shred of my dignity.'

She lifted her chin and pulled back her shoulders in an unconscious imitation of the stance she had taken on the dance floor. 'I acted as if nothing had happened. Danced with him and tried really hard to make polite conversation.'

Her attempt to maintain a calm composure frayed. She drew in a shaky sigh. Her shoulders dropped back down and she slumped on the bed beside her sisters. 'I forced myself not to let him know how much I was hurt, even though what I wanted to do was to hit him round the head and tell him in words unbecoming to a lady just what I thought of him, before bursting into tears and running all the way home.'

Daisy put her arms around her shoulders. 'You should have picked up the heaviest object you could find and crowned the blackguard with it. He would have deserved no less.'

Hazel gulped down the tears that were threatening to escape and gave a small, sad smile. 'I must admit I surprised myself. I think I should go on the stage. After tonight's performance I believe I could rival the famous Lillie Langtry and Sarah Bernhardt with my acting skills.'

Iris put her arms around her two sisters and the three

women held each other close, providing Hazel with much-needed comfort.

They sat in silence for a few moments, then Hazel gave a mirthless laugh. 'What was even worse was on the way home Mother said she and Father had discussed Mr Darkwood during the ball and they have decided to give him permission to officially court me should he ask. Mother said she could see how much he meant to me. She said Father had made enquiries and decided that despite the rumours, which they believe have been exaggerated, he's an honest businessman and known to be honourable in his dealings with others, so they would be proud to have him in the family.'

Hazel closed her eyes briefly to still the unshed tears that were welling up inside her. 'Mother looked so pleased that I finally had a beau and she would be succeeding in her job of marrying off her eldest daughter. It all just added to the humiliation and made me feel so ashamed.'

While Hazel had managed to suppress her own tears the same could not be said of Iris and Daisy, who both had tears running down their cheeks.

'You're not the one who should be ashamed,' Daisy said, brushing at her tears with the back of her hand. 'He is. He should be totally ashamed of his behaviour.'

'Oh, please don't cry,' Hazel said, pulling out a lacy handkerchief from her discarded reticule lying on the bed and handing it to Daisy. 'That cad does not deserve our tears, and I'm determined not to waste any of mine on him.'

Hazel suspected she was once again acting. Would

she really be able to contain the tears that were prick-
ing at her eyes, wanting to fall?

'You're right,' Daisy said, wiping her eyes. 'He
fooled Mother and Father and that, too, is unforgivable. In fact, he fooled all of us,' Daisy said, handing
the handkerchief to Iris.

The two sisters nodded their agreement, as Iris wiped
her eyes and handed the handkerchief back to Hazel.
She defiantly returned it to her reticule, as if making a
statement that she would not cry over Mr Darkwood.

Daisy slowly shook her head. 'He should be on the
stage as well, although he'd have to play the villain.'

'Yes, he certainly had me fooled,' Hazel said. 'I knew
he was up to something, but not this.'

Daisy bit her lower lip in thought. 'No, I mean, just
like Mother and Father, I really thought he was taken
with you, because when we were all in the drawing
room together he was staring at you the whole time and
the look on his face was so affectionate.'

'Well, I suppose he didn't want Mother and Father
to suspect anything,' Hazel said, refusing to even entertain the idea that there could be anything but self-
interest behind anything that man had done.

'Mmm,' Daisy said, as if not entirely convinced.
'And he never once even glanced in Iris's direction.
I've never seen a man do that before.'

About to answer Hazel stopped, closed her mouth
and frowned in thought. They both looked at Iris, who
raised her slim shoulders.

Hazel had to admit, that was unusual behaviour. Men
always noticed Iris. It wasn't vanity on Iris's part. Ev-

eryone in the family was aware of how men stared at her. She had been known to literally stop traffic in the street. She was only seventeen, but everyone could see what a beauty she was and how the moment she had her debut the men would be lining up to ask for her hand. That was the unspoken reason why their mother wanted to get Hazel married off this Season, before her beautiful younger sister came of marriageable age.

'I suppose all that shows is how determined he was,' Hazel finally said. 'Perhaps he didn't notice Iris because he was too busy thinking about the horse he was going to win.'

'Hmm,' Daisy repeated, obviously still not entirely convinced.

'Anyway, it hardly matters,' Hazel cut in before Daisy could formulate any further arguments. 'The man's a pig, a charlatan, a scoundrel. We all know that now. I was just lucky I found out when I did.'

Both sisters nodded and murmured more insults about him being a cad, a bounder, a reprobate.

'At least you'll never see him again,' Daisy said when they had exhausted their list of insults. 'But he really does deserve to be punished.'

Hazel and Iris nodded their agreement.

'Yes, you should send him back his combs with a rude note,' Daisy continued, jumping off the bed and rushing towards Hazel's desk. 'Let's write one now and let him know just what we think of him.'

'Yes, let's,' Iris added, crossing the room. 'You're never going to see him again so you might as well let him know exactly what you think of him.'

Encouraged by her sisters, Hazel joined them at the writing desk. She sat down, pushed back the wooden roll top, pulled a piece of paper out of the drawer, uncapped her inkwell, dipped in her pen, then sat up and looked expectantly at her sisters, the pen poised above the paper. 'Right, what shall we say? It should be really insulting.'

'Yes,' Daisy said. 'Something that lets him know he can't mess around with one of the Springfeld sisters.'

Iris and Daisy gave full expression to their dislike of Mr Darkwood and Hazel scribbled down everything they said as quickly as she could. As the insults became more and more outlandish the girls started giggling, spurred on by each other, each trying to think of even more inventive ways to tell the cad just what they thought of him.

The more outrageous the insults became, the more agonising the misfortunes they wished to befall Mr Darkwood, the more Hazel laughed. Despite knowing Mr Darkwood would never read this letter it was good to write it all down and get all the hurt and anger out of her system.

When they were finished and could think of nothing else to say, she stood up and read out the letter to her sisters, who collapsed back on to Hazel's bed in fits of giggles. Wiping away her tears, now of laughter rather than sorrow, Hazel joined her sisters and climbed up on to her bed. She was so grateful to have them in her life. No matter how cruel the world could be she could always rely on Daisy and Iris to make her feel better.

'Of course I can't send it.'

The two sisters made mock noises of protest as Hazel tore up the letter and let the pieces flutter to the ground.

'What a shame,' Iris said, looking down at the discarded pieces of paper. 'But I suppose you're right. Mother and Father would never forgive us if we really did send such a letter.' She looked up at Hazel. 'But we should do something to punish him. He shouldn't be allowed to get away with this.'

They sat in silence for a moment, each trying to think of what they could do to Mr Darkwood that wouldn't offend their parents. A plan slowly started to formulate in Hazel's mind. She stood up and walked towards the curtained windows, then back again and stopped in front of her waiting sisters. 'It would serve him right if I played him at his own game.'

'How?' they asked together.

'He doesn't know that I know about the bet.'

She walked back to the window, turned and faced her sisters, her hand on her chin as she continued thinking. 'I could use his ignorance against him. If he thinks marrying me is so terrible, maybe that's what I should do.'

'No,' both girls cried out in unison, jumping off the bed at once and rushing over to her.

'You can't do that,' Iris said, taking hold of Hazel's hand, her eyes pleading.

Daisy took her other hand. 'It would be the worst possible thing you could do,' she cried out. 'Please, Hazel, no.'

Hazel laughed. 'I wouldn't actually do it, but I could make him think that I wanted to marry him.'

Iris released her hand and gave her a quizzical look. 'What do you mean?'

'Well, in order to win that dratted horse, he was supposed to fob me off on some other man, but if he failed he would have to marry me himself.'

A few more expressions of *the pig, the cad, the scoundrel* came from her sisters.

'He hasn't managed to find a beau for me yet, so he's going to have to keep trying. If he thinks that I've fallen hopelessly in love with him, that I am expecting to marry him, then he's really going to get frightened. That should be punishment enough for him. He'd realise that not only is he going to lose the bet and lose the horse, but he's going to have to marry someone he doesn't want to. He must have known that there would never be any real obligation to marry me, especially if I didn't want to, but if he thinks that I really, really want to marry him, then he's going to find himself in a terrible quandary.'

Iris drew her eyebrows together. 'But you'd have to pretend to be in love with a man who is a complete scoundrel. You're going to have to act as if you actually enjoy being in the cad's company, when what you really want to do is box him in the ears and let him know just how much you despise him.'

Hazel shrugged. 'I've already proven to myself tonight that I'm a good actress. Well, I'll just have to extend my time on the stage and continue acting for a bit longer until I've completely terrified him and caused him to regret ever making that appalling bet.'

'That's a wonderful idea,' Daisy cried out. 'You're so clever, Hazel.'

They both looked at Iris, who was still frowning. 'It could work, as long as you don't actually fall for him.'

Hazel stared at her sister in disbelief. 'Of course I won't fall for him. Yes, he's very attractive and I was taken in by him at first. But now I know exactly what sort of man he is. I'm no longer deluded by his charm. He might be handsome on the outside, but that's all he is. Inside he's monstrous. The hardest thing is going to be stopping myself from letting him know how much I detest him.'

Iris nodded her agreement. 'You'll have to keep it secret from Mother and Father as well. You know how they expect us to always be demure and modest in public.'

'So you don't ruin your chances of making a good marriage,' the three sisters chorused together in imitation of their mother's voice, then broke into laughter.

'But you're right,' Hazel said with a sigh. 'I can't do anything that might get tongues wagging. Not because Mother might be angry, but because she's right, it could ruin your chances of making a good marriage.'

'No,' both girls cried out.

'I don't intend to marry anyway,' Daisy said, placing her hands emphatically on her hips.

'And any man who cares more about what society says than he does about the woman he is to marry obviously doesn't love her,' Iris said. 'And I will marry for love or not at all. If you do scandalise society, then it will be a good way to test which men are really worth marrying.'

Daisy nodded her agreement and they both smiled at Hazel.

A slow smile crept across Hazel's lips. Mr Darkwood was going to live to regret ever thinking he could toy with one of the Springfeld sisters.

Chapter Ten

Hazel didn't have to wait long to put her plan into action. The next day an invitation arrived at the Springfeld household for Lady Hazel and her chaperon to attend a weekend party at the Kent estate of Mr Lucas Darkwood.

Her parents received the invitation with great excitement. At least, her mother did, while her father did not object. Both were assuming the invitation proved a formal request for Hazel's hand was imminent. Hazel ignored the little stabs of guilt attacking her stomach and forced a smile on to her face as her mother happily discussed the weekend and her father nodded from behind his newspaper.

They agreed that Nathaniel should accompany her, presumably thinking that while their eldest daughter was securing her own future, their twenty-year-old son and heir might also begin laying the groundwork toward finding a suitable marriage partner.

While Hazel hated keeping anything from her parents, she was particularly uncomfortable with hiding things from Nathaniel. In the past they had always shared everything. But she could not tell him what she was up to. He would be as angry as Hazel was at Mr Darkwood's behaviour. Nathaniel was such an open and honest person, even if she told him what she was doing and why, he would not be able to keep up the pretence for the entire weekend. And even worse, there was a danger that he would want to take immediate action to let Mr Darkwood know what he thought of the way his sister had been treated. And that would never do. It would thwart Hazel's own plans for revenge and she was savouring the thought of being the one to make that objectionable man suffer.

In a flurry of activity Hazel had helped her lady's maid pack for the weekend. Her mounting anticipation continued during the train journey from London to Kent. The steam train seemed to take an interminable amount of time and she was so impatient to get started on her adventure. She was even more impatient for it to be over so she could amuse Iris and Daisy with tales of how she had teased and tormented Mr Darkwood, generally making him feel uncomfortable and regretting that he had ever had the audacity to think he could get the better of Lady Hazel Springfeld.

Mr Darkwood's carriage was waiting for them at the station and they were soon rolling through the Kent countryside. They eventually passed through the ornate black-and-gold gates that signalled the entrance to his estate. They travelled down the long, tree-lined path as it wound through parklands and eventually opened up to reveal the house.

Rumours of Mr Darkwood's wealth had not been exaggerated.

Palatial in style and size, his three-storey home sat on the edge of a large lake, where a spectacular fountain sent a plume of water cascading high into the air. The cream stone used in its construction was catching the late afternoon sun, giving it a warm pale ochre hue. Hazel had heard that his father was a self-made man who had bought the home from an impoverished aristocrat. She'd also heard that Mr Darkwood had further added to his father's fortune. Hadn't he said he had interests in mines and other industries?

As she looked out of the carriage window at the imposing facade of the house, the expansive formal gardens and the estate's many acres of farmlands, she could tell he was indeed a man of some substance.

Despite not having a title, it was obvious he was much more affluent, and therefore more powerful, than many of the noble families who still thought they ruled the country.

The carriage drove around the statue of Apollo in front of the house, his bow and arrow pointing up to the heavens. Crunching on the carefully raked gravel, it came to a halt at the entrance where the household was lined up to greet them.

Before the footman could jump down from the front of the carriage, Mr Darkwood had opened the door, lowered the steps and offered his hand to Hazel.

Suddenly her plan started to fray at the edges and

the excitement bubbling inside her turned to churning anxiety. She looked down at him, his arm extended, his grey eyes gazing up at her. Had she really forgotten just how breathtaking he was? Had she forgotten those unnerving smoky-grey eyes? Had she forgotten the sheer masculinity of the man? She froze, only her throat moving as she gulped down her rising anxiety. And most of all, had she really forgotten the effect this man had on her? How he caused quivering spasms to shoot through her body every time he looked at her? It seemed she had.

'Lady Hazel, welcome to my home. I trust you had a pleasant journey,' he said in greeting.

She took his hand and a quiver ran up her arm, lodging itself in the middle of her chest, making it hard to breathe in anything but quick gasps.

'Yes, very pleasant, thank you,' she muttered, willing her legs to start moving. What was she doing? This was a big mistake. When she had been discussing her plans for revenge with her sisters in the safety of her bedroom it had seemed like a good idea, a jolly jest. But now, seeing him in the flesh, it was no longer quite so funny.

How was she going to get the better of this man when simply seeing him again had caused her legs to forget how to walk and her lungs to forget how to breathe properly?

He raised his eyebrows in question and she forced herself to smile and walk down the steps.

'Your home is magnificent,' she said, needing to say something, anything so she did not seem so out of her depth.

He looked over his shoulder and a dark shadow passed over his face. 'I inherited it from my father.' He looked back at her and once again she felt captured by those piercing grey eyes. 'I am pleased that you and your brother could join me this weekend.'

Nathaniel jumped down from the carriage and greeted Mr Darkwood in his usual cheerful manner, providing Hazel with the opportunity to give herself a stern talking-to. She had to pull herself together in order to implement her plan. Falling apart every time he looked at her was not going to help. All she had to do was ignore the sheer vitality of the man, and not let it undermine her determination. Nor should she waste any time speculating on why his demeanour had changed so drastically when he had mentioned his father. Why he suddenly looked so desolate was no concern of hers and she should waste no time in speculation. She had a mission to accomplish. That's what she should be thinking about and that alone.

It was essential to not forget what he had done, how he had humiliated her, how he was still humiliating her. He was using her, laughing at her. He had put her up against a horse in a bet. A horse, for goodness' sake.

Anger reignited within Hazel. Good, she needed to be angry. Needed to keep fanning those flames. What he had done was unforgivable. She just had to remember he was only handsome on the outside. Inside he was a vile man who was playing a cruel game. He deserved to be the subject of her own game playing. He deserved to be treated with the same disdain with which he was treating her.

'I hope I get the opportunity to ride this weekend,' Nathaniel said. 'I hear you have an impressive stable.'

'I'll instruct the groom to ready a horse for you tomorrow morning,' Mr Darkwood replied, much to Nathaniel's pleasure.

At the mention of horses, Nathaniel had inadvertently added fuel to the fire and Hazel's anger blazed stronger. Those damn horses. She was tempted to lash out now. To let Mr Darkwood know she knew all about just how important those horses were to him, more important than her dignity, more important than her feelings.

Hazel drew in a few deep breaths to get her anger under control as Mr Darkwood led her and Nathaniel down the line of people waiting in front of the house. If she was to succeed in punishing Mr Darkwood, she needed to serve out her revenge in a cold, calculated manner so it did the most damage. There was no point simply lashing out at him in rage. That would not cause him to suffer nearly enough. And she intended to make him suffer, slowly and painfully.

'Lady Hazel, Viscount Wentworth, may I introduce my aunt, Mrs Hetty Darkwood. She is the widow of my father's younger brother and lives here with her three daughters.'

Hazel could hear the affection in his voice as he introduced his aunt and Mrs Darkwood sent him a look that could only be described as admiring. It seemed there were people in the world that he treated with respect, but Hazel was not one of them.

The two women curtsied, Nathaniel bowed, and they exchanged greetings.

'It's lovely to meet you, Lady Hazel, Viscount Wentworth,' Mrs Darkwood said. 'I hope you enjoy your stay at the estate.' She turned to three little blonde girls, aged about ten, eight and five. 'May I present my daughters, Lucy, Alice and Minnie.'

With solemn looks on their faces the three girls bobbed deep curtsies, then looked up at Mr Darkwood, smiling and waiting for his approval.

He smiled back at them and Hazel could see the delight on the young girls' faces. They glowed under his approval.

'Very well done,' he said, causing the girls' smiles to grow even larger.

Mrs Darkwood laughed. 'We don't get many visitors out here. The girls have been looking forward to this weekend and have been practising their curtsies.'

Hazel smiled at the girls. 'Well, I don't think I've ever seen curtsies made with such grace and dignity. Have you, Nathaniel?'

Nathaniel adopted a serious look and shook his head. 'Never, and I've seen a lot of curtsies in my time. They were curtsies worthy of being performed in front of Queen Victoria herself.'

The little girls giggled and once again looked up at Mr Darkwood for his approval. The adoration of the girls was obvious to see and for a moment Hazel's anger softened. Perhaps, if those little girls loved him, then he couldn't be all bad.

He led them further down the line and introduced

them to the head servants, who also looked at their master with affection. Hazel's anger further dampened and by the time they reached the end of the line, despite herself, she, too, was starting to see Mr Darkwood in a kinder light. If the girls adored him, and his servants held him in such obvious high esteem, could he be all bad?

The last servant they were introduced to was the stable master and Nathaniel asked him numerous questions about the horses.

Horses. The mere mention of those animals fanned the smouldering flame of Hazel's anger.

While the stable master and Nathaniel chatted, Hazel seethed, relishing the resurgence of her indignation.

If she was to remain focused on her plan, she also had to remain angry with Mr Darkwood. And the perfect way to do that was to keep that brood mare in the forefront of her mind at all times. The animal that was her rival in that insulting bet. She had to remember that Mr Darkwood must be punished for that insult. He might be kind to his servants, his aunt and his cousins, but he had not been kind to her. She was obviously not worthy of the same respect. She was someone he could insult, use and humiliate.

He offered Hazel his arm and she was tempted to swat it away. Instead she forced herself to smile at him. It was time to start her performance. 'I'm so looking forward to this weekend,' she trilled, taking his arm. 'I'd also love to be shown around the house and hear all about it. I'm sure it has a fascinating history. Perhaps you could give me a tour.'

Once again that shadow passed over his face. 'I'm afraid I know little of the house's history,' he said, his voice terse. 'If you want a tour, you would be better to ask Hetty, or even one of the servants.'

'Is this not your family home? Didn't you grow up here? You must know it well,' Hazel asked as they walked up the divided stone staircase which led to the large, intricately carved oak doors and into the entranceway. She was determined to ignore the little voice that was telling her to stop. Talking of the house was obviously annoying him, but wasn't that what she wanted to do, annoy and upset Mr Darkwood?

'It was owned by my father and now it is owned by me, and, yes, I spent my childhood here, but I don't believe I would describe it as a family home. But if you require a tour, I'm sure one can be arranged.'

His terse reply made it apparent that if any tour was to be conducted, he would not be the one doing it. Some other way would have to be found to get him alone so she could convince him she had fallen in love and was merely waiting for the expected proposal.

They entered the house and Hazel looked around the grand, marbled entranceway and up at the large windows, which gave the space a light and airy feel. If this was any indication of how pleasant the house was, then Hazel did indeed want to see more of it.

'Oh, but I'd love it if you could show me around.' She smiled at him. 'This house is beautiful, so warm and welcoming.'

'As I said, I know little of the house's history. I'm sure the head butler would be happy to show you around. He has lived here most of his life. You could almost say it's more his home than it is mine.'

His brusque manner caused Hazel's smile to fade. She turned from admiring the house to look at him. The granite hardness in his eyes, the thin line of his mouth, forced her to lower her gaze. It seemed her insistence of a tour was indeed annoying him, but not in the way Hazel intended. Why would he be so antagonistic about a house, his family home, particularly one so pleasant? Had something happened here that had caused him to become so hostile? Whatever it was, it was something that affected him deeply.

He bowed to Hazel and to Nathaniel, his face still solemn. 'I'll allow you time to freshen up before dinner. Now, if you'll excuse me, I have other guests to attend to.'

Hazel watched him depart, disturbed that she had pushed him so hard on the house tour. She had not meant to offend him. Well, she *had* meant to offend him, that was her sole reason for being here, but not like that.

She drew in a series of deep breaths to calm herself down, determined to ignore what had just happened. There was no point regretting her actions or thinking about why talk of the house should undermine Mr Darkwood's otherwise composed demeanour.

Don't get sidetracked, Hazel reminded herself. *And most definitely don't start worrying about him.*

He wasn't worrying about her. He wasn't caring about her feelings, so she would not care about his. Nothing was going to distract her from the task ahead.

Chapter Eleven

Focus, Hazel reminded her reflection as she sat on the tapestry bench in front of her dressing-table mirror. While Marie-Clare styled her hair, she tried hard not to think about that sudden black look that swept over Mr Darkwood's face whenever she mentioned the house.

The image of his strong jaw tightening, his eyes growing dark and his body tensing would not leave her, as much as she tried to push it away. Something about this house caused him pain. Something had happened here that he was trying to forget.

She shook her head slightly to drive out her thoughts. Whatever that mystery was, it should not be concerning her. There was no point in her speculating about things that did not matter.

She sat up straighter on the bench. It was her pain she needed to think about, not his. Her mission was not to make Mr Darkwood feel better. It was to make him feel worse, to get her revenge. Whatever personal demons were tormenting him, they were *his* demons and she would leave him to battle with them alone.

But why would mention of this house, the very place at which he was hosting a weekend party, cause him to shut down and become even more solemn than he usually was? It certainly couldn't be the house's fault—every part of which she had seen so far, including this room, was beautiful.

She looked around her room to confirm that assessment.

Natural light from the large sash windows bathed the expansive room in sunlight and the room overlooked the delightful gardens and the farmlands beyond. The walls, lined with painted silk, bearing a delightful motif of small, brightly coloured birds, made the room cheerful and inviting, and the plush oriental carpets covering the polished wooden floor added an additional sense of luxury.

Someone, possibly Hetty Darkwood, had thoughtfully placed a large bunch of fresh red roses in a pretty blue-and-white vase on her dressing table and their lovely fresh scent was filling the room. No, there was nothing about this room to object to and nothing about the house that would invoke a dark mood. But something was causing him anguish.

Again, Hazel reminded herself, she was not here to concern herself with anything that might have happened to Mr Darkwood in the past. She was here to make him pay for what he was doing to her here and now.

As if she needed further reinforcement of how she was being treated, she watched Marie-Clare place the silver hair combs in her elaborate coiffure. Those in-

tricately engraved combs were a symbol of Mr Darkwood's abhorrent behaviour towards her.

Her ire started to rise. She'd like to pull those combs
out of her hair, stomp on them or throw them out the
window. But she would do no such thing. Tonight, they
would serve a purpose. Hopefully, wearing them would
cause Mr Darkwood to think she was entranced by his
gift, that she still held him in high regard. And tonight,
she would be convincing him that her feelings for him
were more than just high regard. She would be acting
her heart out, convincing him that she was so hopelessly in love with him that she thought he was on the
cusp of proposing marriage and all he needed was some
determined encouragement from her. And determined
encouragement was what she was going to give him,
overly determined. She smiled at her reflection in satisfaction. She was going to be so determined in her
pursuit of Mr Darkwood that she would reduce him to
a gibbering, panic-stricken wreck of a man. Oh, yes,
he was going to regret ever taking that insulting bet.

Once Marie-Clare had helped her into her corset,
petticoat and lilac gown, Hazel pulled on her elbow-
length gloves and picked up her fan. She was dressed in
her costume, now she was ready for her stage appearance, where she would play the part of a love-struck
maiden and make Mr Darkwood suffer and squirm.

Nathaniel was waiting for her at the top of the long
circular marble staircase that led to the ground floor.
She took his arm and he escorted her down the sweep-
ing staircase to the drawing room, where the door was
opened by a liveried footman.

The large room was already full of men in black evening suits and women in colourful gowns, chatting politely in small groups and taking drinks before dinner. Hazel looked around and once again she could see no reason why anyone would object to such a lovely home.

Although a large room, the cream walls, edged with gold, made it inviting and welcoming. Several large, gilt-edged mirrors reflected light from the crystal chandelier suspended from the ornately carved ceiling. Paintings, featuring pastoral scenes, lined the walls, bringing the outside world inside, and the room was filled with comfortable, modern furniture, rather than the hard-backed, incommodious furniture often found in the country houses of the aristocracy. No, there was nothing about this room that anyone could dislike.

Hazel's gaze moved to her fellow guests. She was pleased to see no sign of the two young debutantes who had taken cruel pleasure in revealing to her Mr Darkwood's despicable bet. Even though her planned behaviour would all be an act, she did not want to put on her performance with those two young women watching and laughing. She took another look round the room just to make sure they were absent and another thought struck her. There was a disproportionate number of males to females present, and, while most of the men were young, the women were of all ages. That was unusual. Weekend parties during the Season were another place for young women to find a suitable husband and the guest list usually consisted of a large number of young, single ladies. She looked around the room again.

In fact, not one of the women present was younger than Hazel and many were quite a bit older.

Had Mr Darkwood deliberately avoided inviting any women who might present her with competition? Her lips pinched together in annoyance. It seemed he had.

How insulting. He had tried to stack the odds in his favour, so she had more chance of meeting a man and of him winning his demeaning bet.

He was hoping to fob her off on one of these men this weekend so he would get that dratted horse. He couldn't possibly invite any pretty young women like those nasty debutantes who had so insulted her at Lady Danson's ball.

Despite their unpleasant personalities, their good looks made them much more desirable catches than Hazel knew she would ever be. They were the sort of women he expected men to be attracted to, the sort of young women *he* would be attracted to.

Well, he was going to pay for that insult as well.

Lucas had planned out the weekend carefully. Rather than inviting men based on their titles or their wealth, he had carefully chosen men who were intelligent and well educated. The guests consisted of men he had known from his university days, their younger brothers and other family members. Unlike Lord Halthorpe and Lord Dallington, these were men who would appreciate Lady Hazel's enquiring mind and her quick wit. In company such as this she would shine rather than be left to languish among the forgotten girls. Although as he looked at her now, she was doing anything but shining. She was standing at the door, scowling at the assembled guests. This was not going to help her find a suitable partner.

He caught her eye. She continued to scowl at him, then her face transformed and she sent him a bright smile. In fact, it was a smile so bright it almost looked artificial. Although that seemed unlikely. Lady Hazel was not one for subterfuge or artifice.

Excusing herself from her brother, she walked across the room, straight towards him, ignoring everyone else present. She was breaking somewhat from protocol, leaving her chaperon behind, but then convention was not what he had come to expect from Lady Hazel.

Once again, she was dressed in a fussy gown that did nothing to show off the curvaceous figure he knew to be hidden under those pleats, flounces, frills, bows and ribbons. She had looked so much more attractive in the simple skirt and blouse she had worn for their ride in Hyde Park and he hoped the other men in the room would also be able to see her hidden womanly charms under all that frippery.

As she walked towards him, despite her smile, her look was almost one of defiance. She no longer had that diffident expression, which had distorted her features when they had first danced together. Nor were her shoulders rounded as if she was trying to make herself smaller and hide herself away. Tonight, she looked proud, confident and, dare he admit it, rather magnificent.

She was also wearing his combs, which looked rather pretty sitting in her dark brown hair. He was pleased that he had chosen well when selecting the gift. He had carefully looked for combs that would sparkle and catch the eye, because Lady Hazel did deserve to catch a man's eye. A good man, one who would love her and make her happy.

'Good evening, Lady Hazel,' he said when she reached him. 'You look lovely tonight.'

He had expected her to blush at his compliment. Instead she held his eyes with a steady gaze, as if assessing him and his words.

'Thank you, Mr Darkwood,' she finally said, then she smiled again. Once again it was a smile that did not reach her eyes and, once again, underlying that smile was a look of defiance. This was also not like Lady Hazel. Her smile was yet another one of her attractive features, as it was so open, so joyful and honest, but tonight her smile was different. She was different.

But nothing was to be gained by analysing Lady Hazel's smile or her behaviour. He needed to concentrate on his plan to find her a suitable beau.

He turned to the man standing beside him. 'Lady Hazel, may I introduce you to Marcus Stanmore, the Earl of Ridgely. He has recently graduated from Oxford, where he took a first in Classics.'

And he would be perfect for you. He's intelligent, friendly, kind and definitely the marrying kind.

She smiled politely at the Earl and Lucas waited for her to become engrossed in conversation with this obviously learned young man. Instead they exchanged a few pleasantries, then she turned her attention back to Lucas.

'As you were somewhat reluctant to give me a tour

of the house, perhaps tomorrow you might like to escort me round the gardens. I'd love to inspect all that they have to offer,' she asked, still sending him that strange, overly friendly smile.

Lucas nodded, despite his reservations. Not only was it rather forward for a young lady to make such a request, but it was not what he wanted. He wanted her to spend as much time as possible with the other men he had invited for the weekend. But at least the gardens held happier memories for him than did the rest of this house. They had provided him with a refuge as a child, a place to escape to, away from the misery of the house, away from his father.

'You might also like to show me the stables,' she added, raising one eyebrow, almost in accusation. 'I hear they are rather important to you.'

In that she was correct. The stables, like the gardens, evoked no unwanted memories. They had not existed in his father's time—something so frivolous that did not make money would hold no interest for him. Since Hetty and the girls had moved in he had visited the house more than he ever had when his father was alive. And now he had started the breeding programme he had even more reason to spend time at his Kent estate. But the memory of his father still haunted him and could assail him at the most unexpected moments.

'I'd be honoured,' he said with a small bow. He looked around the room to see who else he could introduce Lady Hazel to and tried to ignore the tight ache in his stomach that always accompanied thoughts of his father.

Lucas had been reluctant to host this weekend party at his Kent house—it held too many ghosts from his past—but its size made it the perfect location for such a weekend party, particularly as he had invited such a large number of guests.

Although, thanks to Hetty, the house had changed somewhat from how it was when he was a child. Since she had moved in with her daughters, she had turned it into a family home. The laughter and constant chatter of the three girls, and Hetty's loving affectionate manner, helped keep the ghosts at bay, but it was still not a home he had any affection for.

'Wonderful,' Lady Hazel said. She clapped her hands together and that beaming smile grew even larger. 'Then we can spend some time together, just the two of us.'

Lucas looked at her in confusion. Her behaviour tonight was indeed out of character. Clapping her hands? Over a walk round the garden? Most peculiar.

'Yes,' he said slowly, while he assessed her reaction. 'Although this is a party, so I'm sure you'd also like to spend as much time as possible meeting more of the guests.' He turned to the young man still standing beside them. 'Did I mention that the Earl of Ridgely has a first in Classics? Several of his fellow students are also in attendance this weekend, all very learned, fascinating men, whose company you're sure to enjoy.'

Instead of reacting with interest, Lady Hazel merely nodded slightly in a non-committal manner.

Lucas turned to the Earl, hoping he would say something, anything, but instead he smiled, bowed to them

both and moved away, apparently under the impression
that he was intruding. This would not do at all.

'Allow me to introduce you to some more of the
guests.' Lucas looked around at a room full of the men
he was sure she would like to meet, men who enjoyed
intelligent conversation and would not disparage a
woman because she had a fascination for science.

'Oh, no, let's not,' Lady Hazel said, lightly tapping
him on the arm with her fan, before opening it up and
fluttering it in front of her face. 'I'd much rather stay
here and talk to you.'

Lucas looked down at her as she smiled at him and
blinked rapidly. Was she being coquettish? That, too,
was not like her, but her behaviour tonight was not like
her in so many respects.

A terrible thought suddenly struck Lucas. Was she
flirting with him? She was not a flirt, but the batting
eyelashes and the fluttering fan suggested that tonight
she was. Only the coldness in her blue eyes contradicted
this theory. While her lips were spread in a wide smile
fit to burst, the smile had still not reached her eyes,
which almost had a calculating glint. Another characteristic he would not have otherwise attributed to Lady
Hazel. She was the least calculating woman he had ever
met. She had always struck him as somewhat naive
and somewhat unsophisticated. These were delightful,
genuine qualities he found rather attractive and refresh-
ing, particularly in contrast to the jaded cynicism of the
women he usually associated with.

But whatever she was up to he needed to find someone else for her to talk to. Let her flirt, if that was what

she was doing, with a man who would appreciate it. If she was trying to exercise her womanly wiles on him, she was wasting her time. They needed to be directed towards a man in search of a wife.

He looked above her head and scanned the room. She did not want to talk to the Earl of Ridgely, even though he was an eminently suitable young man, but there had to be someone else here who would attract a woman with as lively a mind as Lady Hazel.

'Dr Maffrey, may I present Lady Hazel Springfeld,' he said, turning to one of the men in the nearby group and interrupting him mid-sentence. 'I'm sure she would love to hear about your recent fossil-hunting trip down in Dorset.'

Once again, she smiled politely at Dr Maffrey and exchanged a few pleasantries, then turned back to Lucas. But Maffrey was made of sterner stuff than the Earl of Ridgely and was not going to let her off that easily. He instantly launched into a monologue about his latest discoveries, pleased to have a captive audience.

Lucas knew the man could talk on the subject for hours without pausing for breath, oblivious to the fact that his listeners had almost started to fossilise themselves. It was a desperate move on Lucas's part to introduce her to Maffrey, but at least it distracted her attentions from him.

She was also now surrounded by a group of suitable men. Hopefully, she would catch the eye of one of them and his work this weekend would be done. He could tell Bromley that he had succeeded and he would get that coveted mare.

He continued to watch her anxiously. Instead of immersing herself in the discussion, he could see she was flicking glances in his direction and trying to excuse herself from the persistent Dr Maffrey. This would not do. She needed to talk to these men, not himself. As much as he enjoyed her company, as much as he appreciated her wit and intelligence, and as much as he was coming to find her increasingly attractive—albeit in a somewhat unconventional manner—for so many reasons, not least of which being the bet he was determined to win, it was essential that she attract the admiration of other men, not him.

Chapter Twelve

The gong rang out loudly, halting conversation and signalling that dinner was about to be served.

To Hazel's immense relief Dr Maffrey stopped talking about fossils. The man was obviously an expert in the subject and at any other time Hazel might have found it interesting, but tonight she had more important things to do and she would not let anything or anyone stop her from reaching her goal.

She took Dr Maffrey's momentary silence in reaction to the still-reverberating gong as an opportunity to turn her attention back to Mr Darkwood.

'I assume I'll be sitting next to you at dinner time,' she asked, doing her best impersonation of a flirtatious woman. 'I know that I would like that very much.'

Hazel knew that sitting beside the host would suggest that she was a particularly favoured guest, maybe even one he was courting, and that was exactly what she wanted. Not to be courting Mr Darkwood. Of course she didn't want that, but she wanted him to think that she was under the illusion that they were in fact a couple, that she was someone special in his life.

She stifled a small laugh when a look of concern briefly passed over his face, showing that he, too, thought her suggestion was somewhat presumptuous. It was the same look she had seen when she had mentioned the walk in the garden, the one he had given her when she had avoided talking to that nice, young Earl of Ridgely. It was one that let her know she was taking the right course of action and making him uncomfortable.

And it was a look she hoped to see again and again, all weekend, until Mr Darkwood started to feel cornered and regretted he had ever met Hazel Springfeld and that he had ever thought he could use her to win a stupid horse.

Before he could answer, Hazel gave a false, light laugh and gripped his arm, as if ensuring that should he want to escape from her she would not allow it. 'Of course I'll be sitting next to you. Where else would I be sitting except by your side?'

He looked down at her arm briefly, his impatience clear in his tight expression. Hazel fought not to react to his disapproval, nor her own discomfort that holding his arm was eliciting deep within her. With determination, and teeth gritted in a smile, she tried to ignore that tremble of awareness that rippled through her.

She was not going to succeed if her treacherous body kept undermining her determination. It was essential to remain calm, aloof and focused, and that wasn't going to happen if her heart kept accelerating rapidly and her breath kept catching in her throat in this foolish manner.

Following the instructions he had given her when they first danced together, she drew in a series of deep, calming breaths and exhaled slowly, trying to get her hammering heart under control.

'I thought you might like to sit next to the Earl of Sudbury,' he said. 'He's a very intelligent young man and I believe the two of you have a shared interest in chemistry. And on your other side I had seated a Cambridge don, someone I'm sure you'll find a fascinating dinner companion.'

Hazel pushed her lips into what she hoped was a petulant pout. 'But I want to sit next to you. I don't want to sit next to any silly old earl or boring old don,' she said in a childlike voice.

'The Earl isn't old, he's only twenty-five and the don is a serious man, one who is far from silly,' he all but snapped back.

Hazel's forced smile became genuine as she registered with immense pleasure the annoyance in his voice.

'Oh, but I want to sit next to you.' She looked up at him, affecting that wide-eyed, eyelash-fluttering gaze she had seen so many other young women give men when they were being flirtatious. 'Can't I sit next to you?'

Hazel was sure she heard, or at least she hoped she did, a sigh of exasperation. 'As you wish, Lady Hazel,' he replied in a voice that sounded none too pleased. He signalled to a footman and gave him some whispered instructions.

The couples lined up and Hazel continued to cling on to his arm so that he would have no choice but to escort her into the dining room, even though, as the lady of the house and tonight's hostess, Mrs Hetty Darkwood would be the more natural choice.

They paraded into the dining room. Mr Darkwood took his place behind the seat at the head of the long table and Hazel stood behind the chair at his right. She looked down the table and noticed that due to the imbalance in the sexes, some men were seated next to other men. Mr Darkwood's determination to introduce Hazel to as many eligible men as possible had resulted in an unfortunate break with protocol.

Although, she had to admit, having an imbalance of men to women was the only thing incorrect about this evening's table setting. Either Mr Darkwood, or his aunt, Mrs Darkwood, should be complimented on presenting a stunning table. The dining room's magnificent cut-glass chandelier, suspended over the table, was making the rows of crystal wine glasses and the highly polished silverware sparkle. More candles twinkled in the candelabrum that adorned the centre of the table, along with large displays of lilacs and lilies, which were filling the air with their sweet perfume. The room had the expected opulence found in most grand homes, but unlike the dining rooms of most aristocrats, the walls were not adorned with paintings of the ancestors. Instead, these walls were hung with paintings of thoroughbred horses, some posing proudly, some with colts at their side, some cavorting in fields and others being ridden by brightly clad jockeys.

Hazel sniffed her disapproval. It was so appropriate. For Mr Darkwood horses were much more important than people. If she needed any reminder of why she was here and why she was so angry with him, she just needed to look at those paintings to remember that insulting bet.

Horses. Hmph.

She sniffed to herself, but she would not let him know just how furious she was with him. She drew in a deep breath and forced herself to smile again. No matter how angry she was, she would keep it to herself and continue to pretend she was smitten with this loathsome man.

The footmen pulled out their chairs and, to the sound of shuffling and the swishing of the women's long, flowing gowns, the guests all sat down. Hazel turned once again to Mr Darkwood, that false smile still plastered on her face. 'I hope you don't think I'm monopolising your attention tonight and taking you from your other guests.'

'Of course not,' he said politely, although without a smile as he signalled to the footmen to serve the first course.

'Mother said you were very naughty to monopolise my attention at the last two balls we attended, dancing with me so much.' She sent him an artificially shy look under her lashes. 'Mother said that people will talk and make assumptions. They might even think that you are my intended, but I told her not to worry. They can talk as much as they like and make all the assumptions they choose to. As you said to me, why should we care what other people say or think about us? I certainly don't mind that we are the topic of gossip and speculation and I'm sure you don't either.'

He raised an eyebrow but said nothing, causing Hazel to stifle a laugh. She was repeating back to him what he had said to her at Lady Clarmont's ball, albeit with her own, devious twist.

Everyone began eating their soup while Hazel looked back up the table with mock fascination. 'I wonder how many wedding breakfasts have been hosted in this room. It's the perfect setting, don't you think?'

He froze, his soup spoon halfway to his mouth, then slowly lowered it back to his bowl of lobster bisque. 'I believe my parents' wedding breakfast was hosted here, but none since then, and I obviously did not attend that event, so I don't know whether it is perfect or not.'

His terse voice was making it clear that this was not something he wished to discuss. Good. If it was making him uncomfortable, then, in Hazel's opinion, weddings were the perfect subject for a polite dinner-time discussion.

'Oh, it would be wonderful,' she gushed. 'I just know it. It's such a lovely room. Yes, I can see it now, the room and the table decorated with my favourite flowers.' She placed her hand on her lips as if she had let something slip and gave a mock embarrassed laugh. 'I mean the favourite flowers of the bride.'

He sent her a small frown of disapproval and resumed eating his soup.

'Yes, I think orange blossoms would look splendid, or perhaps white roses. I love the smell of white roses and they're so romantic. What do you think, Mr Dark-wood?'

'I have absolutely no opinion on the subject.'

She looked back along the table. 'Yes, I think white roses would look lovely, particularly if it's to be a spring wedding.'

Hazel continued to smile as she ate her soup, but there was nothing false about her smile now. She was starting to thoroughly enjoy herself.

When she finished she looked at the bowl and drew her eyebrows into a quizzical frown. 'These are lovely bowls, but I think, if I was the lady of the house, I'd go for something a bit more modern.' She looked up at him as if waiting for his opinion on their future dinner service. 'Don't you agree?'

Mr Darkwood made no reply, merely indicated to the head footman that it was time to remove the soup bowls and serve the next course.

When the green salad was served, Hazel turned to the guest on her right as etiquette demanded, still smiling at Mr Darkwood's obvious discomfort. Listening with only half an ear to the man sitting next to her, she continued to think of more annoying things she could say and do that would put the fear of the altar into the duplicitous Mr Darkwood.

She sent him what she hoped was her sunniest smile as the next course of smoked salmon was served. 'Oh, I'm so pleased to be back talking to you, Lucas.' Once again she put her hand to her mouth as if she had made a slip. 'I'm sorry. You don't mind if I call you Lucas, do you? I mean, we are rather special friends now, aren't we?'

Dare she do it? Yes, she dared. She placed her hand lightly on his hand and smiled at him. 'You don't mind, do you, Lucas?'

Touching his hand was perhaps going a step too far. Not because she worried about the effect it might have on him, but because of the effect it was having on her. This was even worse than gripping his arm. With her gloves now removed so she could eat her dinner, it was skin on skin. She could feel the warmth of his body and, as if she had placed her hand too close to the fire, it burned through her. It took all her presence of mind to not quickly pull her hand away as if from an inferno. The heat searing her fingers rushed up her arm, across her chest, up her neck and to her cheeks. All of which she knew must now be resembling a tomato, a beetroot or some other unflattering vegetable.

But did she need to care how she looked? Should she be disconcerted by her blushes? No, not at all. Her blushing reaction would only add to the appearance that she was smitten with Mr Darkwood. That was all for the best, she tried to console herself. It was just annoying that her reaction was not part of her act, but was horribly, uncomfortably real.

He nodded slightly. 'As you wish, Lady Hazel.'

'Oh, good,' she said, gratefully removing her hand and willing her flushed face to stop exposing just how disconcerted she was feeling. 'And you must call me Hazel.'

'I don't think that would be entirely appropriate, Lady Hazel.'

'Oh, I do. I think it's entirely appropriate. It is my name, silly man.' She gave what she hoped was a girlish giggle and tilted her head on the side. 'And, as I said, we are rather special friends now, aren't we?'

He made no response.

'Now come, say it. Say my name.'

She could see the tension gripping his jaw. 'Hazel,' he said through clenched teeth.

'That's much better.' Hazel smiled to herself and commenced eating her salmon. Oh, how she was looking forward to telling Iris and Daisy all the terrible ways she had teased Mr Darkwood. They were going to laugh until they cried.

The plates were cleared away. A course of roast venison was served and Hazel turned to talk to her other dinner companion.

When the empty plates were removed and the dessert of chocolate torte was served, she turned back to Mr Darkwood. Before she could say anything, he asked her about the health of each of her family members. Once that subject had been exhausted and before she could ask any questions of her own, he immediately asked her about what she was reading at the moment and who her favourite authors were.

It was obvious what he was doing. He was trying to distract her and keep the conversation away from uncomfortable topics such as weddings, how she'd redecorate the room if she was the lady of the house, or their so-called close friendship. It was annoying because she

was hoping to torment him just that little bit more with
hints about their impending marriage. Perhaps next she
could even make reference to their future children and
what names she had picked out. That's if he ever gave
her the chance. But at least if he was taking evasive action and trying to steer the conversation in a different
direction, then he must be feeling under attack. That
in itself gave her some satisfaction.

During the cheese course she once again made polite conversation with her other dinner companion, and
tried to speak first when she turned back to Mr Darkwood for the fruit course, but he got in too quickly and
asked her about her father's political career and the new
bills that would be passed through Parliament before it
rose at the end of the Season.

Damn him. Although, it did at least appear that he
thought her intelligent and informed enough to have
an opinion on politics. She had to at least give him
credit for that. Most men she had met during the Season
seemed to think women incapable of having opinions
on something as complex as politics and they most certainly did not want to listen to any views she might hold.

At any other time she might be flattered, but not tonight. A political discussion was hardly ideal fodder for
flirting. She tried to direct the conversation on to more
trivial topics, but he was relentless in his determination
to not let her slip into frivolity. Under usual circum-
stances an in-depth dinnertime conversation would be
just her cup of tea, but she could not see Mr Darkwood
being unnerved by her opinions on Parliamentary re-
form or the extension of voting rights, even if those

opinions were interspersed with girlish giggles and lots of batting of eyelashes.

The final course was cleared away and it was time for the ladies to adjourn and leave the men to their brandy and cigars. Even though she was trying to frighten Mr Darkwood, Hazel did not have the cheek to assume the role of lady of the house and rise first from the table to lead the procession of women out of the dining room. That honour was left to Mrs Hetty Darkwood, seated at the other end of the table, but Hazel managed to quickly slip in behind Mrs Darkwood to be the next one in line leaving the room. That was a position reserved for the second-most important woman present, which as the unmarried daughter of an earl was certainly not Hazel. It would only have been excusable if she really had been Mr Darkwood's intended.

Stifling another giggle, Hazel gave Mr Darkwood a flirtatious little wave as she departed, which she was sure was seen by all the men at the table. They would all now be thinking that Hazel and Mr Darkwood were courting and, even in the unlikely event that any of them actually did want to get to know her better, they would now realise there was no point in pursuing her. As she left the dining room and entered the hall to the drawing room, that stifled laughter escaped.

So far, this weekend was a resounding success. She had just firmly squashed Mr Darkwood's plan to marry her off, while *her* own plan was being executed with the perfect military precision worthy of a leading general.

Chapter Thirteen

Lucas Darkwood continued to stare at the door through which the women had departed. He had a problem. A very big problem. One he was going to have to put to rights as soon as possible. He turned back to the table, where cognac was being served and men were lighting up cigars, then back at the closed door.

Something had happened to transform his funny, sweet, intelligent Hazel Springfeld into a simpering, coquettish woman who no longer had a brain in her head. Her changed behaviour had been somewhat apparent during their last dance together at Lady Danson's ball, but he had put her sudden quiet reserve down to perhaps fatigue at the late hour or over-excitement due to dancing so much with so many men. But neither fatigue nor overexcitement could explain tonight's bizarre behaviour.

He looked at the men seated around the table. They were a group of the most educated, intelligent men he knew and every one of them was single. Hazel should be in her element. She could be discussing a wide array of topics with men who would enjoy her company. Instead she had latched herself on to him with an almost ferocious tenacity and her behaviour was becoming increasingly disturbing.

Lucas was loath to admit it, but there was one explanation for why Lady Hazel was behaving so out of character. That intelligent, sensible woman was doing something extremely senseless. All evidence suggested she had set her sights firmly on him.

The decanter was passed to him and he poured himself a substantial drink, waving away the footman when he offered the cigar box.

Hopefully he was wrong. A woman as rational as Lady Hazel must be able to see that he was not the right man for her. She couldn't possibly be thinking that they could have a future together. He knocked back the rich, spicy drink and poured himself another, trying to convince himself that there had to be another rational answer, but he could think of none.

If he was right, then he would have to make her see that he was not only *not* the marrying kind, but he was not the right man for her for so many reasons. Whereas so many of the men sitting at this table would make her a perfect husband.

Lady Hazel came from a family where love, warmth and joyfulness were second nature. She would expect such behaviour from her future husband and that was something he could never offer a wife. Such a sunny woman as Lady Hazel would wither away like a flower subjected to constant shade if she was married to a man such as him.

If she was to attach herself to anyone, it should be, at the very least, a man who wanted marriage, who wanted children, who could give her the same type of family she was used to, one where there was laughter, warmth and joy.

And then, of course, there was the bet. He poured himself another drink.

He was not going to win if she did not attract the attentions of at least one man before the end of the Season. He had presented her with ample choice. Why, oh, why did she have to throw away an opportunity to find marriage and happiness with a suitable man and waste her time on him?

Lucas looked down the table at Hazel's brother, Nathaniel, who was talking animatedly to a group of men. He was close to his sister. Hopefully, he would be able to explain to Lucas what Lady Hazel was thinking and why she was behaving the way she was. Lucas could only pray that he was wrong, that he had misinterpreted the cause of Lady Hazel's aberrant behaviour.

He rose and walked down to the end of the table. Nathaniel turned in his chair and greeted Lucas with enthusiasm.

'I'm pleased you and your sister were able to join me this weekend,' Lucas said.

'Yes, so am I,' the gregarious young man responded. 'I'm so looking forward to riding tomorrow. I've already introduced myself to the groom and the stable master and they've picked out a suitable horse for me and said it will be ready for me to head out straight after breakfast.'

'Does Lady Hazel ride?' Lucas asked, edging his way into the subject.

Nathaniel laughed. 'No, Hazie isn't too keen on riding, she'd much rather spend her time reading. You should have asked Daisy to join us. She's the sporty one in the family, not Hazie.'

Lucas could hear the affection in his voice when he talked about his sisters, reconfirming Lucas's view that she came from a close family and deserved such a family in her future.

'I was actually surprised Hazie accepted your invitation for this weekend,' Nathaniel continued, declining the footman's offer to refill his cognac balloon.

'Oh, why is that?'

'Well, Hazie isn't one for social events like this. In fact, she usually avoids them like the plague, but she seemed to be enjoying herself this evening.'

Lucas nodded. Enjoying herself perhaps a bit too much in his opinion. 'Did she say anything to you about why she wanted to attend this weekend?'

Please don't let it be because she's expecting a proposal from me.

'No, although Iris and Daisy were also very excited when they saw your invitation, almost as excited as Hazie was herself.'

Lucas controlled the temptation to sigh in exasperation. This did not sound promising. 'Did they say why they were so excited?'

Nathaniel paused and looked thoughtful, then smiled.

'I'm not sure, but something caused her to change in her attitude to attending parties, which I'm pleased about. It's so good to see her having such a good time.'

It seemed the sisters had kept their brother in the dark, but Lucas was becoming more certain that he knew what had caused their excitement. Lady Hazel, the woman he had thought so intelligent, had suddenly lost all sense of reason.

He excused himself and returned to his chair, his suspicions confirmed. Lady Hazel had unfortunately placed more importance on his invitation than it warranted, had seen it as some sort of overture, an expression of his regard for her.

This was indeed a disaster. He did not want to hurt her, but he most certainly did not want her to continue under the mistaken idea that he was seeing her as a potential wife. There was only one thing for it. For Lady Hazel's sake, he was going to have to be cruel to be kind. He was going to have to show her exactly what sort of man he was and shatter any delusions she might have that they had any future together.

To the accompaniment of rustling satin, silk and taffeta, the line of elegantly dressed ladies had walked down the hall and into the drawing room, where tea and biscuits were being served.

While the guests had been dining, the servants had transformed the drawing room. Chairs had been re-arranged and placed in companionable settings to encourage conversation and the fires had been lit around the room. A footman was pouring tea and coffee, while a young maid was handing out cups to the ladies. From the chatter that Hazel could hear around her, it seemed most of the women were acquainted with each other, the mothers, sisters and other relatives of the men who had been invited for the weekend, and many of the men were associated with various universities and other institutes of learning.

They were exactly the sort of people she would normally be excited to meet. She rarely got to associate with people who saw the importance of further education, but unfortunately, this weekend she would have no time to do that. She had other, more important matters to take care of.

Hazel took a cup of tea off the maid, thanked her, crossed the room and settled down in a comfortable wing chair by the crackling fire and smiled with contentment. She took a sip of her tea with satisfaction as she contemplated all the anguish she had caused Mr Darkwood tonight.

Mrs Hetty Darkwood soon joined her, taking the other wing chair beside the fire and sending Hazel a friendly smile.

'This is such fun, isn't it, Lady Hazel,' she said, stirring her tea. 'It's so wonderful to have the house full of people, laughter and conversation. Lucas never hosts parties at the Kent estate and doesn't visit as much as we would like.'

'Oh, do you usually live here by yourself?' Hazel asked before taking a bite of her biscuit.

'Yes, with my three daughters. I'm so grateful to Lucas for letting us stay here. He's our saviour, really.'

Hazel tilted her head in question. 'Saviour? How?'

Mrs Darkwood looked down at the teacup in her hand and sighed lightly. 'My late husband was a wonderful man, but he wasn't successful like his older brother and he certainly wasn't rich, not in the least. When my husband died, we were left with nothing.' She looked up at Hazel, her eyes sad. 'I appealed to old Mr Darkwood for support as we were all but penniless, but he said no.' She drew in a deep breath and exhaled slowly, then smiled again. 'But those days are now over. When Lucas inherited the estate one of the first things he did was contact me and ask me if I would like to live in this beautiful home.' She looked around the room, still smiling. 'He's done so much for us and the girls just adore him.'

Hazel quietly huffed her annoyance. She was pleased that Hetty Darkwood and her girls were being cared for, but she did not want to hear anything good about Mr Darkwood.

'I suppose you have to manage the house and estate for him, do you, Mrs Darkwood?' That would have to explain it. He had merely taken on an unpaid housekeeper and estate manager.

'Oh, please, call me Hetty, everyone does,' she said smiling. 'No, he has a manager to run the estate and a housekeeper to manage the house. It's amazing how someone's life can change. I went from having to work as a char lady and taking in washing just to make ends meet to living a life of luxury. I can still hardly believe it and every morning I wake up and say a little prayer of thanks.'

No, Hazel did not want to hear this.

'But you're stuck out here, in the countryside, away from everyone and everything. That must be very lonely for you.'

'No, I love the countryside and I often have friends of my own to visit, plus Lucas has allocated me a generous allowance so we pop up to London quite a bit and stay at his town house, which the girls love. They much prefer the countryside, but they love going up to London so they can see more of Lucas.' She shook her head and sighed. 'I would once never have thought that such a turn of fortune was possible.'

Damn, damn and damn. Hazel took a sip of her tea, desperately wanting Mr Darkwood to not have one single redeeming feature.

Mrs Darkwood, Hetty, also sipped her tea and then placed it down on the small round table beside her chair. 'Lucas has given us so much. I just wish that he could be happy. That's why I'm so pleased that he wanted to host a party this weekend.'

She gave a small sigh and sent Hazel an appealing look. 'It's not surprising that he can come across as a bit stern at times, I suppose—after a childhood like his anyone would be stern—but it would be wonderful to see him happy. I think that sometimes he's far too serious. He needs to laugh more.'

Don't ask about his childhood, Hazel told herself. *Do not ask any questions about why he is so serious. You haven't liked what you've heard so far. If you keep asking questions you might be even more disappointed. So stay silent.*

'Does Mr Darkwood not often laugh?' she said politely, ignoring her own fierce commands.

'Not really. The girls make him smile, which is lovely, but I rarely see him laugh.'

Hazel puffed herself up with pride. *She* had made Mr Darkwood laugh. An image of him sitting beside her in the carriage as they drove through Hyde Park entered her mind. He had tipped back his head and laughed out loud, amused by her, entertained by what she was telling him.

'No, that's wrong, sometimes he does laugh at the girls' antics,' Hetty said. 'But I never see him laughing with any of the young women he entertains, which is sad.'

Hazel's sense of self-satisfaction burst immediately and she furiously stirred her tea, even though she had not added sugar. She did not need to hear about these *other young women*, did not even want to think about them.

Hetty Darkwood blushed, picked up her teacup and then placed it back down on the table.

Hazel didn't care. Not one iota. She continued to stir her tea rapidly, the liquid spinning round and round, and a small hollow whirlwind forming in the middle.

What of it if he did entertain lots of young ladies? So what if those other young ladies he entertained couldn't make him laugh the way she could? Although, she was sure they did other things for Mr Darkwood that Hazel would never be able to do for him. Not that she wanted to. She did not want to be *entertained* by him, whatever that meant. All she wanted to do was make him pay for treating her so badly.

'Have there been a lot of young ladies?' Hazel was annoyed at herself for wanting to know the answer to that question, but she did. And she was even more annoyed to hear the constricted sound of her voice, which revealed just how upset she was.

As she waited for the answer, the heat of her face increased. Why did she have to keep asking questions? Surely it did not matter whether Mr Darkwood entertained countless young ladies. He could entertain a different one on every night of the week and she wouldn't care, not one little bit. Although that gnawing feeling in the pit of her stomach she was trying hard to ignore suggested she did care and much more than just one little bit.

'Oh, no, not so many,' Hetty replied, also blushing and fumbling with her cup. 'Certainly no one special.'

Hazel took a sip of her thoroughly stirred tea. Even if she did care, it was simply because it reinforced her low opinion of Mr Darkwood. He presumably had an endless number of women in and out of his bed and none of them was special. It was obvious he treated all women despicably, just like her. Although, quite obviously, it was completely different with her. He hadn't invited her to his bed. Hazel almost spluttered on her tea at the absurdity of that idea.

'But it would be lovely if he did settle down with someone special,' Hetty continued. 'Someone who could make a warm and welcoming home for him,

someone who could comfort him and care for him.'
She sent Hazel a knowing look.

Hetty was obviously suggesting that Hazel was just
such a woman. Presumably that was how Hetty saw her.
Not like the other women Mr Darkwood entertained,
who were sure to be beautiful, flirtatious and the sort
of women who could attract a man's eye for qualities
other than their homemaking skills. Well, there was no
way she wanted to be that woman. She did not want to
comfort a man who could treat her in such a cavalier
manner. And she most definitely did not want to make
a welcoming home for him or care for him. Let one of
those other women that he *entertained* do that.

Hazel took a defiant sip of her tea, then sighed. Who
was she trying to convince? Mr Darkwood did not see
her as a potential wife, or, heaven help her, a potential
bedmate. Wasn't that the very reason why she was able
to torment him in such a way? If he did see her as potential wife material, or as a potential lover, then her
scheme would never work.

'You two seemed to be getting on very well at dinner time,' Hetty continued, looking at Hazel over the
rim of her teacup.

Hazel moved uncomfortably in her chair. It was Mr
Darkwood she wanted to fool, not this woman who had
done her no harm and appeared to be a perfectly nice
person. She did not want Hetty Darkwood to get the
wrong idea and think that she was pursuing Mr Darkwood, but nor did she want to let her know that they
meant nothing to each other.

Oh, why did things have to get complicated? Stuck

for an answer, Hazel merely smiled in what she hoped was an enigmatic manner.

'I think Lucas would make a wonderful husband as well and a loving father,' Hetty said. 'My girls adore him. He just needs a good woman to make him see that.'

Please, please stop, Hazel wanted to beseech her. It did not matter whether Mr Darkwood would make a good, bad or indifferent father. She did not want to talk about him like this, did not want to see him as anything other than a despicable man who had treated her appallingly. She would much rather continue to despise Mr Darkwood than think of him as someone who was kind to children and was adored by Hetty's three young daughters. That did not fit in with the image of him she wanted to keep in her mind at all times, the image of a man using her to get a horse, mocking her and humiliating her.

Once again Hazel chose merely to give an enigmatic smile. 'So, how old are your daughters and what do they like to do?' Hazel was interested in hearing about Hetty's children, but she was even more determined to get the subject off Mr Darkwood.

Like all proud mothers it was all the encouragement Hetty needed and she started telling Hazel all about her daughters and their antics. Hazel smiled, laughed and continued to ask questions, enjoying the obvious delight the woman took in her three offspring.

'It's been lovely to have this chat with you, Lady Hazel,' Hetty said, still smiling.

'Oh, please, call me Hazel. And I, too, have enjoyed our chat.'

* * *

The two women had continued to talk and a pleasant half hour or so passed. Then the men started to drift back into the drawing room, bringing with them the smell of cigar smoke and brandy.

A new complication to Hazel's situation became apparent. When Mr Darkwood joined them, she was going to have to recommence teasing and tormenting him with her deliberately clumsy attempts at flirting. But she had no desire to trick the lovely Hetty Darkwood. Hetty had done nothing wrong. It was not her fault that she was related to *that* man. Hazel would not deceive Hetty, yet she did not want to stop tormenting Mr Darkwood. There was only one thing for it. She was going to have to make a tactical retreat and recommence her assault on Mr Darkwood tomorrow when they went for their walk.

After saying goodnight, she left the drawing room and walked down the hall towards the stairs to the bedrooms. The dining-room door opened as she passed and Mr Darkwood emerged, causing Hazel to stop in her tracks.

She drew in an unsteady breath, Hetty's words ringing in her ears. This was an experienced man, a man who entertained countless women, who took countless women to his bed.

He held her captive with his steel-grey eyes, his expression hard. What on earth was she doing? Her game suddenly seemed a very dangerous one.

He walked towards her and she fought the temptation to turn tail and run off down the hall. Instead she closed her eyes and forced herself to remember what he had done to her and why she was here. The image of those two laughing debutantes came into her mind and what he was doing came crashing back in all its embarrassing detail.

She would not be intimidated by him.

Taking another deep breath, she looked down the hall. There was no one else around. Everyone was in the drawing room. The chance to torment him one last time before she retired had presented itself. She would be brave. She would ignore the shiver of warning rippling through her body and would not let this opportunity pass her by.

Chapter Fourteen

Hazel flicked open her fan with as much flourish as she could master and waved it in front of her face.

'Why, Mr Darkwood, you startled me. You naughty boy.'

His brow furrowed and he looked down at her in annoyance. Good. She now had the upper hand. That went some way to settle those disturbing nerves that were skittering inside her. She ignored their ominous warning that she was playing with fire and continued to smile at him.

'Are you retiring for the night, Lady Hazel?' he asked, his voice clipped.

'Well, I did intend to. I thought you weren't going to join me in the drawing room. When you didn't arrive I started to get bored. None of the other men interest me at all.' She pushed out her bottom lip in a childlike pout. 'So I couldn't see any point in staying.'

The furrows between his brows deepened and his jaw clenched so tightly Hazel was sure she could almost hear his teeth grinding together. Even better. That would teach him. He had gone to all this trouble to invite men he could thrust in her direction. Now she had let him know that he had wasted his time. She would not be manipulated by him or anyone else. She would be the winner here, not him.

'In that case I wish you goodnight,' he said with a bow of his head.

He made to walk past her. She halted his progress by placing her hand on his arm and said a silent thank you that her hands were now encased in thick cotton gloves. Touching his hand during dinner without her gloves on had been a disconcerting experience and she had been reluctant to touch him again.

He looked down at her hand and she was tempted to release him. She fought not to give in. Not to him, nor to the feverish heat that had erupted deep within her. It was essential to keep her nerve.

'But I'll be seeing you tomorrow, won't I?' she said, her dry throat making her voice sound cracked. 'You promised to spend the whole day with me, showing me the gardens.' She wasn't sure if he had actually made such a promise and certainly not one that involved spending the *whole* day with her.

He nodded, still staring at her hand. His obvious irritation making her bold, she gripped his arm, clasping the hard muscles slightly tighter.

'I'm dying to see the gardens and it will also give us a chance to get to know each other a little better.' She smiled up at him in what she hoped was a besotted manner and for extra effect once again batted her eyelashes.

'Indeed,' he said, his back ramrod straight, his eyes unflinching.

'Because I think it is time we got to know each other better, don't you?'

He drew in a deep breath and exhaled slowly. 'I thought that we did know each other, but now I'm not so sure.'

Hazel tilted her head. 'Oh, that is a shame and something we must put right,' she said, trying to give him a dewy-eyed look. 'What would you like to know about me?'

His nostrils flared as he drew in a long, slow breath and then exhaled audibly, while Hazel smiled back at him, gazing into his eyes in mock adoration.

He continued to stare at her. Long seconds passed. She faltered, her eyelids blinking rather than fluttering.

Maintaining eye contact would be so much easier if his steel-grey eyes were not boring into her, as if piercing through to her soul.

She forced herself to stop blinking and to not look away, as tempting as that was. Those granite-hard eyes would not undermine her resolve. She would ignore the way his eyes were making her legs weak. He was obviously annoyed with her. That was why he was staring down at her with such intensity, but wasn't making him annoyed part of the plan?

She would also ignore that hint of sadness that was present in his eyes, behind that veneer of arrogant confidence. Hetty had mentioned a hard childhood. Did that explain the flicker of pain she often detected behind his stern countenance?

Despite herself, she blinked again and looked away, trying to dismiss anything and everything she might or might not see in his eyes. Nothing Hetty had said mattered. She could not think about that now.

Once again, she quickly went over everything those young debutantes had said, rekindling the flame of anger that had burnt so brightly when she had first arrived at Mr Darkwood's estate. As if grasping on to a life raft, she held on to that anger before looking back up at him and adopting that false, overly welcoming smile.

'Well, what do you want to know about me?' she repeated as he continued to glare down at her. 'I believe we should be able to share everything with each other now that we are such special friends.'

He shook his head slowly, still staring down at her with unblinking eyes. 'What I do want to know is why are you behaving like this, Lady Hazel? Why are you so different tonight?'

Hazel went to speak, stuttered and stopped. Her hand left his arm and dropped to her side. Why did he have to ask that? It was not a question she could answer honestly. Not without giving herself away. But what was she supposed to say? She swallowed and forced herself to smile ever more brightly.

'Why, whatever do you mean?' she asked, trying to gather her thoughts. 'Different? How?'

'When we first met you were an intelligent woman. Now you're…' he looked over her head 'behaving in a manner unlike yourself.'

Hazel would not allow herself to be side-tracked by the compliment hidden in his stern reprimand. Yes, she was an intelligent woman. Too intelligent to allow him to get away with treating her with contempt.

'Intelligent, that's not much of a compliment to give a young lady,' she said with a little laugh. 'A lady likes to be complimented on her looks and her clothing.'

Go on, I dare you. Reveal your true scheming self. Reveal to me what you really think of me, that I'm someone who is of such little account that she can be used to gain a horse.

His gaze snapped back down to her. 'Is that what you want? To be flattered and praised for your appearance?'

'What young lady doesn't?' she said in a lisping voice, trying to keep the anger out of her response. It was obvious he was unable to compliment her. Right from the very first time he had seen her on the terrace at Lady Clarmont's ball, all she had ever been to him was a means to win that damn horse. He had hardly even seen her as a person with feelings, never mind as a woman one could possibly ever find attractive.

'All right. If that is what you want.' His voice was not that of a man about to compliment a lady. To Hazel it sounded more as though she was about to be admonished for her unacceptable behaviour. 'Lady Hazel, you're not only intelligent, but you're funny and warm. When your smile is genuine, it lights up your face and makes you radiant.'

Hazel gulped. It was a compliment, a lovely compliment, but it was delivered in a disapproving, almost insulting tone.

'You have beautiful eyes that are a stunning shade of blue, almost violet.' He glared down at her. 'Will that do? Is that sufficiently flattering for you or do you require me to admire your figure as well?'

He looked her up and down and Hazel's legs almost gave out underneath her, as his gaze moved slowly over her body.

She swallowed again and wished he'd stop. No, she most certainly did not want him to comment on her figure. The way he was looking at her was bad enough. She didn't need the additional complication of his words. Each part of her body reacted as his caressing eyes stroked over it and she fought to keep her nerve. If this was meant to be a compliment, it was decidedly more unsettling than it was flattering.

His gaze returned to her face. 'Or would you like me to compliment your lips? Those enticing, tempting rosebuds.' He cupped her chin, tilting her head upwards, and ran his thumb along her lower lip.

Blood rushed to her bottom lip, pulsating against the sensitive skin. No longer able to think, Hazel parted her lips and stared up into his arrogant face.

'Is that what you want, Lady Hazel?' he asked, rubbing the pad of his thumb one more time across her swelling lip before removing it. She stared up at him, her lips parted, her breath coming in quick gasps, unable to think, unable to speak.

This could not be happening. She could not let him toy with her like this. Mentally shaking herself, she tried to think through the fog of confusion that was engulfing her. She was here to teach him a lesson. He deserved to be taught a lesson. That would not happen if she let herself be undermined by his arrogant, commanding manner.

She drew in a long, ragged breath to give herself strength. 'If you like those lips so much, why don't you kiss them?' she dared, knowing that he would never do it, knowing he would finally reveal his true, scheming self.

She was wrong. Before she had time to react, his arm encircled her waist and he pulled her close. She gasped, either at the audacity of the man or because the excitement of being in his strong arms was making it hard to breathe. Then his lips came down on hers. He was kissing her, claiming her as if she was his for the taking.

Her mind fought to take control while her treacherous body reacted, loving the way his lips were possessing her.

This should not be happening. She should put up an objection. She should push him away, but she didn't. Being in his arms was frightening, but more than that, it was exhilarating. She knew it was wrong, but was powerless to stop it. And it wasn't because of his superior physical strength, it was because of her own weakness for him.

It was her first kiss and she was in the arms of an expert. Despite what her mind was trying to tell her, it felt good, wickedly good.

Closing her eyes, she stopped trying to do the impossible. Stopped trying to think about what was right or wrong. Instead, she surrendered herself to the sensation of his warm lips hard against hers. With his arms holding her tightly, his masculine taste and scent filling her senses, all she could do now was react. Her arms wrapped themselves tightly around his shoulders. Her body moulded itself into his hard chest. She could feel his heart beating against her breasts, hard, fast, insistent. With her lips, still desperately aware of the touch of his thumb, she kissed him back, revealing her urgent need for him.

He ran his tongue along her bottom lip. She let out a soft moan and instinctively parted her lips, loving the touch of his tongue on her skin. He pulled her in closer, held her tighter, his body crushed against hers. His cheeks, bearing late-night stubble, rubbed against her skin as he kissed her harder.

When his tongue entered her mouth, Hazel's heart pulsated in greater ferocity, pounding throughout her body and intensifying in her most intimate places. An insatiable hunger for him filled her. Her body was crying out for more than his kisses. She wanted him to caress every inch of her body, to take her and relieve her desperate need for him.

His tongue entered her mouth deeper, plundering, probing. Her hands moved from his shoulders, up his neck, to his head. She ran her fingers through his hair, holding him close. Wanting more, needing more, demanding more.

He broke free, untangled her arms from around his head, placed them at her side and stepped back.

'You asked me to kiss you, Lady Hazel. Now that you've got what you wanted will there be anything else you require? More compliments, perhaps?'

She looked up at him, too stunned to speak, her head

reeling, her breath held, her lips still pulsating. It was as if a whirlwind had just picked her up, spun her around, then sent her crashing back to the ground.

He looked down at her, his grey eyes hooded. 'No? Well, in that case, if you'll excuse me, I have other guests to entertain.'

In a daze, Hazel watched him walk away and enter the drawing room, leaving her alone in the hall.

Had that really just happened? She ran a finger along her lips and blinked.

Yes, he had kissed her. But why? He didn't want her. That was obvious. Was he, too, playing some sort of game with her? If he was, he had definitely won that round.

Chapter Fifteen

Hazel so wished her sisters were with her. If they were, then the three of them would have talked it over, discussed what had happened, why it had happened, what he might have been thinking and what she should do now. With her sisters' help, she would have been able to organise her confused thoughts last night and she might just have got a good night's sleep.

Instead, she had hardly slept a wink, tossing and turning, reliving that kiss, going over and over what had happened and trying to think what it meant.

As much as she wanted to, she could not condemn him for kissing her. It had been under her instigation. She had been the one to dare him. But she had expected him to be shocked at her outrageous suggestion. To make an excuse. To tell her it would be inappropriate.

Once he had shown his true colours, then she could have secretly laughed at him and enjoyed his discomfort. She would have succeeded in making him squirm, making him fear that she was in pursuit of him and he had made a serious error of judgement using her for his own gains.

The last thing she had expected was for him to actually take her in his arms. Men like him did not kiss women like her and especially not in the way he had kissed her. She might be inexperienced when it came to men, but that kiss certainly seemed like unbridled passion to her. It was as if, like her, he had lost control. And then he had walked away as if it had meant nothing to him. He had obviously been in complete control after all and knew exactly what he was doing.

But what *was* he doing? Despite going over and over again what had happened, it still made no sense.

Hazel climbed out of bed and pulled the cord to summon her lady's maid. While she waited for Marie-Clare she stared out the window, not seeing the parklands laid out before her, the same thoughts repeatedly whirling through her head.

He did not care for her, of that she was certain. A man like him would never be attracted to a woman like her. That was why her plan to frighten him into thinking she was expecting a marriage proposal was such a good one.

But last night he did not seem frightened. It was Hazel who had been left completely unnerved by that kiss. He had been the one in control and she was the one completely out of her depth.

Marie-Clare arrived, bringing with her a large porcelain pitcher of warm water and a bowl. She placed them on the washstand, and, her mind still distracted,

Hazel washed while her lady's maid organised her clothing for the day.

Despite the intensity of the kiss, she still had no illusions about Mr Darkwood's feelings for her. He did not think of her in *that* way, the way a man thought about a woman he was attracted to. It had not been a kiss from a man who was wooing a young lady and stealing a forbidden kiss. He had kissed her almost in anger, as if warning her that she was playing with fire and, if she didn't stop, she'd get severely burnt.

And burnt was exactly how she felt when he had left her. Every inch of her body had been sizzling. He had ignited something within her she did not know existed. Her entire body had come alive in his arms. Every inch of her had throbbed and ached for him. In his arms she had lost the ability to think, all she could do was feel, feel the touch of his lips, the touch of his body hard up against hers, the intoxicating scent of him, the heavenly taste of him.

She gently touched her lips, then shook her head, trying to drive the memory out of her head.

Had that been his intention? To get her into a state where she was burning for him? If that had been his aim, then he had succeeded. Damn him. That kiss had stripped her of all control and given him complete power over her.

Shame washed through her as she remembered how she had reacted. It would have left him in no doubt just how much she wanted his kisses. And then he had walked away. He had let her know that he had power over her which had reduced her to a panting old maid desperate for a man's touch.

Hazel gripped the facecloth in her hand, anger driving out her embarrassment. That was exactly what he was doing. That was exactly how he saw her. An old maid he could use as part of a bet and then toy with for his own amusement.

He really was a complete cad. He was already humiliating her over the bet and now he was playing another, even crueller game with her. Had he kissed her to let her know what she was missing out on? Was he now laughing at her over that as well?

Or was he merely trying to frighten her off, to make her too alarmed to continue her relentless flirting? Did he think that kissing the old maid would send her running for cover, or, more to his advantage, running into the arms of one of the other, safer, less overtly masculine men attending this weekend's party?

She threw the facecloth into the bowl, causing water to splash over on to the washstand. Well, if that was what he was up to, he didn't know Hazel Springfeld, did he? She had already made up her mind that she would not let him humiliate her and nor was she going to let him intimidate her either.

Instead she would use that kiss to her advantage. Smiling bitterly to herself, she removed her nightgown and pulled on her chemise. In accepting her dare, Mr Darkwood had played straight into her hands. Even if she hadn't known it at the time.

No, that kiss had not signalled her defeat, she told herself emphatically. He might think he had won, that he had frightened her off, but he hadn't. Not one little bit. This was all fitting in perfectly with her plan. A young lady who has been kissed would have every reason to think that a proposal was imminent and that was how she was going to act when she saw Mr Darkwood again.

Marie-Clare pulled out an ornate day dress that Hazel had packed, foolishly hoping to look as attractive as possible.

She smiled at her maid and shook her head. 'I think I'll wear a more sensible outfit today,' she told Marie-Clare. 'The plain grey skirt and the cream blouse will suffice. And don't bother to dress my hair, simply pull it back in a loose bun and tie it with a ribbon.'

'Are you sure, *mademoiselle*?' Marie-Clare said with a barely concealed frown of disapproval. 'That plain style of dress is only fashionable among certain, *serious*, young ladies.'

Hazel smiled. Marie-Clare had said serious with such a disdainful look, one would think it was the worst insult you could give a young lady.

'And your hair,' her lady's maid continued. 'It can be, how do you say, a little bedraggled if not kept under control.'

Exactly. Marie-Clare had described precisely how Hazel wanted to appear. Her simple clothes would depict her as a bluestocking, a woman who cared nothing for fashion. Just the sort of woman a man like Mr Darkwood would never be attracted to. And she just knew what would happen to her riot of curls if they weren't constrained. It would not be long before they would escape their confinement and she would start to look like a music-hall clown, as one rather rude man had once told her.

Mr Darkwood was about to discover just what a mistake he had made. Regret was going to be piled on top of regret. He was going to regret ever making that bet, regret inviting Hazel into his home so he could foist her off on to some other man, and now he was going to severely regret thinking he could toy with her for his own amusement.

Hazel joined the other guests in the breakfast room, full of new-found enthusiasm for the day ahead. She served herself a large breakfast from the silver tureens lined up on the sideboard, took her seat and sat down next to Hetty Darkwood.

Hetty smiled and said good morning. 'Your brother left early to go riding,' she said. 'So Lucas has invited me to join him and act as chaperon when he shows you the gardens.'

Hazel shook out her linen napkin and placed it on her lap. 'That will be lovely,' she said, trying to disguise her annoyance.

'I hope you don't mind, but I've asked the girls as well. They so love spending time with Lucas.'

'Of course I don't mind,' she said, wishing she did not have to lie. As much as she liked Hetty Darkwood, and as much as she would enjoy spending time with her delightful daughters, it was a flaw in the plan. She needed to be able to flirt and frighten Mr Darkwood and she wasn't going to be able to do that if at the same time she was trying to avoid giving Hetty the wrong impression about her feelings for him.

But that was something she would just have to deal with. Her determination was now so fired up, nothing was going to put her off teaching Mr Darkwood a lesson he wouldn't soon forget.

As she ate her breakfast Hazel tried to ignore the praise that Hetty continued to heap on the man she saw as her saviour. Hazel reminded herself that it meant nothing. Yes, it was nice of Mr Darkwood to treat his relatives with such tenderness, but that did not excuse the way he was treating her.

After breakfast Hetty gathered up her excited daughters and they waited for Mr Darkwood at the bottom of the stairs leading to the front door.

It was a perfect day for a walk in the gardens. The sun was shining in a bright blue sky, broken only by fluffy white cumulus clouds. The day was warm and a gentle breeze was causing the leaves on the large trees to rustle slightly. But Hazel cared nothing for that. She wasn't here to enjoy the weather, or to admire the formal gardens and the woodlands. She was here to get her revenge.

The girls' high spirits seemed on the verge of exploding by the time Mr Darkwood arrived. They rushed up the stairs towards him, each trying to grab one of his hands. Then they discovered a dilemma. There were three of them, but Mr Darkwood had only two hands.

After several attempts to overcome the impossible,

Hetty suggested a solution. The girls could run ahead and pick some flowers to give to their cousin.

With squeals of delight the three girls ran off across the grass to the garden, their long blond plaits flying out behind them. Hazel smiled. Their enthusiasm and pure joy of life reminded her of her sisters when they were children.

'Your daughters are lovely,' Hazel said, smiling at Hetty.

'They are, but they're also rather full of energy. If you don't mind, I think I should chase after them as who knows what mischief they'll get up to if left alone. They'll probably strip the garden bare and then I'll have to answer to the gardeners.' She smiled at Mr Darkwood. 'Why don't you take Lady Hazel to see the stables? I'm sure she'd love to see the horses.'

With that, she walked off briskly, leaving the two of them standing alone at the bottom of the steps. Hazel suspected Hetty had an ulterior motive and wanted to give her and Mr Darkwood private time together and suggesting the stables would ensure they were alone in a secluded place.

Hetty had the wrong idea about the two of them, but Hazel wasn't complaining. Not when it was all working out rather nicely. She could put on a performance of adoring Mr Darkwood, of pretending that kiss meant their fate was sealed, without the awkwardness of doing so in front of Hetty.

She looked up at Mr Darkwood, smiling in triumph. He was not smiling. He was looking in the direction of the departing Hetty, an expression on his face of a

man who had just suffered a betrayal. Good, he did
not want to be alone with her. That reassured Hazel
that once again she had control of the situation and
that was the way things were going to stay for the rest
of this weekend.

He looked down at Hazel, drew in a deep breath and
extended his arm towards her. 'Shall we, Lady Hazel?'

Was there an emphasis placed on the word Lady?
Hazel suspected there was. Was he trying to tell her
that, despite what happened last night, they would not
be on familiar, first-name terms? Hazel was sure he
was. Good. He was worried.

She took his arm and they walked along the gravel
path. In terse statements he pointed out various aspects
of the garden, the topiaries, the lines of oak trees and the
rose garden, where Hetty was trying to stop the three
girls from causing too much damage.

Hazel was sure they must look an unlikely couple.
The plainly dressed bluestocking and the elegant country gentleman, attired in a fashionable cream-linen suit,
embroidered waistcoat and silk cravat.

Eventually he led her towards an L-shaped stone
building built around a large courtyard. A young man
was leading a horse back into the stalls, its hooves clip-
clopping on the cobblestones. He tipped his cloth cap
at them as they passed and Mr Darkwood greeted him
by name.

They walked through an arched doorway and into
the stalls, where she was met by the scent of freshly laid
hay, leather and horses. Several horses were looking
out from their stalls and they neighed as if in greeting.

Mr Darkwood approached the first stall and began stroking the horse's neck. His face visibly softened as he patted the animal. Gone was that hardness to his eyes, that arrogant lift of his chin. The animal nuzzled into his shoulder and he smiled.

'This is Captain Sparkles,' he said, still patting the horse's neck.

Hazel walked forward towards the large animal. 'That's an unusual name,' she said, looking up at the dappled grey horse. It was certainly not one she'd expect Lucas Darkwood to pick. She would expect names more like Warrior, Thunder or Caesar. Something much more masculine than Captain Sparkles.

He laughed, still nuzzling against the animal. 'Yes, it's not what I would have called him, but Hetty's girls chose it. Originally it was to be just Sparkles, but I added the Captain so the poor stallion could maintain a bit of his dignity. Such a fine horse deserves some dignity. He's already bred some winners and I think the best is still to come.'

When you win your bet and gain your coveted brood mare.

Suddenly, his affection for his horse did not look so delightful. He might show affection for an animal, but he most certainly did not show such tenderness when it came to humans. At least, that is, when that human was her. She was just here as a means to an end, a way of winning another animal for his stable. No, despite his gentleness with this animal, he was still despicable.

He turned to face Hazel, still smiling. 'I intend to have the best stud farm in the country and Captain

Sparkles is going to help me do it. I just need to mate this majestic animal with the right mare and I'll have an unbeatable winner.'

Damn him. Why did he have to smile at her? She should be concentrating on his words, not that smile. He was talking about that dratted brood mare, remember. Her rival in the bet. She should not be thinking about the way the smile transformed his face. It did not matter that there was a warmth to his smile that she rarely saw. He was usually so serious, as if he was keeping himself in check, refusing to see the joy and pleasure in the world. Despite herself, she knew his smile was something she would like to see so much more of.

She patted the other side of the horse's neck and received a whinny of pleasure as if the horse was saying thank you. She smiled at Captain Sparkles. He really was rather beautiful and she could feel his muscular power, energy and vitality under her fingers.

'There's a lot of research being carried out at present on inheritance and how traits are passed on from one generation to another,' she said, making sure her hand went nowhere near Mr Darkwood's long, stroking fingers on the other side of the horse's neck. 'Scientists have shown how you can breed animals and plants for certain characteristics, but they've found some characteristics are recessive and some are dominant. The only way the recessive characteristic will come through will be if you breed with another animal with that characteristic.'

'There's nothing recessive about my animals,' he

said, his hand stalling, his face affronted. 'They're among the finest, strongest animals in the land.'

Hazel laughed. 'I didn't say weak, I said recessive. Mendel, an Austrian monk, found that pink flowers in peas were dominant and white flowers recessive. If you wanted white flowers you had to breed two peas with white flowers. It didn't mean the white flowers were lesser or weaker flowers.'

He stared at her for a moment, his hand stilled on the horse's neck. 'You know a lot about breeding, do you?'

'No, not really, but I like to read anything and everything about science. And sorry, I do tend to go on about it. Mother's always telling me off about that. I didn't mean to bore you.' She looked up at him and smiled, then mentally kicked herself. Boring him was exactly what she wanted to do.

'I've already told you, you don't bore me. And I'd never be bored by someone talking about breeding horses.'

She went back to stroking the horse's neck. Oh, well, if that's what he wanted, that was what he would get. 'By breeding two successful horses you increase your chances of getting a winner, but there's no guarantee. There might also be recessive genes that both parents have that you're unaware of.'

She gave a little, embarrassed laugh. 'Just look at my family if you want proof of that. You've met my sister Iris, haven't you? It's hard to believe we come from the same parents. She's so beautiful and graceful and I'm... well, I'm me.' She gave another laugh.

'Don't do that,' he said, his voice stern.

She pulled her hand away from the horse's neck. 'Sorry, am I upsetting him?'

'I don't mean that. Captain Sparkles loves to be stroked. I mean, don't talk about yourself like that. There are enough people in this world who are happiest when they're making others feel bad about themselves. You don't need to do their job for them by insulting yourself.'

Hazel shrugged. 'I'm not insulting myself. I'm just speaking the truth.'

'If you're just speaking the truth, why don't you focus on your attractive features? Last night I told you that your eyes are a pretty shade of blue and you have a beautiful smile. I meant what I said. But these are things you choose to ignore.'

Hazel looked up at him in stunned surprise. Last night these descriptions were not said as compliments. They were almost hurled at her like insults. Now they were being used almost as a reprimand for her self-deprecation. Either way, they were still compliments and were unnerving.

She gave a little laugh to cover her discomfort.

'What's so funny?' he asked.

Hazel shrugged and tentatively went back to stroking the horse. Nothing about this was the least bit funny. Far from it. Once again, he was making her feel uncomfortable. It was supposed to be the other way round. Her plan was already starting to unravel and if it was not to completely fall apart, she needed to rethink her tactics so she could gain the upper hand. And that wasn't going to happen if he kept complimenting her.

Chapter Sixteen

Lucas needed to get control of this situation and that wouldn't be achieved by complimenting Lady Hazel, but he could not abide her habit of criticising herself. The more time he spent with her the more he had come to realise that she had an undeserved low opinion of the way she looked. She had a unique beauty that in many ways made her more attractive than young women conventionally thought of as good looking. If he could see that, then she must be able to as well and she should stop constantly disparaging herself.

But making Lady Hazel see her inner beauty was not what he was here for. He was here to nip her flirting in the bud, to make her see just what a waste of time it was to set her sights on a man who could offer her nothing. And now was the perfect time to do that.

He looked back at Captain Sparkles as he gathered his thoughts.

He had been annoyed when last night she had all but forced him to agree to take this walk with her. Then, after that kiss, his regret in agreeing to show her the garden was compounded. It would be wisest to put as much distance between himself and the lady as possible, not spend more time with her and certainly not time alone.

He looked down at her, still softly stroking the horse's neck with her long, elegant fingers.

He had been annoyed with Hetty for disappearing and leaving them alone together, but perhaps it was all for the best. He would be able to tell her clearly and precisely why she needed to stop this pursuit of him. She needed to direct her attentions elsewhere, to a more appropriate man, and not just because he still wanted to win his bet.

But that wasn't going to happen if he kept complimenting her.

He had tried to direct her attentions towards the other men last night, but last night had been nothing short of a disaster and he had compounded that disaster by kissing her. That was something that must never happen again. What he had been thinking when he kissed her Lucas had no idea, although he suspected it was lack of thought which had resulted in that unfortunate outcome.

When she dared him to kiss her he should have simply walked away. Why he hadn't, he didn't know. All he did know for certain was that their kiss had continued to torment him throughout the sleepless night. He also knew that once he had her in his arms he had been lost. It had taken every ounce of self-control he could master to eventually pull away from her, to remember himself, to remember that he was not supposed to be encouraging Lady Hazel, but letting her see the folly of her flirtatious behaviour.

Instead he had discovered what it was like to kiss those tempting lips. There had been so much untapped passion in her, passion that had been released by his kiss. Her lips had seared into his, her skin had been so soft and inviting, her warm, curvaceous body had felt so good pressed up against him. Everything about kissing her had felt so right. Too right. It had elicited such strong emotions from him, emotions he had never experienced before, emotions he did not know what to do with. He had wanted to frighten her off, but it was he who had been frightened. But he would not think of that now, nor would he remember that kiss. Now was the time to set Lady Hazel straight and let her know she was wasting her time.

That would only happen with plain speaking, not with compliments. She needed to know the truth about what sort of man he was, why they were so unsuited to each other and why she should be directing her attentions elsewhere.

He continued stroking Captain Sparkles, not looking at Lady Hazel.

'One trait everyone in your family seems to have inherited is the ability to be happy,' he said, keeping his voice as steady as possible while leading the conversation in the direction he wanted it to go. 'I'm sure that's a characteristic you'd like to pass on to your own children one day.'

She shrugged one shoulder. 'I don't know if happiness is an inherited characteristic or something you learn from being around happy people. My parents are happy people who wanted to make a pleasant home for their children.' She paused in stroking the horse's neck and looked up at him. 'So, what was your family life like?' she asked, her voice soft and quiet.

Lucas looked out of the door of the stable and released a slow sigh. As painful as it was, it was time to tell her the truth, to let her know what sort of man he was and why he was so wrong for her.

'Not a happy one.' He looked back down into Lady Hazel's compassionate blue eyes. 'I most certainly would not say that my father was able to pass on a tendency to be joyful and the ability to provide a pleasant home to his offspring.'

'What was your father like?'

Lucas placed his hand on the edge of Captain Sparkles's stall to steady himself as painful memories of his father crashed back in. 'Cold is the best way to describe that man. Being around him was like being in a permanent winter.' He looked out through the arched door of the stables towards where the house stood. 'He even refused to have fires in the house for much of the winter. I often thought it was so the house would be as cold and miserable as he was.'

'That must have been very hard for you,' she said in a gentle voice. 'And what of your mother, what was she like?'

He drew in a faltering breath. 'I hardly remember her. She left when I was only a few years old. I suspect he never loved her and only married her for her dowry, her connections and her title. He always referred to her as *that Italian contessa*, with disdain, and he told me she had never wanted me. He said that was why she ran off and left me behind.'

'I'm sure that wasn't true,' she gasped.

He nodded. 'No, it wasn't, but as a child I believed him. When I was at university, I was contacted by one of her relatives who wanted to let me know of her passing. He told me it was my father's cruelty that had driven her out. She hadn't taken me with her because she knew that if she took the son and heir he would track her down wherever she was and drag me back. Apparently, she had written to me often, but I never saw the letters. Presumably my father destroyed them.'

He felt her hand gently touch his arm and he drew in another painful breath.

'Your mother loved you,' she said quietly.

If his mother had loved him, he didn't know. He had certainly had no experience of what love was like.

'But at least I got to leave this house when I was seven,' he said.

'When you were seven? Where did you go?'

'I went to boarding school.' Lucas gritted his teeth at the memory of that school, where there was no more warmth to be found than at his home. The cold showers and chilly dorm rooms were only part of the misery. There was also the relentless bullying of the older boys on the younger, weaker pupils, and the harshness of some of the masters, who were as unhappy as their students. 'I only came back to this house during the term breaks and I avoided even that whenever I could.'

He looked down at her. 'And your Austrian monk

was right about inherited characteristics. I'm just like my father. I have no intention of creating a happy family home for a wife and children. That is one of the many reasons why I will never marry, will never have children. I will not subject any woman to the marriage my mother had with my father, nor will I subject any children to the life I experienced.'

Now she knew exactly what sort of background he came from, exactly what sort of life he would make for any woman foolish enough to want to marry him. It was not the sort of life a sensible woman like Hazel Springfeld would want.

She looked up at him, tears glistening in her eyes. 'You're not your father, Lucas. The way you treat Hetty and her girls proves that. Hetty almost worships you for the kindness you have shown her, and the girls adore you. Hetty said you often laugh with them and play with them. They love you and I suspect you love them as well. You're not your father.'

'Hetty isn't my wife. The girls are not my children,' he snapped back, annoyed that she hadn't taken in the full meaning of his words. 'I will not be marrying anyone, Lady Hazel,' he said, staring intently into her eyes, so she would know that he meant he would not be marrying her. 'I will not subject any woman to the life my mother lived, or any children to the sort of childhood I had.'

She nodded slowly. 'I can see why you would feel like that after all you've been through. You did not deserve that childhood, Lucas, no one did. All children should be raised surrounded by warmth and happiness.'

He looked up, over her head, at the house that had been constantly shrouded in a funereal pall and had contained not a moment's warmth or happiness. He had never spoken of his childhood before, could hardly bear to even think of it. Now that he had, it was as if he was back there. Back to being a frightened, vulnerable child. That was something he could not abide. He was not a child and he would never be vulnerable or frightened again.

'All children, all people, deserve to be loved,' she murmured, her hand moving from his arm to gently stroke his cheek. 'Including you.'

Her hand moving round the back of his head, she lifted herself up on tiptoes and gently kissed his cheek. Desperate for the warmth she was offering, desperate to feel anything other than the pain that was consuming him, he wrapped his arms around her, pulled her towards him and kissed her back, not on the cheek but on her waiting lips. Nor was it a gentle kiss. He was desperate for her, desperate for the comfort she could provide. He needed the solace of her warm body, to lose himself in her, to forget his crippling pain. He needed her to make him feel strong again. To feel like a man.

Forcing her lips apart, he plunged into her mouth with his tongue, letting the feel of her soft lips on his and her feminine taste drive out all other thoughts.

She melded herself into his body and he held her tighter. So tight he knew she must be able to feel his arousal against her legs, to feel how strong his need for her was. Pleasure flooded through him as she rubbed herself against him, her breasts touching his chest, her hips hard against his, her legs moving against his thighs.

His hands stroked down her back to her buttocks, cupping them and holding her firmly against him. Her back arched, her buttocks moving sensually under his hands, feeding the fire of his desire, making it more powerful, more insistent.

He wanted her, out of her clothes, laid out before him, offering herself to him, making him feel like the strong man he knew himself to be. He pulled the ribbon out of her hair and tossed it to the ground, freeing her locks and letting the riot of curls fall around her face, giving her a wanton look that was driving him mad with need.

Cupping her chin, he looked down at her. She was so beautiful, wild and untamed as she gazed back up at him.

Her eyes were glazed and hooded with desire, her lips were parted in invitation and the flush on her face and neck told him she wanted this as much as he did. Kissing her again, he plundered her mouth with his tongue, taking satisfaction in her moans of pleasure.

Moving from her lips, he nuzzled into her neck, kissing the soft, vulnerable flesh. She tilted her head back to give him access. As he kissed a line along her neck, he felt her pulse, throbbing in her throat. She tasted so good. Her feminine scent of vanilla and spring flowers filled his senses like a powerful narcotic, making him desperate for more, much more.

Her breath was coming in faster and faster gasps. He looked down at her breasts, rising and falling under the blouse with each panting breath. He wanted to caress them, to lick and kiss them. Pulling her blouse out of her skirt, he slid his hand under the fabric, gripped her cotton chemise and pulled down her only protection from his caresses.

Taking her breast in his hand, he released his own moan of pleasure as he cupped the full, feminine mound. Running his thumb across the peak, he smiled as it tightened, becoming hard under his touch.

He looked down into her face. Her eyes were closed, her head tilted back, her lips parted as she gasped in time to his caresses. He knew he could take her now. He could strip her of her clothes, lay her down on the straw and make love to her, here in the stables. She would put up no objection. Her arousal was as evident as his own. She wanted him as much as he wanted her.

Kissing her parted lips again, he increased the pressure on her lovely breast, taking hold of the tight nipple between his thumb and finger and gently squeezing, loving the way her moans grew louder until they became cries of pleasure. His tongue entered her mouth again, probing, wanting to possess her. To his immense satisfaction, she entered into the erotic joust, her tongue moving, first tentatively, then with a demanding need that matched his own.

His excitement reaching fever pitch, he kissed her harder, entered her deeper, unable to stop the passion she was evoking in him.

He wanted this woman. Wanted to do more than just kiss and caress her. He wanted to make love to her, now, to lose himself deep inside her warm body.

'You're so beautiful,' he murmured, reaching down

and taking hold of the bottom of her blouse so he could pull it off her and expose her beautiful, curvaceous body to his gaze.

She lowered her arms to allow him easier access and gazed up at him. Her blue eyes were so dark they appeared black, her face and neck were flushed, her breath was coming fast and shallow as she waited in anticipation.

'Lucas,' she murmured softly, her hands reaching out to him. 'You deserve to be loved. I could love you.'

Love.

As if struck by a thunderbolt, hitting him with its full force out of a blue sky, Lucas was repelled backwards. He did not want her love. He did not want anyone's love. He did not need or deserve love.

What was he doing?

He stared at her, suddenly able to see clearly what had previously been obscured by the fog of his desire. He was seducing an innocent young woman. Had he really become such a reprobate? She was not the type to indulge in a passing dalliance, she was not his type of woman. He did not want to marry her, or any other woman, but that was exactly what he would have to do if he had finished what he had started.

'I'm so sorry,' he mumbled, stepping forward and fumbling to pull down her blouse.

His behaviour was unforgivable. He had been about to use her to satisfy his own carnal needs. She did not deserve this. She deserved a man who she could love and who could love her in return. And that man was not him.

She stepped back from him, her cheeks still pink, her eyes wide, looking up at him in a confused appeal.

Damn it all, she still looked so beautiful, so desirable. Her lips had that plumped-up, recently kissed look, her hair was loose and wild around her face as if she had just been bedded. Her chest was still rising and falling rapidly, making him think of those beautiful soft mounds under her blouse, of the hard buds he had so much wanted to take in his mouth.

He let out a groan and closed his eyes. Despite how much he knew it to be wrong, he still wanted her.

'I'm sorry,' he murmured again, opening his eyes.

Turning her back on him, she stuffed her blouse back into her skirt.

He bent down to retrieve her ribbon. 'I'm so sorry, Lady Hazel,' he repeated, hopelessly. 'I did not mean to kiss you. I should not have kissed you. I'm sorry.' He knew his apology did nothing to undo the damage he had done, but he was at a loss to know what else to say, what to do, only knowing that no words were sufficient to make right his unforgivable wrong.

She turned to face him, her eyes lowered, staring at the ribbon in his outstretched hand, as if unsure what it was and why he was offering it to her.

'I've given you the wrong impression and for that I'm sorry,' he stumbled on. 'I don't want to marry you, Lady Hazel. I don't want to marry anyone.'

She looked up at him, her face slowly hardening, then she grabbed the ribbon out of his hand, took hold of her hair and quickly tied it back in a knot behind her head.

'Yes, you should be sorry,' she fired at him, her

words sharp. 'I know you don't want to marry me and I don't want to marry you. You're a despicable man.'

It was no more than he deserved. After kissing her in such a manner she was quite within her rights to demand that he do the honourable thing and ask for her hand. But then, Lady Hazel was a sensible woman, and now she could not be under any illusion about what sort of man he was, what an unacceptable husband a man like him would make.

'You're right. I know I'm despicable. Worse than despicable. I should never have kissed you. It was unforgivable.'

She glared at him, her blue eyes cold and angry. Her fury was to be expected and he waited for the full extent of her wrath to be unleashed on him.

'I don't mean that,' she shouted as she gestured towards where they had been standing when he had kissed and caressed her. 'I mean, I know all about your bet. That is what is unforgivable. That is why you are a despicable man.'

Lucas stared back at her, suddenly struck dumb as he took in the full implications of her words.

Chapter Seventeen

Hazel glared up at him, his furrowed brow and tight lips reflecting her own confusion. How had that happened? Again?

She pulled the roughly tied ribbon out of her hair, winding it around her hand as she fought to organise her thoughts. She could hardly believe it. Had they really kissed, or had it just been a dream and now she was back to reality? As she looked up at a man who was staring down at her with a bewildered expression, it was easier to believe it had been a dream.

But her dishevelled hair, roughly tucked-in blouse and dislodged chemise were tangible reminders that it had been no dream.

Lucas Darkwood had kissed her again, caressed her, with the passion of a man possessed. And she had loved it. Had loved the touch of him. Had loved the sense of power that had flowed through her. Had loved knowing that his desire for her was unstoppable. At least she had thought it unstoppable. Now she knew different. Her unguarded words, uttered without thought, had been enough to cause him to reject her. Again. How could she be so stupid? Why had she said she could love him? She did not love him. Could not love him.

She reached up and grabbed her hair, once again fiercely tying it back behind her head with the ribbon, trying to put the wayward locks into some sort of order, just as she was trying to bring order to her wayward thoughts. Anger raged through her. Anger at herself, anger at him, an anger so fierce it was almost winning the war it was waging against her intense sense of embarrassment and shame.

Pushing down her still rucked-up blouse, she also tried to push away the mortifying thoughts that were rushing through her head. She had all but told Lucas Darkwood that she loved him. He was a man who had used her as part of a bet, who had seen her as a joke, who had now tried to seduce her in a stable, of all places. How could she possibly think she could love such a man? It was ridiculous. She was ridiculous.

She smoothed down her skirt and discreetly tried to pull up her chemise above her still-sensitive breasts and restore it to its proper place.

This was surely all his fault, she thought, attempting to console herself. She had done nothing wrong. She had nothing to reprimand herself for. This had all started because of his bet. This was his fault, not hers.

Her words had stopped the kiss from going any further and thank goodness for that. Heaven knew what might have happened if he hadn't stopped. She might this very moment be in his arms. He might still be kissing her. His hands might still be caressing her. He had almost removed her blouse, he might have continued and…

She mentally held up her hands to stop her wandering thoughts, refusing to allow her mind to go any further. She would not think about what might have happened, what she might have allowed him to do, what she might have wanted him to do.

Instead she clung on to her anger, convincing herself that she would have come to her senses before things went too far. She had accompanied him into this stable with the intention of teaching him a lesson, to show him she was someone he could not toy with. And wasn't that what she had just done? Her words had shocked him, otherwise he wouldn't be standing watching her while she brought order to her disordered clothing, a look of remorse distorting his handsome face.

Hazel could almost convince herself that everything that had happened between them had been a deliberate ploy on her part, all part of her plan to get even with him. Almost.

She smoothed down her skirt one more time, then looked at him and glowered. Before she left, she would give him one last piece of her mind and leave him in no doubt that she was not some innocent dupe that he had toyed with.

'You thought you were being so clever, that you were fooling me, but I've known about the bet all along,' she fired at him. 'You weren't fooling me in the slightest.'

'I'm so sorry,' he said shaking his head. 'For the bet.

For everything,' he repeated, his voice ragged. 'And I should never have kissed you.'

Hazel wished he would stop saying that. She could almost convince herself that she was not humiliated by his rejection, but not if he kept insisting he regretted their kiss.

'And I'm sorry, too,' she shot back. 'Sorry I ever met you.' Hazel knew she was sounding petulant, but with her emotions jumping rapidly between desire, embarrassment and anger, she hardly knew what she was saying, never mind how she was saying it. All she knew was she had to get away from this man and get control of the turmoil that was gripping her.

Before he could say another word, she turned abruptly and all but ran out of the stables. If she put some distance between them maybe, just maybe, she'd also be able to run away from her own shame and confusion.

Almost at the arched doorway, he caught up with her, grabbed her arm and spun her around to face him.

'I can explain everything,' he said, a fervent note in his voice. 'Don't leave like this. You must give me a chance to explain.'

'I don't *have* to do anything and I don't want your explanations,' she said, trying to pull free from him, trying to ignore the effect the touch of his hand was having on her nervous system and trying to ignore the way her traitorous body was loving being so near to him again. 'What you did was unforgivable.'

And the way I reacted to your kiss was even more unforgivable.

'I'm sorry, you're right. I should never have kissed you last night and I certainly should not have kissed you again today. I don't know what came over me. But what I said was true. I can't offer you the life you want. I can't offer you love. You need to marry a man who will love you and make you happy, and that's not me.'

Hazel tried to laugh with disdain, to prove she did not care about his kisses or his rejection of her, but her laughter caught in her throat. 'I don't mean that...that kiss,' she hissed back. 'I don't care about that. I mean your bet. There is no justification for putting me up against a horse in a bet. That is unforgivable.'

She drew in a deep breath, trying to organise her thoughts, to get them clear in her mind, to make him understand how offensive his behaviour had been. 'You want me to marry another man so you can win a stupid bet, of all things. That's the only reason you have paid me any attention. That's the only reason you invited me here this weekend.'

At least he had the decency to look ashamed, but Hazel would show him no mercy. What she had said was true. A man like him would never pay attention to a woman like her. He had, but for one reason only: because he wanted to win a horse. That was unforgivable, but what was even more unforgivable was the way he had made her feel. When she was in his arms, for one moment she had forgotten about that bet, forgotten that she could never attract a man like him. And in forgetting she had made herself vulnerable and exposed her need for him. It had taken his rejection to remind her of the truth. And that was even more unforgivable.

She glared back at him, forcing herself to remember that bet, to feed her anger so it could overpower her humiliation.

'And poor you,' she jeered. 'If you lost the bet you would have to suffer the horror of asking me to marry you. As if I would want to marry a man like you. You seem to be under the illusion that you are either such a marvellous catch that no woman could resist you, or you thought I was so desperate that I would marry any man who would have me, even one who has behaved as despicably as you. Well, you're wrong. I would never marry a man like you.'

He stared at her, his eyes imploring. 'I am so sorry, Hazel, I didn't mean—'

'Yes, you did. You meant to make that bet. Nobody forced you to do it. You just didn't care whether I got hurt or not, or whether you humiliated me in the process.' She pulled at her arm again.

'No, that wasn't it. I was sure I would—'

She held up her free hand to stop his flow of words. 'I don't want to hear your outrageous excuses. What you did was unforgivable. But I had the last laugh.' She gave a small, stifled laugh to try to prove her point.

'I was playing you at your own game. That's why I came to this house party. That's why I've been pretending to be attracted to you. It was all pretence. As if I would really behave this way if I wasn't having a joke at your expense.'

She looked him up and down as if his handsome appearance disgusted her. 'I wanted to make you panic, to think that you were going to lose the bet and would have to marry me. It was all just a big joke for me as well. I was laughing at you.'

He released her arm, his face suddenly hard, but Hazel would not be deterred by his change in countenance. Her anger was up, bubbling towards boiling point, consuming her, overriding her embarrassment and making her reckless.

'You had no right to treat me like that,' she said, her voice raised. 'You have no right to treat anyone the way you have treated me. All women, no matter who they are, even if they're not great beauties, should be treated with respect, not as property to be bartered and put up as a stake in a bet.'

'You're wrong, Hazel,' he said quietly. 'It wasn't like that.'

'No, you're the one who's wrong. Your friends are wrong. I still had a choice and believe me, Mr Darkwood, I would not have married you. I would even have preferred to marry old Lord Dallington than you. He might be abhorrent, but at least he's honest. I know that he only cares about my dowry. Whereas you have lied to me from the moment I met you. I believe that makes Lord Dallington a better catch than you would ever be.'

'I'm sorry,' he repeated, his arms hanging loose at his sides, his broad shoulders drooping.

Good. He was ashamed of himself. And so he should be, but that didn't mean that Hazel was going to accept his apology, that she would forgive him for what he had done.

'Are you? Or are you merely sorry that you were found out?'

He didn't answer.

'Yes, I thought so.' Hazel turned and strode out through the archway, her boots clicking on the cobblestones as she marched across the courtyard. All embarrassment was now forgotten. Rage coursed through her, not just for Mr Darkwood, but for every man who had ever treated her disrespectfully because they thought it didn't matter, because they thought *she* didn't matter.

'I never meant for you to be hurt,' he called out.

She stopped in her tracks, turned and strode back to the stables, her blazing anger still unquenched.

'I'm not hurt,' she threw at him. 'I'm just disgusted by you and your behaviour. And I doubt that you really are sorry. I suspect that's just another lie. You never thought about whether I might get hurt. You didn't think about me at all. I was just a means to an end for you. All you were thinking about was your stud farm, winning that horse and getting the better of Lord Bromley.'

'That's not true, Hazel.' He drew in a deep breath, looked down, then slowly looked back at her. 'That's not entirely true,' he added, his voice constrained.

'Well, perhaps when you have to tell Lord Bromley that you have lost and that you're going to have to come up with some forfeit of equal value to the horror of being married to me, then you really will be sorry.'

'What I did was wrong, but I *was* thinking of you. I wanted to help you. I was hoping you would meet a man who would appreciate you, would give you the future you deserve.'

'Help me. Help me,' Hazel spluttered out, unable to believe the man's audacity. 'You don't help someone by humiliating them. You don't help someone by tricking them, laughing at them, making sport of them for the entertainment of your friends.'

'I did none of those things,' he said back, his voice rising. 'I made the bet because I believed it would benefit both of us. I would win the horse and you would meet a suitable man, and possibly even marry him. I could not see the harm in that.'

Hazel glared back at him, trying to think of a suitable comeback. How could he not see the harm he had caused? The harm he was still causing.

'I knew that I would win, that's why I took the bet,' he said quietly, reaching out his hand towards her.

She looked at his hand, took a step back and glowered up at him. 'How could you possibly know that?'

'Because I always win.'

She laughed at him, a laugh that held no humour. 'Oh, really? Can you not hear how arrogant you sound?'

'I also knew that as soon as other men saw you the way I do, then you would have your choice of beaux.'

'Do not do that,' she seethed. 'Do not try to charm and flatter me. It won't work.'

'I'm not trying to flatter you or charm you. I'm telling you the truth. I knew that once other men realised you were an attractive, intelligent, lovely young woman then they would treat you differently and you would stop running away from them. You would stop acting like a wallflower, but as a young woman who expected men to court her.'

'Oh, so this was all for my benefit, was it? How magnanimous of you.' She placed her hands on her hips, determined not to believe a word he was saying, determined not to be swayed by his flattery. 'Even if that is true, which I doubt very much that it is, it does not justify what you did. You used me as part of a bet so you could win a horse.'

He drew in a deep breath and exhaled slowly. 'You're right. My behaviour was unforgivable and you have every right to hate me.'

'Well, good then,' Hazel said, his capitulation leaving nowhere for her to direct her rage. 'And now I can see no reason for me to remain in this house a moment longer.'

She hesitated, as if waiting for him to make another objection. When none came, she stormed off, still expecting to hear him calling out to her to stop. When no call came, she rounded the corner and rushed up the pathway, her boots kicking up the gravel as she all but ran towards the house.

Determined to maintain her anger towards that loathsome man, she fled up the stairway towards her bedroom, and rang for her lady's maid so they could start packing immediately. She just wished the anger coursing through her body was the only thing she was feeling, that her lips weren't still tingling from his kiss, that her body didn't still bear the imprint of where his hands had caressed her and her heart wasn't aching as if it had been torn out of her chest.

Chapter Eighteen

'And then I said to him, "I know about the bet." You should have seen his face. He looked like a collapsed soufflé.'

Hazel's sisters laughed loudly, just as she expected them to do.

When she had set out for Mr Darkwood's estate, she had promised to return with funny stories to entertain her sisters about how she had teased and tormented Mr Darkwood and made him suffer for daring to behave in such a cavalier manner towards her. And that was exactly what she was doing. She hadn't exactly lied to Daisy and Iris. She had just left out a few pertinent facts, such as the kiss in the hall and the kiss in the stables. If she had included them, she would not have been able to turn the entire enterprise into an amusing anecdote.

It was so much easier to pretend it had all been a jolly good jape than to admit the truth. Not that her sisters would react with anything other than compassion if they knew what had really happened. It was more that she was reluctant to tell the truth to herself.

She did not want to be sad. She did not want to wallow in self-pity and she most certainly did not want to recall that kiss over and over again.

And yet, when she was alone that was exactly what she did. Her mind would not do as it was told. It kept reliving the way he had taken her in his arms. She kept remembering how he looked just before he kissed her, like a man who was in the thrall of passion. Even, dare she think it, like a man who was in love.

A shiver ran through her as she recalled the fire in his eyes. It wasn't just passion she could see, it was also affection. Was it any wonder that she had said what she said? Was it really a surprise that she had let down her guard and asked him to let her love him? And with that one sentence she had broken the spell and ended everything.

Then reality had come crashing down on her. He had made it abundantly clear that she was wrong, that he did not share her feelings. She had made herself vulnerable, had exposed her need for him and he had rejected her. For that she could never forgive him.

She forced herself to laugh again. 'And then I put my nose in the air, turned my back on him and walked away, leaving him standing in the stable, his mouth open, his eyes bulging.' She did a comical impersonation of the man she had just described, one that looked nothing like Mr Darkwood. 'It was then that he realised I had got the better of him and thwarted any chance of him winning his bet.'

Daisy and Iris both clapped their hands in excitement, smiling in admiration at her daring.

Hazel chose not to tell them that he had then asked for her forgiveness. Something which she had refused to give him, not just because of her anger over the bet, but because of her own embarrassment at what she had done and said.

Nor did she choose to tell her sisters about what she had learnt about the terrible childhood he had suffered. She did not want them to feel pity for him. And she most certainly did not want them to see him as a good man, a man who had provided a home for Hetty and her children. These were parts of the story Hazel tried hard to tell not even herself. She wanted to see him as a villain, someone who had treated her badly, and to forget everything that did not fit into that judgement of his character. Unfortunately, they kept popping into her head, undermining her resolve to despise him.

'Serves him right,' Daisy said.

'Yes,' Iris added. 'He'll think twice before treating any other woman badly.'

Hazel nodded, although had Mr Darkwood really treated her so badly? He had said that he expected to win the bet and, when he did, it would mean she'd have attracted the attention of a man, possibly one who wanted to marry her.

Was that such a bad thing? It was what she had been trying and failing to do for the last five Seasons. And hadn't he invited men to his party who he had thought she would want to meet? Men who shared her passion for learning. Men she was unlikely to meet at places like a society ball.

And at the last ball she had attended, thanks to him, she had danced nearly every dance, something she hadn't done before. He had given her confidence, made her feel attractive, so much so that she had been relaxed when she danced, had enjoyed herself. No one's toes had been crushed to pieces under her unruly feet. She had been happy.

But none of that mattered now. She was still furious with him. Not because of the bet. That no longer mattered. Not just because he had rejected her, although that still caused a level of shame and embarrassment that was almost unbearable. She was furious because he had kissed her. He had shown her what it was like to be kissed, to lose herself in a passionate encounter, to feel things she had not known it was possible to feel. Her fifth Season was almost over. She would soon be officially left on the shelf. If she attended a ball next Season it would be as her sister's unmarried companion, not as a young lady seeking a beau. Once that fate was something she was prepared to accept, but now that she knew what she was missing out on, it filled her with a deep remorse that could consume her if not kept firmly under control.

She gave herself a little shake and smiled at her sisters. This self-pity was unacceptable. It was exactly what she had told herself she would not do. It had to stop.

They continued to ask her questions, revelling in what they saw as Mr Darkwood getting his deserved comeuppance. So Hazel continued with her story of how she had made him suffer, how she had come out of the weekend triumphant, while Mr Darkwood had been left behind, defeated, his plans sabotaged, his bet in tatters.

A knock on the door drew Hazel's attention from her laughing, chattering sisters and Marie-Clare entered. 'A letter and a package for you, my lady,' she said with a curtsy before departing.

Hazel opened the box and saw a small posy. The girls gathered around to look at the pretty circle of miniature roses. She opened the letter, then quickly closed it when she saw the signature. It was from him.

'It looks as though you've got an admirer,' Daisy said. 'What has he written? Is it a love note? A poem? Is it from one of the other men who attended the weekend at Mr Darkwood's estate?'

Hazel drew in a deep breath and quickly read the note then screwed it up. 'No, it's a letter from *him*. An apology.'

'Oh,' both girls said at once, looking up at Hazel, then back down at the letter crumpled in her hands.

'So, he's sorry for what he did.' Daisy took the letter out of Hazel's hands, smoothed it flat and read the contents. She looked up at Hazel, her brow furrowed. 'Perhaps he's not as terrible a man as we first thought.'

Hazel pulled the letter out of her hand, screwed it up and threw it towards the empty fireplace. 'Yes, he is. He probably just doesn't want word to get out about how badly he's behaved.'

Iris picked up the discarded letter from the floor, smoothed it out and read it. She, too, looked at Hazel with a furrowed brow. 'He does sound genuinely contrite and it is rather a lovely letter.' She looked back down at the paper in her hand. 'He says he would like to meet with you again. Perhaps you should, so you can hear what he has to say.''

'Never,' Hazel said, pulling the letter out of Iris's hands and tearing it up. She clasped hold of the pieces, as if fearful the girls would take the tiny pieces and try to put them back together.

The two sisters stared at her, no longer laughing. 'And what does he mean by never forgetting the moment you shared?' Iris asked.

She shook her head and shrugged. 'I don't know, perhaps he misinterpreted all my fake flirting and thought I really was attracted to him.' She forced herself to smile and tried to ignore her blushing cheeks. 'But I showed him, didn't I? I had the last laugh.'

Neither sister gave her the hoped-for laugh. They continued to stare at her and she could see the concern on their faces. She walked over to the fireplace and threw the pieces into the empty grate. 'But it doesn't matter what he meant because I never want to see him again.'

He might be sorry for what he did, but she would still never forgive him for making her tell him she could love him.

She stopped walking, her legs suddenly weak, remembering what she had said to him, how she had said it, with such heartfelt sincerity. How could she forgive him for causing her to say such a thing? That—more than the kiss, more than the bet, more than the rejection—was unforgivable and the reason she never wanted to see him again. She had opened herself up to him and he had all but pushed her away. He had made it clear he did not want her and was repelled by her offer.

She had just been caught up in the moment, the passion and the desire to make him see that he could be loved, that the world was not always as cruel as it had been when he was a child.

Of course she did not love him and she never wanted to think of that moment, or those words she had so thoughtlessly uttered, ever again.

She tried to think of something funny to say, failed and sank down on to the chair beside the fireplace. Her sisters rushed over to her and wrapped her in their arms.

'I'm sorry, Hazel,' Daisy said. 'He obviously hurt you, and of course you shouldn't forgive him. But hopefully you can soon forget all about this.'

'Yes,' Iris added. 'Don't give that man another thought. He acted appallingly. You put him in his place and taught him a lesson. Now he's feeling guilty and so he should. You're right to not want to see him again. It's much better to just forget all about him.'

Hazel smiled at her two sisters, loving them for their kindness and wishing that forgetting all about him was as easy as tearing up his letter.

Letters kept coming and Hazel tried to ignore them all. She wanted to rip them up unread, to throw them into the fire so they would be consumed by flames before she could read the contents. But an annoying part of her wouldn't let her do that. Instead she read each one, digesting his apologies, his claims that he never wanted to hurt her. After reading each letter she wanted to shout at him *but you did hurt me, caused me more pain than I thought it possible to feel.*

Instead she put them away in her drawer, unable to rip them up the way she had the first letter. And fool that she was, she would take them out and read them again, as if wanting to torment herself all over again.

While she kept the letters, she gave away the engraved hair combs to a grateful Marie-Clare and the chambermaid loved the gift of the posy of flowers.

Her mother had politely questioned her about the letters she kept receiving and her reasons for returning early from Mr Darkwood's house party. She had also, ever so delicately, asked her whether they were likely to receive a visit from Mr Darkwood. The unspoken question being, was he going to ask for Hazel's hand? Nathaniel had apparently alluded to Hazel and Mr Darkwood seemingly getting on rather well at the house party, which had fanned her mother's hopes.

Hazel had managed to put her off, telling her that, yes, she had been slightly taken with Mr Darkwood, but had decided that a man with his reputation was not for her. Her mother had looked disappointed, but had accepted Hazel's decision. She explained the letters away as correspondence regarding a fossil-finding expedition in Dorset, which as expected, her mother wanted to know no more about. While she hated lying, she convinced herself it was all in a good cause.

At breakfast time, Hazel was finding herself anxiously waiting for a letter from Mr Darkwood. On the mornings none arrived, she would mentally kick herself for being disappointed. Instead, she should be pleased he was finally getting the message that she did not want to hear from him, did not want to read his excuses and explanations.

So it was with a mixture of irritation and anticipation she watched her father as he agonisingly slowly picked up the morning post piled up beside his plate on the breakfast table, sorted through them and handed them out to his wife and children.

When he passed her an envelope bearing Mr Darkwood's strong handwriting, her fingers tingled as she held his note, before she reined in her emotions and slit the envelope open, with as much detached nonchalance as she could muster.

Instead of a letter, the envelope contained two tickets. They were for a lecture on the principles of hydroelectricity. Hazel stared at them. This was quite different from the posy of roses. What was she supposed to do with such a gift?

No one else in the household would appreciate the tickets, so there was no point giving them away. But it was a subject Hazel found fascinating. She had read about this method of generating electricity which could bring light and heat to homes throughout the country. It was a revolutionary idea that could change society and a subject she wanted to learn more about. But did she really want to accept a present from that man?

She stared at the two tickets while the rest of the family continued to eat, chat and read their own mail.

If she went, she would have to take a chaperon. It

would be cruel to make Marie-Clare sit through some-thing she would find completely boring, so she would have to give the second ticket to Nathaniel.

She flicked the tickets between her fingers. The lec-ture was something she really wanted to attend. And just because she might accept the tickets did not mean she had forgiven Mr Darkwood, did it? Of course it didn't. It was the lecture she was interested in, not for-giving him. Nor did it mean that she would have to see Mr Darkwood again.

He hadn't included a note this time. He hadn't men-tioned that he would be attending the lecture. He hadn't even said it was his way of apologising. It was simply a gift of two rather hard-to-come-by tickets to a scien-tific lecture on a topic he would know she would find fascinating.

He was unlikely to attend such an event himself. When had he ever expressed any real interest in sci-ence? And even if he did attend the lecture, it did not mean she had to talk to him. Well, apart from perhaps a polite thank you, but that was all.

Yes, she would go to the lecture. It seemed he had won a small victory and ever so slightly overcome her resistance to him. Giving away the flowers and combs had been easy to do, but these she could not part with.

'I've received tickets to a talk I wish to attend,' Hazel informed her family, choosing not to discuss who they had come from. 'Perhaps Nathaniel could escort me.'

Nathaniel put down his knife and fork and reached out his hand to see what the tickets were for.

'Hmm, sounds a bit dull,' he said. 'But, yes, if you

want to go, Hazie, I'll escort you. It might cheer you up a bit. You've been so down since we returned from Lucas Darkwood's estate.'

Daisy and Iris sent her supportive smiles while Nathaniel went back to devouring his kippers.

'Thank you, Nathaniel,' she said.

'Yes, you have been rather down of late, Hazel,' her mother said. 'That's not like you. You're not sickening for anything, are you?'

'No, not at all. I'm in the best of health.' Hazel gave what she hoped was her sunniest smile to prove her robust good health.

'Hmm,' was all her mother replied, still looking at her with concern. 'Maybe this lecture thing will take you out of yourself.'

Hazel hoped the same. Despite her determination not to wallow in self-pity, she knew that was exactly what she had been doing and it needed to stop.

Perhaps her mother was right. Perhaps this lecture was just what she needed to take her out of herself.

Chapter Nineteen

On the evening of the lecture, Nathaniel and Hazel joined the line of people entering the stone building where it was to be held. Surrounded by the burble of voices from the excited crowd, they handed over their tickets and took their seats in the lecture hall. The stage was set up with various intriguing apparatus, strange contraptions, wheels, light bulbs and other paraphernalia. It looked as though they were in for more than just a speech—they were going to receive a demonstration as well. The chatter around them was filled with speculation about what might be about to happen. Such demonstrations in America were reportedly as much sideshows as scientific lectures and the props on stage had the excited crowd expecting that they, too, were in for quite a spectacle.

Hazel looked around the audience, telling herself she was just curious to see who else might have attended. The crowd was made up mainly of men. They came from all walks of life. There were men in top hats, bowler hats and cloth caps, plus a few women. But there was one person who was not present. Mr Darkwood.

Good. Hazel turned back to face the front. She did not want to see that man again and was pleased he was not in attendance. More people entered the auditorium and shuffled along to take their seats. She looked over her shoulder. Once again there was no sign of Lucas Darkwood and once again she told herself how pleased she was.

The lecturer came on to the stage to thunderous applause. The expectant crowd hushed and the lecture began. Hazel knew it was a fascinating topic and she should be riveted by everything she was hearing and seeing. The flashes of electricity, the wheels spinning and the light show should have had her gasping along with the rest of the crowd.

She also knew she should not be taking furtive looks over her shoulder to see if he had arrived late. Especially as she kept reminding herself she did not want to see him again.

The lecture over, Hazel stood up, picked up her reticule and made to leave. Then she saw him. Standing at the back of the lecture room, leaning against a stone pillar. Suddenly, it was as if Hazel, too, was made of stone. Unable to move she stood in the middle of the aisle, struggling to breathe properly. Had she really forgotten just how handsome he was? She thought her memory had exaggerated, but if anything, she had diminished his commanding presence.

'Hazie, you're holding everyone up,' Nathaniel said.

She looked behind her and saw a line of impatient patrons wanting to exit.

'Oh, yes, sorry. I was just thinking about the lecture and I quite forgot myself.' Clutching her bag tightly in her hand, she moved past the now-empty chairs and down the centre aisle, not looking at Lucas Darkwood.

It would be so tempting to creep out without speaking to him, to pretend she hadn't seen him. But he had seen her staring at him like a startled rabbit. She could not pass by him without, at the very least, thanking him for the tickets. That would be unpardonable rudeness.

Although, to her shame, she was tempted to be rude. It would certainly be a lot easier than actually speaking to him and risking exposing just how much he affected her. Hazel gripped her reticule more tightly and gritted her teeth, determined to get this over and done with as quickly and as painlessly as possible.

Seeing her again brought it all back, just how lovely she was. His unconventional beauty. Kissing her had been wrong, he knew that, but how could he condemn himself for such an action? She was like no other woman he had met before and no other woman had affected him the way she did.

But his behaviour had offended her and making amends was demanded. Her eyes were downcast as she walked up the aisle. Was she really going to pretend she hadn't seen him, to not even acknowledge him?

At least she had accepted the tickets. Hopefully, that suggested she was at least no longer furious with him.

Finally, she looked up. He smiled at her. She stopped

walking, once again holding up the departing patrons, and sent him a small, pinched smile. Her brother followed her gaze to see who she was smiling at. He saw Lucas, gave him an effusive smile and took his sister's arm to lead her over to him.

Thank goodness she had taken her brother as her chaperon, and not her stand-offish maid, or they might not have had the opportunity to converse again.

Nathaniel gave him a hearty handshake and Hazel bobbed a small curtsy, barely looking at him.

'Did you enjoy the lecture?' he asked them both.

'Well, I still don't understand how it all works.' Nathaniel laughed. 'But I enjoyed the flashing lights, the spinning wheels and all those lightning cracks. Great fun.'

'And you, Lady Hazel?' he asked, with uncharacteristic diffidence.

'Yes, it was fascinating and thank you for the tickets.' Her voice was quiet.

Lucas struggled for something to say in response. He was suddenly awkward, like a young, inexperienced youth speaking to a girl for the first time. This had never happened before, even when he was a youth. He knew Hazel was angry, considered him beneath contempt, but she wouldn't be the first woman who had felt like that. Other women had been angry with him, expecting more emotionally than he was prepared to give, but their wrath had never caused this level of discomfort and had certainly not made him act in such an awkward manner.

Nor had he ever before gone to so much trouble to

redeem himself to a young woman. He had never before
sent repeated letters all but begging for her forgiveness.
But with Hazel it was important to him that she forgive. Although there seemed little chance of that, if the
pinched expression on her face was anything to go by.

'I would be honoured if the two of you would join
me for supper at Claridge's so we can discuss the lecture,' he said. He could not let this be the end to it. He
could not let her just walk away, despising him the way
she did.

Although how he was going to discuss the lecture
he did not know. After a long debate with himself over
whether he should attend the lecture or not, he had finally arrived late and had hardly taken in a word of
what the lecturer had said.

He had been so pleased to see her seated in the
crowded auditorium. While the audience gasped and
applauded he had seen nothing of what was happening
on the stage, his attention focused entirely on Hazel.

And now that he had seen her again, it was not
enough to just know she had accepted his gift, he
needed to talk to her, to try to at least explain himself
one last time.

Her eyebrows drew together. 'Oh, no, I think…'

'We'd be delighted,' Nathaniel enthused. 'Won't we,
Hazie?' He smiled at his sister, then turned to Lucas before she responded. 'Hazie enjoys nothing better than
talking about things like this.' He gestured towards the
stage with a twirling arm, as if it encompassed the entire field of scientific research.

'Good, then I'll arrange for my carriage to take us there.'

Lucas rushed out, quickly found his coachman and instructed him to bring the coach to the front door, then he hurried back to the lecture hall. He had almost expected Lady Hazel to have disappeared and was relieved to see her waiting inside the entranceway with her brother.

They drove through the busy, chaotic London streets, with Nathaniel chatting with great animation, while a silent Lady Hazel stared out of the window.

When they arrived at the hotel, a waiter ushered them to a table in the busy dining room, where many of the other people who had attended the lecture were also taking supper.

He tried to make polite conversation with Lady Hazel while they waited for their meal to arrive, but her one-word answers made it clear she was not in the mood for conversation. But Nathaniel filled in the gaps, chatting away and seemingly oblivious to the tension between his sister and Lucas.

While they sipped their wine, Nathaniel continued to do most of the talking until he spotted a friend across the room, made his apologies and quickly departed.

An uncomfortable silence descended while Lucas fought to think of something, anything, to say, but the words to express what he was feeling eluded him, particularly as he had no idea what it was he was actually feeling.

Over the last month, he had gone over and over all the things he wanted to say to her if he ever saw her again. Now he had the opportunity and he was suddenly tongue-tied. Something else he had never experienced before.

'I'm so pleased you accepted my tickets and the invitation to supper,' he finally said, determined to end the silence before it stretched out beyond breaking point.

'It was kind of you to send them. Thank you.'

They sank back into an even more uncomfortable silence.

'I thought the lecture would be something you would appreciate,' he finally said. 'The tickets were my way of saying sorry for the way I treated you. The tickets and the flowers, and, you know, all that...' His voice petered out. He really had turned into a bumbling schoolboy.

She gave a small laugh and her cheeks turned pink. 'I realised they were supposed to be an apology. Don't worry. I would not be so stupid as to think they were tokens of affection.' Her cheeks grew a darker shade of red. 'After everything that has happened there is obviously little affection between us.'

She might have accepted the tickets, but it was obvious she was a long way from accepting his apology. Perhaps she never would, but he at least had to try, even if his attempts were becoming increasingly awkward.

'Despite all that has happened, I would like to think that one day we could be friends, or at least if not friends, that we could be cordial to each other.'

She sat up straighter in her seat. 'I would like to think I would always be cordial to everyone.' An edge of primness had entered her voice.

'And that one day we could be friends?' Lucas knew

it was more than he should ask for, more than he deserved.

She shrugged her shoulder, picked up a small cake and placed it on her plate, then stared at it, as if reluctant to even look at him.

'I can see you have not forgiven me for what happened.' He looked down at his plate and drew in a deep breath to give himself strength then looked back up at her. 'For that bet. For that kiss.'

She looked up at him. 'There's nothing to forgive. It was nothing. I've forgotten about it already.'

Lucas doubted that. Her tense behaviour made a lie to her claim. And he most certainly could not forget their kiss. He had kissed a lot of women in his life, forgotten most of them, but he knew he would never forget kissing Lady Hazel Springfeld.

It hadn't just been the kiss that had made it so memorable, as passionate as it had been, but his reaction. The warmth and closeness that had flooded through him when he held her in his arms was unlike anything he had ever experienced before. He had felt so close to her, physically and emotionally. It had been wrong to kiss her, but at the time, nothing had felt more right. But it *had* been wrong and it would be selfish to think otherwise. Lady Hazel should be kissed by a man who loved her. She should be made love to by a man who had married her and wanted to devote the rest of his life to her. That man would never be him. She deserved a man who could give her a warm, welcoming, happy home. Someone who could provide her with a life like the one she was used to. And that was not him.

'I'm surprised you have forgotten our kiss,' he said quietly, almost to himself as he ran his finger around the top of his glass. 'Because I haven't.'

He looked at her, at those big blue eyes staring back at him in stunned surprise.

'Kissing you was an unforgettable experience,' he continued. 'I know I shouldn't have done it, but I have no regrets for myself. My only regret is that I upset you.'

She shook her head slowly from side to side, her eyes growing even bigger. 'You don't regret it?'

He shook his head. 'Kissing you was unlike anything I have ever experienced before.' He knew he was sounding like an unsophisticated youth, not a man who had kissed so many women he had lost count, but that was how she made him feel, as though she was the first woman he had ever kissed. 'It was wrong, I know that, but it felt so right at the time. But I never meant to upset you.'

A slow smile crept across her lips and she put her fingers on them as if to stop it. 'I wasn't upset and I don't regret it either.'

She lowered her hand, letting that lovely smile shine on him. 'I rather enjoyed it.' She bit the edge of her top lip as if the words had escaped but continued to smile at him. 'It was rather exciting.'

He smiled back, wishing he could repeat their kiss right now, right here, regardless of who was watching. 'It was, wasn't it.'

They continued to smile at each other, enjoying their secret. The tension Lucas had been carrying round in his shoulders for the last month started to release its painful grip. With his shoulders relaxed he could suddenly breathe more easily. But there was still something else he needed to apologise for, something else he needed to be honest with her about.

'The day after you left my estate, I contacted Lord Bromley and told him the bet was off.'

Her smile died and her expression closed down, as if shutters were being lowered and firmly locked tight. 'Well, I suppose you had no choice in the matter, did you, considering that you weren't going to win?' She tilted up her chin and looked around the room, as if no longer wanting to discuss the subject.

He shook his head. 'That hardly mattered and maybe I still would have won. In fact, several men at the party had asked about you, said they were disappointed you had left before they had had a chance to get to know you better.'

Her lips pulled down, as if she did not believe him.

'If I had still been determined to win, I would have told Lord Bromley about them. That was all that was required to win. If Bromley had spoken to those men, then he would have had no choice but to admit defeat, but I knew you were right. The bet had been insulting. I had not thought of your feelings. I'd only been concerned about winning.'

Once again, her eyes had grown large in surprise. She blinked a few times as if considering what he was saying. 'So, what did Lord Bromley expect in return? What forfeiture did you have to make?'

He waved his hand as if that was of no importance.

'What was it? I want to know.'

He paused.

'Well?'

'I had to surrender my entire stud farm to him, all the horses.'

Her hand shot back to her mouth. 'Oh, I'm so sorry. That will be the end of your dreams of breeding champion horses.'

He waved a hand in dismissal. 'Unfortunately, yes, but it was a price I was more than prepared to pay and no less than I deserved.'

'But what of Captain Sparkles? Did you have to give him to Lord Bromley as well?' Concern was now etched on her face, but it was for his horse, not for him.

He nodded.

'But the girls must have been heartbroken.'

'Hmm, yes, they were upset,' he said, trying not to remember their sad faces as Captain Sparkles was led away. 'But I compensated them by buying them each a pony and organising riding lessons. And once Lord Bromley has grown bored of boasting to everyone of his victory, I will buy Captain Sparkles back from him. No doubt he'll ask a highly inflated price, but so be it.'

She reached across the table and placed her hand on his. 'Oh, Lucas, I am so sorry. I never meant for that to happen.'

'None of this was your fault. I brought it all on myself. It was all due to my arrogance and, as you so rightly said, my lack of concern about another's feelings. I'm just sorry I didn't call Bromley out on the spot when he suggested that appalling bet, rather than behaving in the disreputable manner that I did.'

She continued to frown. 'Poor Captain Sparkles.'

He covered her hand with his own and smiled at her in reassurance. Their gazes met and held. His fingers entwined with hers. He felt as though he could stay like this for ever, just holding her hand, looking into those lovely blue eyes.

She sent him a small smile. 'I suppose I should feel complimented. Instead of being valued at the price of one horse, it seems my value has increased to that of an entire stable of horses.'

'Your value is immeasurable,' he murmured. 'And you taught me a valuable lesson. Achieving a dream should not come at the expense of someone else. I should never have accepted that bet.'

'No, you shouldn't. Although, as you said, you did expect to win. You did expect to find me a beau.'

'It did not seem to me to be much of a challenge,' he murmured.

He continued to gaze into her eyes and watched a delightful blush spread across her cheeks.

'My mother has found it a challenge,' she said with a little embarrassed laugh. 'Otherwise I wouldn't still be unmarried at the advanced age of twenty-three.'

'It's because she keeps introducing you to men like Halthorpe and Dallington. Men you have no desire to marry.'

Men who don't appreciate you the way I do.

Nathaniel rushed up to the table, interrupting them. Her hand shot back from his and disappeared under the table. She lowered her eyes, took a few breaths, then looked up at her brother and smiled.

'Hazie, I've just been talking to the lecturer, Professor Smythe,' he enthused, looking over his shoulder to where a group of men were standing, listening with rapt attention to the lecturer.

'Come over, I'll introduce you to him. You, too, Mr Darkwood. He really is quite entertaining.'

The spell had been broken between them, but Lucas told himself he should not be disappointed. All he wanted was Lady Hazel's forgiveness, for them to be on more friendly terms, and he had achieved that. He did not want more from her, so had no right to be disappointed that she was no longer gazing up at him with something that looked suspiciously like adoration. In fact, he should be grateful for the interruption. It would be unforgivable if he did anything to suggest there could ever be anything more between them than just friendship.

They stood up, followed Nathaniel across the room and joined the group.

He looked at the assembled men. These were the sort of men that Hazel should be gazing at with adoration. They were the sort of men he had invited to his weekend party. Learned men who could offer a young, intelligent woman a future.

Nathaniel introduced them and Lady Hazel told the lecturer how much she had enjoyed the talk. Lucas could see the surprise on the older man's face when she started asking him thoughtful questions about turbines, generators and storage capacities.

To his intense annoyance, the other men in the group were also giving every appearance of being impressed by Hazel and, even worse, he recognised that look on several of their faces. It wasn't Lady Hazel's intellectual prowess they were showing their appreciation of.

He had no right to be jealous, if that was what the bile rising in his throat and the tightness in his jaw was. He'd never experienced jealousy before and he shouldn't be experiencing it now. He didn't want her. He didn't want to marry her, or any woman. One of these men could offer her what he could not. He should be happy that they were paying her attention. But as he glared at the other men, he knew it wasn't happiness that was coursing through his veins.

Chapter Twenty

Lucas forced his rigid lips into something resembling a smile, trying to convince himself he was pleased that these men were enjoying her company. He had her forgiveness. They were now on friendly terms. His guilt had been assuaged. Now he should be happy for her and pleased she had these men's attention.

She asked the lecturer another question and the men all gazed at her in obvious admiration. The tension in Lucas's shoulders returned and his smile became harder to maintain.

That unfamiliar feeling gripped him more tightly. It was no longer guilt that was consuming him. It was something else, something much worse.

What was wrong with him? Was he so like his father that he begrudged her happiness? Was he so like his father that he had no real intention to make amends for his bad behaviour? Was he such a cad that even though he didn't want her for himself, he didn't want any other man to have her? Could he really be so reprehensible?

It seemed he was an even worse man than his father.

Or was it that he did want her? The thought hit him like a punch in the stomach and he suppressed a shocked gasp. Of course he did not want her. He wanted no one.

She looked over at him, still smiling that lovely, genuine smile, and despite his confused state he smiled back.

He knew that he rarely smiled, but with her, smiling was the natural response. How could he not, when confronted with such a delightful smile? Unlike so many other young women, her smile never contained artifice. She had flirted with him during the weekend party, but even that had not been due to coquettishness, but had been her attempt to get even with him for his outlandish bet. She had been determined to teach him a lesson and she had succeeded. She had made him see how badly he had behaved, what an inconsiderate cad he was.

And at the time he had suspected there was more to her flirting than just coquettishness. He had known she was not like that. She was no coquette. She was honest and open. What you saw with Hazel Springfeld was what you got and he had to admit, he was liking what he saw, more and more.

He realised he was still smiling at her like some sort of adoring puppy, turned his gaze quickly to the lecturer and began nodding, as if fascinated with whatever it was the man was discussing. It seemed he wasn't immune from adopting some artifice himself when it suited him. That, too, was something he had never experienced before. Guilt, jealousy and now subterfuge, not to mention confusion. What was happening to him?

Hazel Springfeld was causing him to act out of character, like a man he hardly knew.

Another man joined the group and introduced himself as a meteorologist, which caused the topic of conversation to instantly change, with questions flying at the newcomer, including ones from Lady Hazel. She was obviously enjoying herself.

Smiling, her eyes shining with pleasure, she was obviously more comfortable in the company of these educated men than she ever was at a society ball. There she had been a wallflower. Now that she could relax and be herself she was like a beautiful rose in full bloom. Here she was the centre of all these men's attention.

That was good. Wasn't it? Of course it was. The tickets had been a gift she appreciated and now, thanks to him inviting her to supper, she was enjoying herself in the company of men who appreciated her for who she was, not for her dowry or her title or anything else she might bring to a marriage.

She was in her element and had presumably forgotten all about him and his bad behaviour. He was achieving what he had set out to do, making amends. He should be satisfied with this outcome.

So why did he want to drag her away from this group of men who were rabbiting on endlessly about weather patterns and cloud formations? Was he really so much like his father that he could not stand to see other people enjoying themselves?

The group was joined by the lecturer's young assistant. Damn him. Why did he have to be young and so good-looking? He instantly got into a deep conversation with Lady Hazel and Lucas could see just how much she was enjoying the young man's attentions. Was the man flirting with her? What right had he to flirt with her when Lady Hazel was his guest?

'If you would like to learn more about the subject, you must visit our study and laboratory at the scientific institute,' the assistant said, causing Lucas to grit his teeth.

'Oh, yes, that would be a delight.' She smiled at Lucas as if it was he who was responsible for this invitation. Lucas attempted to smile back, his teeth clenched so tightly his jaw was starting to ache. He knew he was acting like a spoilt child, but he did not want other men inviting her anywhere, even if it was just an innocuous scientific institute.

'In fact,' the assistant continued, 'we're looking to employ someone to do some clerical work, aren't we, Professor Smythe?'

The older man nodded. 'Indeed, we are.'

'It's nothing particularly exciting, just filing and whatnot, but would that be something that would interest you, Lady Hazel?'

Her smile grew wider, showing just how much it would interest her.

'The wages are rather low, I'm afraid,' the professor added, 'but it would mean you were part of the team and you could sit in on lectures if you wanted to.'

Hazel clapped her hands together and turned to look at Lucas, her eyes shining with excitement.

Lucas swallowed to try to ease the fiery bile that had once again risen up his throat. 'I'm not sure if that would be entirely appropriate,' Lucas said, hearing the censorious note in his voice.

Her smile faded.

He had no right to tell Lady Hazel what she could or could not do, but somehow he was incapable of stopping himself. 'I'm sure your parents would not approve of you working for wages.'

She nodded and sighed slightly. 'Oh, yes, you're right.'

She looked so crestfallen and Lucas knew he should be ashamed of himself, not feeling as if he had won a victory. His intention was to make amends to Lady Hazel, not to put obstacles in the way of her happiness. Was he really such an appalling man?

'I know,' she said, her face brightening up. 'I won't take wages. I'll do it as a volunteer. No one objects to a lady doing volunteer work.'

'An excellent idea, Lady Hazel,' that annoying assistant said with a bow.

Bile rose back up his throat and the tension in his jaw increased. He should let this go, let her have this happiness. He had no right to interfere.

'But you would need a chaperon,' Lucas said, ignoring the commands of his brain. He looked at the young assistant, feeling an absurd sense of victory over a rival. He did not want her spending time alone with this man. It might have once been his goal to introduce her to someone suitable, someone for whom there might be a mutual attraction, someone, heaven help him, that she might even possibly marry, but he did not want that now.

'You're right, again,' she said, nodding. She turned

to the assistant and the professor. 'Thank you for the offer. I'll ask my mother, but I'm afraid Mr Darkwood is right—she might not approve.'

Like the cad he knew himself to be, Lucas smiled with satisfaction at the disappointed assistant. Then he looked at Lady Hazel. She was no longer smiling. Her eyes, which moments ago had been bright and shining, were now dulled by disappointment. She was standing quietly, her hands clasped in front of her, instead of enthusiastically asking questions.

Had he really sunk this low? Was he really prepared to ruin her dreams because of an inexcusable jealousy? A jealousy he had no right to feel. So what if something developed between her and the young assistant? He had no right to prevent it from happening, had no right to stand in her way of finding happiness.

He swallowed down the bile. 'I'm sure there will be a way round it,' he said reluctantly. 'Perhaps your mother will come up with a solution. There might be other women working at the institute who can act as a chaperon. Perhaps Nathaniel will be able to accompany you to and from the office.'

He looked around to see what Nathaniel thought of this arrangement and spotted him talking to some friends across the room. It seemed he wasn't taking his role of chaperon terribly seriously tonight, so might not be the best of choices to protect his sister from the advances of amorous young assistants.

He looked back at Lady Hazel. Her lovely smile had returned and her eyes once again sparked with pleasure as if he had bestowed on her a fabulous gift. If she knew the uncharitable thoughts that had been going through his head when he made that suggestion, she certainly would not be smiling at him like that.

'Yes, I'll speak to my mother. I'm sure I can make her agree,' Lady Hazel said to the professor and his assistant.

'Then I will wait to hear from you,' the assistant said with a bow before departing.

The scientific conversation resumed and slowly other members of the group drifted off. Finally, the professor also made his goodbyes, but not without once more reminding Lady Hazel about his offer of a job and saying he was looking forward to her joining the team.

'Oh, it's so exciting,' she said to Lucas once they were alone. 'I can't thank you enough for bringing me here this evening.'

He nodded, guilt tarnishing any pleasure he might have taken from her exuberant thanks.

Nathaniel joined them and Lucas excused himself to arrange for his carriage to be brought around to the front of the hotel.

The trip back through the London streets was a stark contrast from their journey to the hotel. Instead of sitting in sullen silence, Lady Hazel was now brimming with excitement, while her brother said nothing, just smiled at his sister, and Lucas looked out of the window at the chaotic passing parade of coaches, horses, pedestrians and men on bicycles.

She chatted with enthusiasm throughout the journey about everything the professor and the other men had said. When she had exhausted herself, she paused, drew in a breath and smiled at him.

'Oh, this has been such a wonderful evening. I don't know when I have enjoyed myself so much. Thank you, Mr Darkwood. I think I can honestly say all is now forgiven and forgotten.'

'Forgiven and forgotten?' her brother asked.

'Oh, it's nothing, Nathaniel, just a small disagreement between Mr Darkwood and myself.'

Wasn't that exactly what Lucas wanted to hear? So why did he feel even worse now than he had when she was so angry with him? Was it because another man had made her happy, other men whose company she had enjoyed? Was it because she could reduce what had happened between them to *a small disagreement*?

'I'm pleased you enjoyed the lecture,' he said, trying to keep all rancour out of his voice.

'Oh, I did. And to think I might soon be working at a laboratory and attending lectures.'

'That's if your mother agrees and can find you a suitable chaperon,' Lucas reminded her, hoping, despite himself, that this would not be achieved.

'I'm sure Mother will work something out. She can be quite resourceful.'

'Mmm,' he murmured and looked out of the carriage window again. *And if she thinks there's a possibility of marrying off her eldest daughter, she will no doubt become extremely resourceful.*

He turned back to face Lady Hazel, his face etched with fake concern.

'I wonder whether your mother will mind you mixing with people outside your class.' He clung on to this idea as if he had been thrown a lifeline. Hopefully, her mother would see the same danger in her associating with these scientists as Lucas did, that she might marry one. Although Lucas cared little whether they had a title or not and he suspected her mother wouldn't either. Proof of that was her mother not objecting when Lucas invited Hazel to a weekend party. Hazel's mother had to be aware that he had no title. He was getting desperate in his objections to her new job and he knew it.

'That won't be a problem,' Nathaniel said. 'While none of the men we met today had titles, many of them were younger sons or related in other ways to some of the country's most prominent and respectable families. I'm sure when I point that out to Mother, she will be more than happy for Hazie to mix with them.'

Damn that young man. Why did he have to come as Lady Hazel's chaperon and not her lady's maid, who kept her opinions to herself.

'I'm sure none of that matters anyway,' Lady Hazel said. 'I'm only going there to work in an office and hopefully to attend lectures. It's not like going to a social event.'

No, it's worse, because these are people who are more likely to appreciate your intelligence than the sort of men you have been meeting at society balls.

Lucas was still seething when his carriage pulled up outside her home. He jumped out, helped her down the small steps and escorted her up the pathway. Nathaniel said his goodbyes and disappeared into the house, leaving them at the door, the liveried footman standing to attention just inside the open door.

He was reluctant to say goodbye. Would this be the last time he would see Lady Hazel? Now that he had achieved his goal, he had gained her forgiveness, that was all he required from her. He could now put this entire episode behind him. There was no reason for them to ever see each other again. It wasn't as if he was courting her, the very idea of such a thing was absurd. Wasn't it?

'Thank you, Mr Darkwood, I had a wonderful time,' she said and bobbed a small curtsy.

'I'm pleased you enjoyed yourself and I wish you good luck for your future,' he said, trying hard to mean it.

She tilted her head in question. 'My future?'

'Your job, the lectures.'

And all those damn men you are likely to meet.

'Oh, yes, and thank you for that as well. If you hadn't invited us for supper, that would never have happened.'

That was something Lucas knew only too well and didn't he now regret it.

'And are we now friends?' Lucas said, feeling somewhat awkward. When had he ever wanted to be friends with a woman?

'Of course we are.'

He should be pleased by her reply. Yet the heaviness that had settled on his chest suggested he wanted more from her, even though he had no right to expect it, particularly as there was nothing more he could offer her.

They remained standing on the doorstep, both seemingly reluctant to leave. Finally, she nodded goodbye and headed through the doorway. Lucas watched her go, his eyes drawn to the swishing of her skirts, the swaying of her hips. He should be pleased with the way things had turned out. They were now friends, all was forgiven and they were both able to go back to their own lives. And yet, as the footman closed the door on him, he couldn't help but feel he had just let something precious slip through his hands.

Chapter Twenty-One

Hazel knew she should be happy. She had everything she wanted. At least, everything she would have wanted prior to meeting Lucas Darkwood.

Yes, she had once dreamed of marriage and children, but that had been when she made her debut. It was a dream that had started to dim by the end of her first Season. By her fifth she knew it was unlikely to happen and the sensible thing to do was to put such dreams aside. She had become increasingly reconciled to being content as an unmarried woman, one with nice hobbies, who chaperoned her unmarried sisters and eventually cared for her ageing parents.

That is, until *he* came into her life. In the short time she had known him he had reignited that small spark of hope, the one that made her believe that she, too, would one day experience love, marriage and having a family of her own. He had caused her to dream again, to dream of being in love with him and being loved by him.

It was a dream that had been extinguished as quickly

as it had been ignited. He had kissed her, then he had immediately rejected her. Now she was determined to be a realist, to be happy with her life just the way it was. She was no longer angry with Mr Darkwood, at least not for the way he had treated her. She still harboured resentment towards him for the way she felt about him, but she could hardly blame him for being handsome and charming. It was not his fault that, like a senseless naive, young girl, her head had been turned by a man who was unavailable to her.

They had parted on good terms. Had agreed to be friends and she should be content with that. There was no point pining for what you never had and never could have.

But one thing she did have, one thing that brought her immense joy, was her job.

She looked around the professor's crowded office, at the wooden desk, chairs and large filing cabinets pushed up against the walls. It was messy, it was cramped and, until she had got busy with a feather duster, it had smelt of dust, but she loved being here.

She had a real job. She smiled to herself. Well, it was almost a real job. Her parents had agreed she could work in the office on condition it was a voluntary position. The idea of an earl's daughter doing paid work was a step too far for them. But after a brief discussion they had come to the conclusion that it would be nice for Hazel to have a hobby outside the home. She knew how to interpret that. They had decided that there was now no possibility of her ever marrying. The Season was almost over. She was twenty-three years old, would be turning twenty-four before the start of the next Season. Next Season her beautiful sister Iris would make her debut, putting Hazel further in the shadows. There was little chance of a woman of her advanced age finding a suitable husband, so a little hobby would have to do as a substitute.

As for having a chaperon, to her surprise, that seemed to give them less concern than having a job. Nathaniel or one of the servants were to walk her to and from the office, and while she was working, a friend of the family who worked in the same building had been instructed to pop in occasionally to keep an eye on her. Again, Hazel interpreted that as meaning her parents were confident no one would be after her virtue, so it was perfectly safe. And as she would soon be off the marriage market, spending time unchaperoned would not cause the same scandal that it would have when she was actively seeking a husband.

While she couldn't describe the job as riveting—it mainly consisted of filing reports and experimental results—the professor had been true to his word. She was given plenty of leeway and she was able to spend as much time as she liked reading the papers she was filing. As a result, she was becoming quite the expert on a wide range of scientific endeavours.

She was also allowed to sit in on lectures. Obviously, she would not be able to study for a degree, no women did that, but she would be able to learn, study and mix with people who saw scientific exploration as exciting, not something that elicited stifled yawns.

Yes, she should be ecstatic at the way things had

turned out. But she wasn't. Lucas Darkwood had ruined everything. Hazel hadn't admitted it to her sisters, could barely admit it to herself, but the evidence could not be ignored. It was evident in her thoughts, in her dreams, in her constant state of agitation. She had tried to ignore it. Had tried to explain away what she was thinking and feeling as anger, confusion, regret, anything except what it really was.

She was in love with Mr Lucas Darkwood. And it was a hopeless love. She, fool that she was, had fallen in love with a man whose good looks and wealth meant he could pick any woman he wanted. And to make things worse, he didn't want any woman. Well, at least, not as a wife. But more importantly, he didn't want her. He had kissed her, yes, but that was all and that was because she had all but thrown herself at him. He wanted no more from her and had nothing to offer her, certainly not his love, certainly not marriage.

She picked up another pile of papers that the professor had dumped on a seat in the middle of the office and began scanning them to see where they should be filed.

This was what she should be doing. Concentrating on her wonderful new job. Throwing herself into her studies and forgetting about that man. She should forget about that kiss, forget about how he had made her feel, and forget all about those smoky-grey eyes that could cause her to melt when he looked at her. She had to stop thinking about the touch of his lips on hers. She had to completely put out of her mind what it was like being held in his strong arms. She had to never again dream about the touch of his hard, muscular body pressed up against hers. She most certainly should not remember the delicious taste of him when she kissed him back, the sensation of the rough skin of his cheeks rubbing against hers, or that intoxicating masculine scent of his. No, she had to put all such thoughts firmly out of her mind.

She closed her eyes and drew in a slow, steady breath to regain the composure that thinking of that kiss had so easily stripped away from her.

And now, in the middle of this office, was most certainly not the appropriate time to think of that. She opened the filing cabinet, pushed in the papers and closed it with a decisive clunk. She was a new woman now, she reminded herself for the umpteenth time. She was part of the new breed of women who didn't just sit around all day taking tea and gossiping. She was part of the working world, a professional woman, and she should act accordingly.

And the professor was so thankful for all that she was doing. When she'd first arrived, papers had been piled everywhere, on desks, chairs and in toppling stacks on his desk. She had quickly got to work, reorganised the chaotic filing system and tidied away the clutter. He had been so pleased with the way she had organised everything and every time he was able to find what he was looking for without having to fumble through countless papers, he would thank her again and tell her he didn't know how he had managed before she started working for him.

Now that there was some semblance of order in the office she had less to do. That meant she could bury herself in the research papers and pass the day exactly where she wanted to be, reading about the latest scientific discoveries. Well, that was one of the places she wanted to be. She would not think about the other place, the place that involved being enfolded in Lucas Darkwood's arms. No, she would not think of that. Ever again.

Mr Darkwood would not be thinking about kissing her, of that she was certain. He had said he did not regret it, but by now he probably hardly even remembered it had happened. Why would he? He had probably kissed countless women, whereas she had only ever been kissed by one man. That was what made this so foolish, made *her* so foolish.

She picked up another pile of research papers, scanned through them and then stared absent-mindedly out the window at the busy street below.

If what was happening to her was a scientific experiment, Hazel knew the evidence would prove she had fallen in love with Mr Darkwood, but what did she really know of love? He was the first man who had paid her any heed. He was certainly the first man who had kissed her. Was that the only reason she had fallen for him so hopelessly, because she didn't know any better?

She looked back down at the papers in her hands. It was a definite possibility, but she had no way of knowing for sure.

If only a scientist really had made a study of love and the workings of the human heart, she might know the answer. Hazel was sure that would be a fascinating area of research and would answer questions that had plagued men and women since the beginning of time.

But enough of that. Hazel focused on the papers in her hand and told herself, once again, not to think of that man, that kiss, or the meaning of love.

She sighed. Knowing that was an order she would never be able to follow.

Retreating in the face of defeat was a new experience for Lucas Darkwood. But that was exactly what he had done. He had not experienced defeat before, not until he had been defeated by Lord Bromley. And now he had retreated from society to his house in Kent, where he could bury himself in the countryside.

London, with all its distractions, could not hold his attention. He had no desire to see any of the women he usually passed his spare time with. Even his business interests didn't hold much attraction. Defeating other men at business, proving that he was better, more successful than them, particularly those who had been born to wealth and privilege, had always given him a great deal of satisfaction. But no longer.

So he had retreated to the place of his miserable childhood, where he could wallow in his present misery. He had planned to spend as much time as he needed in solitude, licking his wounds and cutting himself off from the world. But solitude was impossible when you had three active, excitable girls running round the house. Being miserable was difficult to maintain when they filled the once cold and gloomy house with their laughter and playfulness.

Even if he was feeling empty inside, he had to maintain a false sense of joviality in front of the girls. He would do nothing to ruin their carefree, childish joy. He had learnt from his father how misery was infectious and he did not want to infect his lovely cousins with his own gloom and doom. But when he was alone the full weight of his misery would descend on him like a black cloud blocking out the sunlight.

And what was worse, he knew he had no right to feel like this. He had lost the bet, but he no longer cared about that, it was not the cause of his discontent. His only regret was that he had taken the bet in the first place, but he had learnt his lesson. He now knew better than to risk hurting other people for his own gain.

He had thought his unsettled state was because he had offended Lady Hazel and she was angry with him. But now he had her forgiveness. He had thought that was the cause of his agitation. To try to drive thoughts of her away he had sought her out, sent her presents and letters. Now that she had said she was no longer angry with him he should be satisfied. He should be able to go back to how he was before he met Lady Hazel Springfeld.

But that had not happened. He was just as agitated, just as discontented as he had been before her forgiveness. It was a vexatious state, but he was sure time away, time in which he could recuperate would be all that he needed to eventually drive out those thoughts of her that kept tormenting him.

'It's lovely that you're spending time here, Lucas,' Hetty said to him one morning over breakfast. 'And the girls just love spending time with you. But I was wondering whether you might not be hiding from something.'

Lucas looked up at her from reading the morning newspaper and frowned. 'Nonsense, I'm just having a break in the countryside.'

'Hmm, and yet, apart from taking the girls out for walks, you don't seem to be spending much time enjoying the countryside. If you don't mind me saying, you seem to be spending a lot of time moping.'

Lucas frowned at her. Defeat, retreat and now moping. These were things he did not do. Or at least he had never done before.

'I believe I might know the reason for you hiding away in the countryside,' Hetty said.

'I'm not hiding,' Lucas responded as evenly as he could before taking a sip of his coffee.

'Well, then, I believe I know the reason for your sudden desire to get in touch with nature.' She gave a little laugh. 'I believe, Lucas, you have done what you thought you would never do. You have fallen in love.'

Lucas nearly spluttered on his coffee. He placed the cup down in the saucer with a decisive clink and sent Hetty an incredulous look. He most certainly had not fallen in love. The idea was preposterous. Love meant commitment, marriage, possibly even children. That was not for him. And yet...

He picked up his cup again, then placed it back in the saucer. No, it was ludicrous. A man like him falling in love with a woman like her. Never.

Hetty raised her eyebrows, waiting for his response.

'I am not the sort of man who falls in love,' he said with as much conviction as he could muster.

'There's no such thing. There are men who have fallen in love and men who have yet to fall in love, but there are not men who can't fall in love. You used to be a man who was yet to fall in love. Now you're a man who *has* fallen in love.' She smiled at him, obviously very pleased with herself for making this observation.

'Well? I'm right, aren't I?' she probed.

He released a sigh of frustration and was about to tell her that she was wrong, very wrong, then thought better of it. He had been lying to himself for so long now that it was becoming second nature, but she was right. As impossible as he would once have thought it, he had now joined the ranks of men who had succumbed to that illogical emotion. Why else had he reacted with that pitiful act of jealousy when she had been talking to the young assistant? Why else had he secreted himself away in the countryside, except as a way of hiding away until he was free of the thoughts and feelings that were consuming him. Feelings that quite possibly were, in fact, love.

'Perhaps you're right,' he said. 'But even if I have, there's nothing to be done about it. It will pass and that will be that.'

Hetty shook her head slowly, staring at him as if he were a strange creature, the likes of which she had never encountered before. 'But why would you want it to pass? You've fallen in love with a wonderful young woman who would make you a loving wife. You should be embracing this glorious state, not wanting it to pass as though it's some sort of illness.'

An illness described it perfectly. He had become infected by a condition he didn't want, had never sought and now wanted to be rid of. He did not want to be thinking about Hazel Springfeld day and night. He did not want to be whipping himself up into a froth of jealousy at the thought of her with another man, of her talking and laughing with some young assistant professor or any other learned man. He wanted to be back to the way he was before he had ever met Lady Hazel.

And Hetty was right. The object of his love was a wonderful young woman, one who would make someone the perfect wife, but that man would not be him.

'I will not be embracing this supposedly wonderful state,' he said, shaking out his newspaper. 'I do not want to be in love with Hazel Springfeld. I do not want to marry her. What could I offer a woman like her? Nothing. You're right, she is a wonderful young woman. As was my mother by all accounts. And look what happened to her. No woman should have to endure what my mother did.'

Hetty stared at him as if he had just grown horns. 'Lucas, you are not your father,' she said slowly as if he had suddenly become dim-witted.

'Aren't I? I believe there are more similarities between us than differences, but I prefer not to discuss them.' He stared at the newspaper, the black letters a blur before his eyes.

He had no intention of telling Hetty just how badly he had treated Hazel, how he had used her and made her the subject of a bet. Nor did Hetty need to know just how enraged Hazel had been with him. And rightly so. It was only her gracious nature that had resulted in her finally forgiving the unforgivable.

He tried to read the print, hoping that Hetty would realise that was the last word on the subject. He was wrong.

'Let's compare you with your father and see how much alike you really are.'

He looked at her over the top of the paper. She was tapping her chin with her forefinger as if giving the subject serious consideration.

'Your father did not care if my children and I lived in poverty. We're family, the closest family he had after you, but he didn't do a thing to help us, despite his wealth. When you heard about our plight you immediately took us in and gave us a lovely home to live in and made provision for my daughters' futures.'

Lucas merely hmphed in reply. It was the least any man would do. He had a large estate and more than enough money to support Hetty and her girls. That proved nothing.

'Your father married your mother because she brought with her an enormous dowry and a title,' Hetty continued. 'You don't care about such things. You'd love Hazel Springfeld even if she was a pauper with no title.'

Lucas merely scowled again. That hardly meant a thing either. Lady Hazel did have a title, so Hetty's claim was mere supposition.

'Your father was determined to make this house as miserable and cold as he was. You've ensured my daughters are happy and are having a wonderful child-hood.'

Lucas smiled at that. Hadn't Hazel said the same thing? Then he frowned again. That, too, meant nothing. It was Hetty who ensured this house was a happy one, not him.

'Your father despised people who were warm, open and loving. You've fallen in love with a woman because these are the very qualities she possesses.'

Hetty stared at him, waiting for a response. Instead he merely shook his head. Even if what she said had a kernel of truth to it, it wasn't the full story. If Hetty knew the full truth about how he had treated Hazel, she wouldn't be saying such things. He was tempted to tell her that even his father hadn't stooped as low as betting a woman's future against a horse, but was disinclined to share anything that might be insulting to Lady Hazel.

'It's not as simple as that,' he said instead.

'Yes, it is. Don't let your father's miserable ways continue to taint your life, Lucas. You have a chance of happiness, real happiness. You should be grabbing it with both hands, not pushing it away.'

Lucas slowly folded up his newspaper, then drew in a deep breath. 'It's not my happiness I'm worried about, it's Lady Hazel's. I don't want to make any woman miserable the way my father made my mother miserable.' He had already hurt Lady Hazel once. He did not want to risk doing anything that would ever hurt her again.

Hetty shook her head and sighed. 'You are not your father and a marriage to Hazel Springfeld would not be like the marriage between your parents.'

Lucas stared at her and slowly shook his head. She was wrong. All his life his behaviour had been defined by his father. And he *was* just like him. Lucas knew he did not have the capacity for easy laughter the way other men did. He had never had any desire to create a welcoming home. He rarely entertained. He had only hosted a recent house party because he wanted to win a horse, not because he had any desire to welcome people into his home. And he had never had a desire to tie himself to one woman, to become a father himself.

'I am like my father,' he said, a definitive statement. 'And I prove that every day. Look how much I care about constantly making more and more money, just like him. I'm determined to win at all costs, just like him. I'm ruthless in business, just like him.'

Although since his retreat to the country he had lost interest in either making more money or winning in business, but he was certain that was merely a temporary situation. It had to be.

'You're not mean, like him,' Hetty responded. 'And what you really prove to me, every day, is that you're capable of love. Your father never loved anyone in his life. You love my daughters and they love you back. You make them happy and you take pleasure in their happiness. Just because your father deprived you of a happy childhood, doesn't mean that you should deprive yourself of a happy future.'

Lucas picked up his newspaper, rustled it as if he intended to concentrate on the words, even though the print was a blur. 'You should be encouraging me not to marry and have children. After all, that will mean your girls will inherit everything. They're sensible girls. I'm sure one will marry a man capable of one day running the estate and the businesses.'

Hetty pulled down his paper and glared at him. 'Neither me nor my girls would want to benefit from someone else's unhappiness. We all want you to be happy. We want you to make Lady Hazel happy.'

Lucas placed the newspaper on the table and sighed. It seemed only the full truth would stop her badgering. 'It is too much of a risk, Hetty,' he said, pain gripping his stomach. 'I can't do it. What if you're wrong? What if I do end up just like my father? What if I do hurt her? What if I do make her miserable?'

She placed her hand gently on his arm, her face concerned.

He drew in a deep breath and slowly exhaled. 'I don't want to risk making Hazel unhappy, and I certainly don't want to risk making our children miserable.'

Our children.

Lucas could easily imagine Hazel as a mother, her children running around the estate, playing with their older cousins, but he could not imagine himself as a father, except as a stern, aloof man in the background that everyone feared and avoided.

'You're afraid,' Hetty said, quietly.

Lucas was about to deny it, then realised that, yes, he was afraid. Very afraid. He had been afraid of nothing in his adult life. Once he was old enough, he had stopped fearing his father's wrath and had stood up to him. He had stood up to the bullies at school, had stood up to the scorn of members of the aristocracy who thought he wasn't good enough because he didn't have a title or the supposedly correct background, and he had stood up to the most ruthless of business rivals. None of them had scared him. But the thought of making Hazel unhappy, of making his children unhappy, of being a bad husband or father, that terrified him.

'Yes, I am. And that's a good reason why I shouldn't marry Lady Hazel. She doesn't need a man who is frightened of responsibility. She needs a man who will be strong and supportive.'

'She needs a man who loves her and wants the best for her, and that's you, Lucas. Being afraid is a good reason why you should marry her.'

Lucas looked at her incredulously. He had never heard anything so absurd. Men should be strong, frightened of nothing, and until now he had taken pride in being exactly that sort of man.

She patted his hand gently. 'It once again proves you are not like your father. Do you think your father ever feared that he might make someone unhappy? Do you think he was frightened that he might ruin your mother's life when he married her? When you were born, was he worried that he might not be a good father, that you might not be a happy child and have a good childhood? Of course he didn't because he didn't care. You are afraid because you do care. And because you care you'll do everything in your power to make sure your fears don't come true.'

Lucas stared back at Hetty, trying to formulate an argument that would prove her wrong.

'Being afraid shows you will try hard to be a good, loving husband and a good, loving father,' she added.

'But—'

Lucas was prevented from proving her wrong by the girls, who burst into the room, carrying a frog they had found down by the lake. The frog escaped from Alice's hands and began jumping round the breakfast table, croaking as it did so, much to the girls' pleasure.

'Can we keep him? Can we keep him?' they chorused together, looking from their mother to Lucas.

'I think he'd rather live down by the lake,' Hetty said, laughing as she cornered the poor frog beside the milk jug, picked him up with a grimace and handed him to Alice, who placed the still-croaking frog in her pocket. 'Perhaps you can return him there and you can just visit him each day.'

'But we want a pet.' Lucy pouted.

'You each have a pony,' Lucas reminded them.

'Yes, and we love them to pieces, but we can't have them in the house,' Minnie said, then looked expectantly at her mother. 'Can we?'

Hetty laughed. 'No, you can't have the ponies in the house.'

'That's why we want Froggy,' Alice responded. 'He'd much rather live in a lovely house with us than in a stupid lake and we'll take really good care of him.'

'Your mother's right,' Lucas said, trying to adopt a voice of authority. 'Frogs like to live in water, not in a young girl's pockets. If you want a pet, a dog or a cat would be a better option.'

Three young faces turned in his direction and stared

up at him, their eyes large and expectant. 'Oh, can we?' Lucy said. 'I want a cat. One that will have lots of kittens.'

'No, a dog, a puppy, would be much better. Then we can take him for walks and teach him tricks,' Minnie said, to the nodding enthusiasm of the other two girls.

'But a cat would also be lovely,' Alice added. 'She would curl up on our laps and they have such nice soft fur that you can stroke.'

'No, a puppy,' Minnie said.

Lucas raised his hands in defeat. 'Well, I think the estate is big enough for both. Perhaps we should get a cat and a dog, but no frogs.'

A loud cheer erupted from the girls, louder than one would expect from such small children. Alice took Froggy out of her pocket. 'Right, let's get you back to the lake, where you belong.'

The three girls rushed out of the room, their excited chatter turning to an argument about what names would best suit their future pets.

Hetty looked from the door through which the noisy girls had departed and back at Lucas, her eyebrows raised.

'What?' he asked. 'They wanted pets and I was right. There's plenty of room in the house and on the estate. We could probably have several dogs and several cats, a troop of kittens and puppies, and we'd hardly notice.'

'That's not what I'm smiling at. You said you wouldn't be a good father. That you would make your children miserable. My daughters don't seem miserable to me. You'd make a wonderful father, Lucas. You'd make a wonderful husband. Don't let your father deny you the chance of future happiness.'

Lucas picked up his paper, smiling to himself. Hetty might just be right. Although, there was still one problem that Hetty had not considered. There was no guarantee that Lady Hazel would see him as a potentially good husband and father, but there was only one way to find out.

Chapter Twenty-Two

Hazel paused in her filing and looked out of the window, a pile of reports nestled in the crook of her arm. Something had drawn her to the window. She had lots of work to do and should not be spending time idly staring at the passing world.

Once again, she had arrived in the morning to piles of papers on top of desks, chairs and stacked up on the floor. She had plenty to keep her occupied, but now that she was looking out the window, now that she could see what had drawn her attention, she was incapable of moving.

Lucas Darkwood was outside, pacing backwards and forward, seemingly talking to himself. Was he lost? He walked past the building, turned and walked back. Then he stopped and looked up. She jumped back, so he wouldn't see her, nearly dropping her pile of papers.

Tentatively, she took a step forward, took hold of the curtain and peeped out the edge of the window.

He was still there, but now he was walking up the

stone stairs that led to the building's foyer. Was he coming to see her? She quickly put down the files and looked around the room for a mirror. Of course there wasn't one. The professor was not the sort of man to care about his appearance. Most of the time he was so distracted he looked as if he had hardly bothered to brush his hair before arriving for work in the morning.

With no way of seeing her appearance, she touched her hair to reassure herself that it was still in place and smoothed down her skirt. Then she picked up her files and went over to the cabinets. If he was indeed coming to see her, she wanted to appear as busy as possible. She did not want him to think she had been watching him. Nor did she want him to see how easily he could cause her to become flustered.

Because flustered was exactly what she was. It would be so much easier if she never saw Mr Darkwood again. She had been trying so hard to put him out of her mind, but to no avail. One day, she was certain, her obsessive thoughts would clear and she would be free. One day she would realise it had been a long time since she had thought of Lucas Darkwood, that he was no longer constantly in her thoughts. She just wished that day would hurry up and arrive.

She looked back at the window, at the door, then down at the papers in her hands, unsure what to do with herself. She both hoped and dreaded that he really was here to see her. Spending time with him after the lecture had been so enjoyable that she had briefly been tempted to try to see him again. She had wondered if maybe he would attend the few balls that were left in the Season. Maybe he would dance with her again. Perhaps he would take her hand again the way he had at the restaurant. Maybe he would look into her eyes again, with such affection. Maybe, just maybe, he might kiss her again. Hadn't he said he didn't regret what he had done, even though he knew it was wrong?

Such thoughts would whirl around in her head until reality hit her, harder each time, pulling her back and reminding her of the folly of drifting off into such fantasies. None of these things were likely to happen again. He did not usually attend balls and, if he did, now that the bet was over, there was no point in him dancing with her.

Now that she had given him her forgiveness there had been no more letters, no more gifts. Nothing. And that was all for the best. She had realised that she was never going to get over him if she saw him again. While spending time with him after the lecture had been wonderful, it had only made the realisation that he could never be hers all the more painful.

Much to her mother's chagrin she had declined to attend the last few balls of the Season. Meeting a potential beau at this stage was unlikely, so what was the point of putting herself through that ordeal? Even if a man did show interest in her, it would be wasted on her. How could she return any other man's attention when she was always thinking about Lucas Darkwood? And it would have been even worse if Mr Darkwood had actually attended one of those balls. How would she have coped if he had danced with another woman? The answer to that was obvious, she would not have coped.

No, her decision to avoid seeing him again was a sensible one. It was the only way she would ever be free.

And now it looked as though she would see him again anyway. She looked towards the door. Why was he here in this building? Was it to see her, or was he visiting another office?

She picked up another pile of papers that had been left stacked up on the desk, tried to read them so she would know what to file them under, but could make no sense of what she was reading. She put them back down on the desk, once more smoothed down her skirt, took in a deep breath and picked up the papers again.

She turned from the desk and the papers fell out of her arms, scattering into a disorderly mess on the floor. Lucas Darkwood was standing at the door, his body filling the frame.

'Oh,' Hazel blurted out as her stomach suddenly lurched, 'it's you.' She mentally chastised herself for stating the obvious and sounding so foolish. She knew he was coming so why was she acting so surprised? But he *was* a surprise. Seeing him again was surprising.

'Yes, it's me,' he said and smiled. He moved towards her and she was unable to stop herself from taking a series of small steps backwards, her back now up against the cabinets. He bent down, picked up the discarded papers, shuffled them into a more orderly pile and placed them on the desk.

'I need to speak to you, Hazel. Is now a good time?'

No, Hazel wanted to say. *No time would be good for me to talk to you again. Not when I'm trying so hard to forget you.* Instead, she shrugged her shoulders and tried to ignore her body's frantic reaction to his presence. It was important for her to at least try to maintain a modicum of nonchalance, even though the heat on her cheeks was revealing exactly how unnerved she was.

They stared at each other for a moment. He looked uncomfortable. That could not possibly be the case. Mr Darkwood never looked uncomfortable. He picked up the papers again, shuffled them into an even neater pile, placed them back on the desk, then looked back at Hazel.

'Lady Hazel,' he said, then hesitated and drew in a deep breath.

It was difficult to believe, but he looked as awkward as Hazel felt.

'Lady Hazel,' he repeated. 'There is something I must confess to you.'

Hazel's already furiously pounding heart increased its tempo until she was sure the beating sound must be filling the room. What on earth could he possibly have to confess to her?

'I have already apologised for that atrocious bet.'

She nodded, not wanting to think about that now. Not wanting to think about it ever again. Until she put that entire incident behind her, she was not going to heal. Mentioning it only reminded her that she had fallen hopelessly in love with a man who had once treated her so badly.

'The bet was part of my thoughtless behaviour. I've always wanted to win and I was determined to win that bet as well, determined to win that horse, determined that I would have the best stud farm in the country and that my horses would win every major race on the racing calendar.'

Hazel nodded again. That was hardly a confession. He wasn't telling her anything she didn't already know.

'My behaviour was unforgivable and you were so gracious to forgive me for it.'

Hazel waited. Surely that wasn't the reason for his visit. Was there some other unforgivable behaviour he was seeking forgiveness for? She hoped he wouldn't mention that kiss.

Please don't mention that kiss. I want to do the impossible and forget all about it.

'What I didn't realise was in taking on that bet I was chasing the wrong things,' he continued. 'In trying to win, I lost the only thing that is important to me.'

She waited nervously while he drew in another ragged breath and exhaled slowly.

'Captain Sparkles?' she asked as a prompt.

He smiled, that lovely enchanting smile that lit up his face, and for a moment she forgot what he was talking about, instead allowing herself to be bathed in the glow of that smile.

'I lost you.'

Hazel's breath caught in her throat. Had she heard correctly, or had she been so dazzled by that smile that she had momentarily lost her sense of reason?

He took a step towards her, his hands reaching out. 'Until I met you, I didn't realise what I had been doing. I've spent my lifetime trying to protect myself from pain. I had closed down, created a hard exterior so that nothing could get through it. But you did.'

He looked down at the floor, as if giving himself the courage to continue, then looked up at her, his eyes beseeching her to understand. 'I chose not to admit that I was falling in love with you. I couldn't admit it. If I did, it would mean I'd have to let down my defences. I'd have to let you in. I'd have to open myself up to pain, risk being hurt, and that wasn't a risk I was prepared to take. Until now. Now that I've admitted that I love you I've realised that you have to risk pain.'

'You love me?' Hazel asked. Now she was sure she must have misheard. Had he really said he loved her or was it another tormenting dream?

'Yes, Hazel, I love you. I wish I was a poet so I could truly express in beautiful words the depth of my love for you. But all I can do is tell you, in my own clumsy way, how you have changed me. You've changed my world. You've made me see the world differently, in a warmer, more caring light. Before I met you, it was as if I was living under a grey cloud. You brought sunshine into my life. You made me see the possibility of happiness.'

He looked down and drew in another breath. 'And that's just one of the many reasons why I love you.'

'Oh,' was all Hazel could respond, her voice little more than a gasp.

'That was what I wanted to confess. I know I've probably left it too late, that I've done too much damage, but I still wanted to say it. You've probably moved on from me by now and left me in the past. I saw how those men reacted to you when we were at Claridge's. Perhaps you've now got men lining up to court you.'

Hazel nodded, shook her head, then nodded again.

It was true that one of the scientists had been paying her a lot of attention and perhaps she might have once been flattered by that, but after knowing Lucas Darkwood no other man could compare. He had ruined her. That kiss had ruined her. Not her reputation, as no one had heard about the kiss, and she doubted anyone would believe it if they did hear, but he had ruined her for ever wanting another man. It was him or no one and as she thought she couldn't have him, she had decided it would be no one.

'If there is someone else, then I'll wish you all the best and leave you alone. I just hope he appreciates you for who you are, realises you are perfect exactly as you are and doesn't try to change you in any way.'

He looked at her, his eyes sad.

'No, there's no one else,' she said quietly.

She could almost see the tension lift from his shoulders.

'In that case, will you give me the chance to prove that I am worthy of you? I don't know if I could ever make you love me, especially after everything I've done, but, Hazel, would you at least let me try?'

Hazel stared back at him in disbelief. Him? Unworthy? Of her love?

'I know I have no right to ask this of you,' he continued, 'but I beg you, allow me to love you, to court you. Allow me the opportunity to convince you that I can make you happy. I want to make you happy with all my heart. I want to bring even more light and joy into your life, just as you've brought light and joy into mine. I love you, Hazel, and I want the opportunity to do everything I can to convince you to love me.'

Hazel continued to stare back at him, still not entirely believing this was real and not some illusion conjured up by her fevered brain. But if it was an illusion, she had nothing to lose by making a confession of her own. 'Oh, no, that won't be necessary,' she said, shaking her head.

He suddenly looked crestfallen and nodded slowly and solemnly. 'I understand. I was hoping to show you that I was a changed man. That you had changed me, but, you're right, after all that I've done, it was too much to hope for.'

Hazel shook her head rapidly, stepped forward and grabbed hold of his arms, desperate to make him understand. 'No, I mean it won't be necessary for you to try to convince me to love you because I already do. I love you, Lucas Darkwood.'

Now that she had said those words out loud, Hazel loved the sound of them and she said them once again, just to hear how they sounded. 'I love you, Lucas.'

His face transformed in front of her. Once again, a smile lit up his face, causing his grey eyes to crinkle at the edges in that way she adored so much. 'You can't know how happy it makes me to hear you say that. But I still don't feel worthy of your love. I want the chance to prove to you that I am now a better man. I want to make amends for all that I have done. Will you allow me to court you, Hazel, so that one day, once I've proven myself to be a good man, a worthy man, you might consent to marrying me?'

Hazel's hands shot to her mouth, then she slowly lowered them. 'Oh, Lucas I've always known that deep down you're a good man.' She gave a little laugh. 'And I certainly know that you're a good kisser. I think I could fall in love with you for that alone. In fact, I think it was your kisses that made me fall in love with you.'

He smiled at her. 'In that case...' He took her in his arms and kissed her. Hazel could feel the passion in his lips, the love, the affection. She was being kissed by a man who loved her, who she loved in return. Hazel didn't know whether it was possible to feel happier, her entire body seemed to be singing with joy.

He drew back from her, his lips close to her ear. 'I want to make you happy, Hazel. To make you feel loved. Will you teach me how to do that? With you as my tutor I'm sure I can be a man capable of giving and receiving love, a man capable of great happiness.'

She nodded, wanting him to kiss her again. He obliged, following her unspoken command by kissing her lightly on her neck as she purred with pleasure.

'With you as my tutor I'm sure I will learn how to make our home a happy one for our children.'

Our children. She stood back and looked at him in surprise. 'Oh, and we're going to have a lot of children, are we?'

He looked down at her and smiled, a delightful, cheeky smile. 'Well, I'd like to have as many little Hazels as possible, all studying hard and learning everything they can about the way the world works. Who knows, maybe things will change and one of them will be the first woman to graduate with a science degree.'

His face suddenly became serious. 'So, may I ask your father for permission to court you, with the intention of us eventually marrying?'

Hazel nodded her head vigorously. 'Oh, yes, the sooner the better.'

'Good, then let's finish what we started at my estate.'

He turned from her and moved towards the door. Hazel's smile died. He couldn't be leaving, could he? Not now. He couldn't just leave after only one kiss, not when she wanted so much more from him.

Instead he shut the door, turned the key and the lock clicked.

He paused at the door and smiled at her. Then in two quick strides was across the room and she was in his arms. Her arms went around his neck as he kissed her with a passion that was all-consuming, that drove out all thoughts but one. She was in love with this man and he was in love with her, and this was where she was going to spend the rest of her life, in the arms of this wonderful man. Hazel's happiness was complete.

Epilogue

For many people heaven consisted of chubby cherubs sitting on fluffy white clouds, playing harps while a celestial choir of angels filled the air with their ethereal music.

For Lucas Darkwood, heaven was standing at the altar of a small country church and watching in expectation as his lovely bride walked slowly up the aisle towards him on the arm of her father. Heaven was knowing that this wonderful young lady would soon be his wife and his life would be complete.

He smiled at Hazel. She had never looked more beautiful, dressed in a flowing white gown and smiling with pure happiness, her lovely blue eyes sparkling, reflecting the happiness he was feeling.

The simplicity of her gown showed off her curvaceous beauty and Lucas briefly wondered whether it was appropriate to experience lust when standing at an altar. But how could he not. His beautiful, confident bride had thrown out the demands of fashion, those flounces, frills, bustles and padding that gave other women the illusion of an hourglass figure. His bride needed no such embellishments, not when her womanly curves were all her own.

Far too slowly his angel moved towards him, her smiling sisters following behind, while Hetty's daughters threw petals on the aisle, and occasionally at each other as if they were having a snow fight.

The girls had been so excited to take part in the wedding and they looked adorable in their matching pink dresses, with wreaths of flowers circling their blond heads.

Only the father was seeing this as a solemn occasion, although even he was having the occasional lapse in seriousness, patting his daughter's hand and sending her secret winks.

Lucas was sure he had to be the luckiest man in the world. He was no longer involved in breeding horses and would now never be toasting his winning horse at Ascot. The men at his club thought him a loser, someone who not only couldn't win a bet and take the horse that he had vowed would be his, but had conceded easily to Lord Bromley's demands and given him everything he wanted. Then to compound their belief that he was a loser, he had paid Bromley an excessive amount of money to buy back Captain Sparkles. But Lucas knew he was the winner.

He had discovered what it was like to love and be loved, what it was like to be happy. Hazel had brought such warmth and joy into his life, and nothing could ever beat that.

She joined him in front of the altar. Her father handed her over to Lucas and then sat down beside Hazel's smiling, sobbing mother. The vicar began the service and Lucas wished the man would hurry up. He wanted to be a married man, he wanted Hazel to be his wife and for them to start their lives together.

Their courtship had been a brief one, both quickly agreeing that they knew they wanted to be married as soon as possible. They knew they were in love, knew they wanted to spend their lives together, so why waste time? He had asked Hazel's father for her hand. He had given his consent and Lucas had instantly been welcomed into the Springfeld family as if he had always belonged there.

Now he just had to get through this interminable service. Tomorrow they would be travelling to the Continent for a month-long honeymoon. Lucas had never travelled before, had never seen the point, and would once have been unable to understand why anyone would consider taking such a long time away from their business merely for the sake of enjoying themselves. But that was the old Lucas Darkwood. Now he wanted to enjoy as much time with Hazel as he could. They would tour Italy and France, spending the days exploring the sites and the evenings entwined in each other's arms, exploring each other's bodies.

He looked down at his wife-to-be and smiled as the vicar continued reading out the service. He was anxious to get his beautiful bride to himself.

Once they returned from their honeymoon they would set up house in London, so Hazel could continue to attend her lectures. Even though she would not be able to graduate with a science degree, he was sure his clever wife would be able to make good use of everything she learnt. She had talked of tutoring other women, maybe setting up a school, and the professor had suggested that she might one day work with him with his research.

The vicar asked him if he took Hazel for his wife and he gave an emphatic *I do*. Of course he took this beautiful, clever woman to be his wife. It was hard to believe he had once thought he would never marry, but then, that was before he met Hazel Springfeld, the woman who had changed everything.

Finally, the vicar pronounced them man and wife. Lucas knew he was indeed in heaven when he was told he could now kiss his bride. She looked up at him and smiled. For the sake of propriety and the watching guests he kissed her lightly on the lips. He would save his passion for when they were alone.

To the accompaniment of the ringing bells they left the church hand in hand. Hetty, the girls and his new family surrounded them, accompanied by their usual constant chatter, laughter and much kissing of cheeks. Lucas couldn't stop smiling as he was embraced in the warmth and happiness of this loving family.

'Welcome to the family, my boy,' the Earl of Springfeld said, shaking Lucas's hand.

'Yes, welcome,' his new mother-in-law echoed. 'I feel so proud that you're now part of the family.' She turned to look at Hazel, who was being hugged by her two sisters.

'Hopefully seeing how happy marriage has made Hazel will change Iris and Daisy's minds,' Lady Springfeld continued in a more serious tone. 'They seem to have decided they don't want to marry, but I'll soon get those foolish notions out of their heads.' She turned back to Lucas and smiled. 'I know you'll make a loving husband for Hazel and you two will be wonderful parents.

She kissed him on the cheek and went and joined her daughters. Hazel looked over at him and smiled, a beautiful, radiant smile, and then she walked over to him.

While the guests showered them with rose petals, he took his wife in his arms once again and kissed her, causing the family to break into noisy cheering and applause. Yes, he certainly was in heaven.

* * * * *